# SPEAK NO EVIL

SALLY RIGBY

TOP
DRAWER
PRESS

CRIME FICTION BOOKS

Edited by Emma Mitchell of @ Creating Perfection.

Cover Design by Stuart Bache of Books Covered

# GET ANOTHER BOOK FOR FREE!

To instantly receive **Nowhere to Hide,** a free novella from the Detective Sebastian Clifford series, featuring DC Lucinda Bird when she first joined CID, sign up for Sally Rigby's free author newsletter at www.sallyrigby.com.

# Chapter 1

Catherine Cooper walked into the social services meeting room for a conference regarding Lacey, the child she'd been fostering over the last few weeks. It was the strangest case she'd ever come across and the police were no closer to solving it. Government agencies had been working hard to find the parents but, so far, with no success. Lacey, the name given to her by the social worker in charge of the case, and which the child was already answering to, had been found alone sitting on a bench in front of the Old Grammar School in Market Harborough's High Street. Despite the weather, all she was wearing was an ill-fitting pink short-sleeved cotton dress. She had scuffed sandals on her feet, and around her neck hung a sign made of cardboard. The words *Speak No Evil* were handwritten on it, in black felt-tip pen.

The poor little mite hadn't said a word since she'd been found. Catherine had fostered regularly over the years and at the moment didn't have any children apart from Lacey, which she was pleased about as she doubted the introverted child would have been able to cope with it. Bangs or unexpected noises made her jump and press her hands over her ears. The only person Lacey would interact with was Catherine, and even then she hadn't really let her guard down and would only nod or shake her head in answer to any questions. The child would back away from Pete, Catherine's husband, if he came anywhere near and would run and hide if anyone knocked on the door.

Although Lacey hadn't yet spoken, she ate whatever meal was put in front of her and had been taught to use cutlery correctly. She had far better table manners than most children of her age. Catherine had offered her biscuits and sweets, but the child refused them, turning her head until they'd been taken away. It was almost as if she was frightened, but that made no sense to Catherine.

Lacey had only been with them for a short while, but it had been decided that a case conference should be held now to make a decision regarding her future. Catherine sat at the large round table in the meeting room. She'd been there many times in the past, as she'd been regularly used as a foster carer, in particular for those children who had emotional and physical difficulties. Throughout the years, over fifty children had been in the care of her and Pete.

She scanned the people around the table, recognising most of them from when she'd taken Lacey to visit them or when they'd come around to the house to see the child in a more relaxed setting. Next to her was the psychologist, Dr Miranda Watkins, whom she'd met several times in the past when they'd fostered a little boy who screamed non-stop from morning to night. She'd been able to help, much to Catherine's relief, as he'd been one of the hardest children they'd dealt with. The child had been one of twelve siblings, with only nine years between the eldest and the youngest. The screaming had been a learnt behaviour. It was the only way he could command any attention. Even if it was negative.

Lacey differed from other children they'd looked after. She wasn't hard to deal with. In fact, she was no trouble at all. But her lack of childlike behaviour was heartbreaking. Dr Watkins had tried hard to break down Lacey's barrier and had already seen her several times. But she couldn't get anything from her. She'd given Lacey crayons to colour with, toys to play with, and had spoken to her at length. But the child had remained seated with her head bowed, ignoring everything going on around her. It was pitiful to watch. Catherine had wondered if Lacey wasn't understanding what was being said to her. That perhaps she was foreign, or had some learning difficulties. But her eyes showed understanding, and at home she'd always do as she was asked to. There was something far deeper going on which the little girl wouldn't, or couldn't, divulge. Catherine hoped that one day, she might relax enough to confide in her.

There was also a specialist police officer seated at the table, but Catherine couldn't remember her name, despite wracking her brain. They'd only met once before, when the police had reported on the investigation at the initial meeting.

On Catherine's right was the health visitor, Daphne Wright, a kind, experienced nurse who had visited them at home every week since Lacey's arrival.

At the head of the table, with a thick Manilla folder in front of her, and appearing to be in charge, was a woman Catherine hadn't encountered before.

'May I have everyone's attention,' the woman said. 'Thank you for coming along to the case conference. For those who don't know me, I'm Valerie Clarke, senior social worker, and I'll be chairing the meeting today regarding Lacey's future. Where's Stephen? He—'

The door opened and the social worker, Stephen Shaw, who was new to the area but with whom Catherine had the most contact, came rushing in.

'Sorry, I'm late. I got caught up in sorting out a residential care application for a client. Have I missed anything?' He sat on an empty chair next to the health visitor.

'No, I was about to ask everyone to introduce themselves before we discuss what, if any, progress has been made with the child.'

After they'd done that, the chair turned to Dr Watkins and asked for her assessment.

'I need to continue seeing Lacey and hope to gain her trust. It's hard to make an accurate assessment, but it's likely that she's suffering from abandonment issues. Whatever situation she was in before she was left, it would've been one she was accustomed to. Even in situations of abuse, children away from their familiar surroundings will suffer.'

'Has there been any change in the child's behaviour?' Valerie asked.

'I've observed Lacey interacting with Mrs Cooper and have noticed that she's beginning to relate to her. But it's a slow process.'

'I've heard excellent reports about St Joseph's residential home for children. Lacey would have therapeutic support and care twenty-four-seven. Would that help her development and be a better environment for her to be in?' the police officer asked.

Surely, they couldn't think that would be better than what Catherine and Pete were doing? That was ridiculous.

'I don't believe so, not in this case. It's my suggestion that we do nothing to upset the status quo, as it could be disastrous for Lacey and her successful integration into society,' Dr Watkins said.

Catherine relaxed her tense muscles. She knew deep down that she was doing a good job with Lacey, as far as anyone could, but if Dr Watkins had expressed a different view, then the child could've been taken away from her. Without question, that was the wrong thing for the child's well-being.

'Thank you, Miranda, your views are noted. What about her health, Daphne?' Valerie turned to the health visitor.

'When she was first brought into care, we got permission to give her X-rays, scans and have her bloods taken. She was in good health, a little undernourished, but not overly so, and her age was determined to be between six and seven. She had no injuries on her body, and there was no sign of any old ones either. All tests have come back negative and there were no traces of her having been drugged. Physically, there's nothing wrong with her.'

'That's good to hear as it means we're not concerned about her health. We can concentrate on her social and mental well-being. Mrs Cooper, you've been with Lacey more than anyone else, what can you add to this assessment?'

Catherine sucked in a breath, wanting to appear competent and objective in her response.

'She is quiet, as Dr Watkins pointed out, especially when we're out and meeting other people. I don't mean verbally, because she doesn't speak. But in all of her behaviour. She doesn't run upstairs, for example, or make a noise while eating. Everything she does is done deliberately and quietly. There are definite signs that she understands what's going on around her. It's apparent in her eyes, and her responses. She always does as I ask and, unlike other children we've fostered, never quibbles when it's time for bed.'

'Is she able to do anything for herself?' Valerie Clarke asked.

'Yes, there are many things with which she doesn't require assistance. She gets herself up and dressed, and will brush her teeth in the morning and evening before she goes to bed, without being asked, and requiring no help. In fact, she's the first one up in the morning. Most days I'll find her dressed and sitting on the sofa in the lounge when I come downstairs to make breakfast. She has excellent table manners and, if anything, she's advanced for her years. She eats whatever I put in front of her, apart from treats and snacks. If I offer those, she tenses and turns her head. It's as if she's scared of them, or doesn't recognise them for what they are. I don't push her at all.'

'It's certainly a tricky case. Has Lacey made any attempt to speak to you since she's been in your care?'

'Not directly, but in her sleep she mutters. I haven't been able to work out exactly what she's saying, but the rhythm and tone of her speech is almost like she's saying her prayers. I'd wondered whether she'd come from a religious background, but other than when she's asleep there's no further evidence of this. She doesn't attempt to say prayers before her meals, which she might have done if her family were devout.'

'Miranda, do you have any comment to make regarding this behaviour?'

'I'd need to witness it before making any assessment, which isn't possible as it takes place while she's sleeping.'

'Could Mrs Cooper video Lacey when it happens?' Daphne asked.

'I'm not sure about the ethics of that,' Catherine said. 'Also, it doesn't happen all the time and might only last a few seconds. It would mean sitting in her room every night with my phone to capture it and that's not practical.'

'I agree,' Valerie said. 'Does Lacey watch the television or look at books?'

'She'll sometimes pick up a book and turn the pages. I don't know whether she's reading the words or looking at the pictures, though. When I read to her, she sits still with her hands in her lap and her head tilted towards me, clearly listening. But there's no sign if she's enjoying the stories. Her face remains expressionless. It's the same with the television. I put on children's shows for her and she stares at what's on, but whether she enjoys them, I can't say.'

'In your opinion, is Lacey intellectually challenged?' Valerie asked.

It was a question that early on Catherine had asked herself, but she knew the answer to that now.

'I don't believe so, although I'm no expert. Lacey may not speak at all, but from her responses I'm convinced she knows exactly what's going on around her.'

'That's good to know. Where are we on tracking down the parents?' Valerie asked, turning to the police officer.

'The investigation's ongoing, but so far coming up blank, despite a national appeal and cross-checking the missing persons databases. Interpol has been alerted, but they too have nothing. Those who have come forward claiming they know who Lacey is aren't anything to do with her. We were able to establish that straight away, as we didn't publicise anything about the sign left around her neck.'

'And let's make sure that piece of information remains confidential,' Valerie said.

'We will,' the police officer said.

'Before we make our decision, does anyone else have any questions for Mrs Cooper?' Valerie asked.

Catherine stared at each person in turn as they shook their heads and said no.

'In that case, are you prepared to continue fostering Lacey?' Valerie asked, looking directly at her.

A question that she didn't even have to consider what her answer would be. The little girl needed her.

'Absolutely. I think it would be extremely harmful if we were to move her again. She's only just getting used to us.'

'We'll need to consider schooling, if she is around six years old, which the doctors believe, but not yet. We'll wait until we next meet.'

'I'm a qualified primary school teacher and taught for several years until we began fostering. I can homeschool her when the time's right.'

Catherine glanced at Dr Watkins, who was nodding her agreement. Together they would do what's best for Lacey.

'Thank you for what you've done so far. After listening to what everyone has to say, I propose that we leave Lacey with Mrs Cooper for now, and meet again in six months. I would ask you all to continue assessing the child over this period so we have a clearer picture of her current and future progress. At that time, we'll be able to make a more informed decision regarding her future. Are you in agreement, Stephen?' she asked the social worker.

'Yes. I'd recommend that she stays with Mrs Cooper, who's doing a superb job.'

'Thank you all for attending. I look forward to seeing you all again soon.'

Catherine left the conference room and breathed a sigh

of relief. She'd already grown fond of the little girl and knew living with her and Pete would be the best place for her if she was to overcome whatever had happened to her in the past.

Further disruptions could do irreversible damage.

# Chapter 2

*Twelve Months Later*

'Come on, Lacey,' Detective Constable Lucinda "Birdie" Bird said. 'Let's leave Auntie Catherine to pay for the birthday cards she's bought, and we'll go to the café down the road and get a takeaway ice cream.' She held out her hand and the little girl, who'd been looking at a jigsaw puzzle on the table in front of her, gripped it. 'I'm having a mint choc chip cone. Would you like the same? I bet you would.'

The little girl looked at her and nodded, her lips turning up into a smile, revealing a gap where her front two teeth used to be until they'd fallen out a week ago. After telling her aunt where they were going, the two of them walked outside onto the busy High Street. It was bustling with people, and Lacey squeezed Birdie's fingers and stood very close to her as they headed down the street. It was Saturday and there was bound to be a queue.

Despite having lived with Birdie's mum's sister, Catherine, for twelve months since she'd been abandoned, the girl was still very quiet. She seldom spoke, although over the last few months they'd started to get a few more words out of her. For some reason, Lacey had taken a shine to Birdie, and whenever she visited, the little girl would sit next to her and hold her hand. It was Birdie who'd introduced her to ice cream, as the child had appeared not to know what it was. But now, whenever it was offered, she'd wolf it down.

Lacey was a bright child and Birdie's aunt had been giving her lessons most days. Already she was advanced for her age in both maths and English and Auntie Catherine was convinced someone had taught her before, as she already knew so much. Yet, whoever it was hadn't made themselves known to the authorities.

It had been decided by the psychologist, social worker, and Auntie Catherine that Lacey wasn't ready to go to school and mix with other children. They believed she wouldn't cope in a normal classroom because she was so reserved and the other children might tease her, and do untold damage. Lacey was well-behaved and her manners were impeccable. Most days she'd sit quietly playing or reading and she was already tackling books that were way beyond her years.

According to Auntie Catherine, Lacey was *too* well-behaved for a child of her age, and she'd wondered whether that was through fear of being naughty and what the consequences would be. Birdie shuddered at the thought of someone mistreating the child she'd grown so fond of. If she got her hands on them, she'd … Lacey tugged at her hand, pulling her towards the café where they were going to buy their ice creams, and distracting Birdie from her thoughts.

They continued down the street when Lacey stopped dead in her tracks, almost causing Birdie to trip right over her.

'What's wrong, Lacey? Are you okay?' Birdie crouched

down to the child's level, scanning the area, unable to see anything out of the ordinary.

Lacey's eyes were wide, and she was staring at something on the other side of the road a few yards down from where the Old Grammar School was situated. Her entire body shook, and she appeared oblivious to anything else around her. Trickling down her leg was a yellow stream. The poor thing had wet herself.

Birdie had never known her to do that before.

What on earth had happened?

Still at Lacey's level, Birdie tried to see what the child was fixated on, but there was nothing out of the ordinary. Cars driving past. Cars parked. Families walking. People on their own. No one was staring in their direction. Or acting suspiciously. So what had caused such a reaction?

Birdie pulled out some tissues from her handbag and wiped Lacey's legs. All the time the little girl remained still, like a statue, her face pale and expressionless.

Had she seen someone, or something, related to her past? What else could it be? It wasn't as if she went out anywhere without Birdie or her aunt. She didn't know anyone. During the investigation after she'd been abandoned, nobody had come forward claiming they knew her. Or, at least, nobody genuine. There had been the usual time-wasters, or worse, people who wanted a young child for reasons that made Birdie shudder.

At the last case conference, six months ago, Auntie Catherine had said she wanted to continue fostering Lacey because they'd established a good relationship. They'd established routine that had resulted in the child becoming much securer in her environment than she had been. To uproot the child would have been disastrous. Lacey would never have coped.

'Lacey, tell me what's wrong?'

The child didn't seem to hear her.

'You're safe now. I'm with you. No one's going to hurt you.' She pulled Lacey towards her into a hug. 'What did you see that upset you?' she asked softly.

Lacey went rigid in Birdie's arms, her breathing shallow and erratic.

'Do you want to go back home?' Birdie asked, not wanting to push the child for more information, as she was so distraught.

Lacey turned her head to face Birdie, her eyes glassy with tears. 'Yes, please,' she whispered.

'Well, that's what we'll do, then. Straight away. Let's find Auntie Catherine and tell her where we're going. We'll take the key from her so she can carry on with her shopping.'

Birdie turned Lacey around until they were facing the way they'd come and couldn't see whatever had captured her attention.

'I don't want to be on my own. Please stay with me,' the little girl said, squeezing Birdie's hand even tighter.

Birdie swallowed hard. That had to be the most Lacey had ever spoken in one go in all the time she'd known her.

'I'll always be here for you, sweetheart, and will never leave you on your own. Never. Do you understand?'

'Yes,' she whispered.

They hurried back to the shop they'd just left and met Auntie Catherine as she was coming out. 'What's happened?' Her brow furrowed as she glanced at Birdie and then down at Lacey, whose green and plaid skirt was wet at the front.

'A minor accident. Nothing to worry about. I'm going to take Lacey home so she can have a wash and change. I'll stay with her while you carry on with your shopping.' Over the top of the little girl's head, so she couldn't see, Birdie mouthed 'Something bad's happened.'

Her aunt gave a nod to acknowledge she'd understood. 'Okay, off you both go. Here's the key.' She opened her bag and handed it to Birdie. 'I won't be long. Make sure to have the kettle on, as I'll need a strong cuppa when I get back. Why did I chose a Saturday to shop when I can't stand the crowds? I'll see you both soon. Next stop is the bakery to buy some jam doughnuts for us all to have later.'

Her aunt took off down the street, in the opposite direction from where she lived, and the route Birdie and Lacey were going to take.

'Are you okay to walk back?' Birdie asked Lacey. They could catch the bus. It was only a couple of stops, but she doubted Lacey would want to sit down while wet.

Lacey nodded. It was only a ten-minute walk to where her aunt lived. Birdie put the key in her pocket and took the little girl's hand. They headed up High Street, turned right into Bowden Lane, and then left into Burnmill Road.

The child was silent while they were walking, and Birdie found her mind wandering to her own birth mother. She'd been adopted at six months, and although she loved her parents and brothers and had a great relationship with them all, something inside was pushing her to discover more about her background.

She'd already started looking but had a setback after applying to put her name on the Adoption Contact Register. She'd been informed her birth mother had requested that she was not to be contacted.

Why?

Birdie wanted to know what had caused this response, but the staff at the register were prohibited from telling her anything. They couldn't even tell her the date her mother had sent in the request.

She wouldn't let that stop her from finding out where her mother was, though, even if they never met face to face.

But for now, Lacey had to be her top priority. Whatever she'd seen, this incident was proof that there was something in the area that was connected to her.

The police investigation had been put to bed after they'd come to a dead end. They couldn't find any family members or anyone, in fact, who knew anything about the child. Because they were unable to ID Lacey, it meant they couldn't locate her dental or doctor's records. Or any school records. It was as if she hadn't existed before she was found in the town centre.

Lacey, being so uncommunicative, hadn't helped either, but that wasn't her fault. It was frustrating for Birdie that the investigation had ended, but she understood the reasons. Other, more pressing, cases had demanded their attention. There was only a finite number of hours in the working day, and cases went down in priority after a certain amount of time with no success.

This incident could be a breakthrough. It had affected Lacey badly. Maybe they should reopen Lacey's case. Who, or what, had she seen? Was it someone who had harmed her in the past? What sort of treatment had she been subjected to that caused her to be so frightened? Lacey might not have shown signs of any physical abuse, but that didn't mean she hadn't been the victim of emotional trauma.

They owed it to the little girl to find out about her background. Even if she didn't contact her family again, Birdie hated the thought of Lacey growing up feeling like she did ... that there something was missing in her life.

# Chapter 3

Birdie parked mid-way between two white parking lines in the station car park, but didn't have time to straighten up. She jumped out of the car, grabbing her jacket and handbag from the passenger seat, and flew into work at a rate of knots. Her hair, which she hadn't had time to brush and tie back that morning, was flying out in all directions and whipped across her face and into her mouth.

'Morning,' she shouted to the sergeant on the front desk on her way past.

'One day, Birdie. Just one day, you might make it in on time,' he called out, laughing.

'Well, you know me. I'm predictable.'

Which made her seem really boring. Not a look she wanted to cultivate.

She ran upstairs, taking them two at a time, into the office she shared with the other officers in CID, and plonked herself down on a chair next to her partner, Detective Constable Neil Branch, aka Twiggy. According to the clock on the wall, she'd made it with two minutes to spare before their boss, Sergeant Jack

Weston, came in to do the daily briefing. You could set your watch by him, so she knew he wouldn't be late.

'You cut that a bit fine, didn't you?' Twiggy said, grinning in her direction.

'Nothing like stating the obvious, Twig.'

'I'd have put money on us watching Sarge having a go at you for missing the morning briefing again.'

'I don't miss it that often.'

'Liar. Where were you this morning, anyway? Did you have some early morning rendezvous?'

'I wish. I can't believe I slept in again. I'd made such a concerted effort to be here early by setting three alarms and putting out my clothes for the day before I went to bed.' She let out a frustrated sigh.

'I can. Out late last night, were we?'

Far from it. Birdie's problem last night was being unable to sleep because of worrying about Lacey and trying to work out how she was going to convince Sarge to let her investigate the case again.

'I had cricket practice and then went for a quiet drink with the team. I had an early night so you can't blame my social life this time.'

'If you ask me, your track record speaks for itself.'

'Says Mr Perfect.' She flicked his arm with her fingers. 'I hope Sarge is in a good mood this morning. I want to speak to him about something important.'

'You're off to a good start by being here before him. What's it about?'

Should she tell him? She might as well. It wasn't as if he'd make any difference to Sarge's decision.

'I want him to reopen the case of Lacey, the child who was found twelve months ago in the middle of town. Do you remember her?'

'Yeah. She went to live with your aunt. Is she still there?'

'Yes, and I was out with them both on Saturday when something happened, which sent Lacey into a total state of shock. I couldn't see what it was, but it was enough to cause her to wet herself.'

'Children often have accidents. Mine did. I wouldn't worry about it.'

'This was different. It wasn't a case of her needing to go and not being able to hold it. Something shocked her enough for it to happen. Trust me on this. I know her very well. Normally, she's quiet and isn't fazed by what's happening around her. I don't want this to set her back, she's been progressing so well recently.'

'That's good.'

'Right? And that's why we should take another look at the case. If only to discover what affected her so badly on Saturday and hope we can prevent it from happening again.'

'Good luck in trying to persuade Sarge to let you investigate. Everyone's so busy at the moment, what with Rambo still being off with his broken leg.'

'I still can't believe he broke it so badly from tripping over a tiny toy car.'

'He was too busy chasing the kids doing a runner to notice what was on the path. But at least we arrested the little shits later. It would've been even worse if they'd got away with it.'

'When's he coming back to work?'

Being such a small team, it only took one of them to be off sick or on leave for it to make a big difference. Sometimes, Sarge would call in officers from other Leicestershire stations to work with them, but for some reason, this time he hadn't bothered. Either that, or there wasn't anyone available.

'No idea, but it's got to be at least a couple more weeks as it's only been ten days since it happened.'

'Let's hope Sarge puts him on desk duty. Save us having to take turns answering the phone.'

'But that still keeps him off the streets, and why you've got more chance of flying to the moon than getting Sarge to agree to you working on Lacey's case.'

'I don't care what you say. I'm still going to ask him.'

Even though she had more than a sneaking suspicion that her partner was right. It would take a miracle for Sarge to agree.

'Don't hold your breath, because you know what he's like. I bet you a sausage roll he says no you can't do it. In fact, make that two, my tummy's already rumbling.' He patted his protruding stomach, which she'd swear was getting rounder by the day.

'Don't tell me. Evie's got you on another diet. What is it this time?'

Ever since Birdie had joined CID a few years ago, Twiggy's wife had been trying to get him to shed a few pounds. Every time a new diet came out, he was put on it. Not that they ever worked. How could they when he didn't stick to them. Then again, if he was left to his own devices, he'd be twice the size he was now.

'The Paleo diet, which means eating the food they ate ten thousand years ago. I ask you, do I look like a bloody caveman?' He groaned.

'If you stuck to it instead of cheating, then she wouldn't be on your case the whole time. I still don't get how she doesn't realise you cheat at work. I've seen you creep into the office on your days off to snack.'

'No, I don't,' Twiggy protested.

'Yeah, right. And …' Her attention was distracted by Sarge walking into the room, so she turned to face him.

'Morning, team.' He scanned the room. 'Where's Sparkle?'

Birdie glanced over at DC Gemma Litton's desk which was on the other side of the room. She hadn't even noticed the officer was missing.

'Um …' Twiggy said.

The door opened, and the Sparkle flew in. 'Sorry, Sarge, I got stuck behind a massive lorry this morning.'

'You should've left earlier, then. Sit down and let me get on. I haven't got all day.'

Birdie forced back a giggle. It made a change for someone else to be on the receiving end of Sarge's short fuse.

'Yes, Sarge.'

'Tiny. Did anything come in overnight?' Sarge asked DC Aleki Tuala, whose desk was adjacent to Sparkle's.

'No, Sarge. It was quiet.'

'Good. That's what I like to hear on a Monday morning. Twiggy, what are you doing today?'

'Birdie and I are heading out to interview someone who's come forward about the carjackings. Supposedly they were nearly a victim of one at the weekend.'

'Nearly? What does that mean?'

'That's what we'll find out,' Sarge.'

'Let's hope they have something we can use. We're desperate for a break on this case, as the DI keeps reminding me. Sparkle?'

'I'm in court this morning, Sarge, testifying in the factory arson case.'

'We can do without that when we're a man down. Okay. Tiny, what about you?'

'I'm waiting for forensics to come back on the robbery in The Headlands. I'll be in and out today.'

'Right. I expect a productive day from all of you. I'll see you tomorrow morning, if not before. And make sure you're on time, Sparkle.' He wagged his finger in her direction.

'It was a one-off, it won't happen again,' Sparkle said, her brow furrowed.

It was mean of Sarge to have a go at her. She was always on time. Almost always.

'Make sure it doesn't.' He gathered his folders from the desk and as he turned to leave, Birdie jumped out of her seat and ran over to him.

'Sarge, hang on a minute. Can I have a word?'

'What about? I'm in a hurry. DI Curtis is due here in half an hour for a meeting and I need to access some performance stats from the system.'

Curtis was the one person who could turn the tables on Sarge and have him worried. The DI was his boss, and he split his time between the stations at Wigston and Market Harborough. Fortunately for all of them, Wigston was Curtis's actual base, which meant he spent more time there than at Market Harborough.

'I won't keep you long, promise. I'd like us to reopen the case of Lacey, the little girl who was found abandoned by the Old Grammar School twelve months ago.'

He folded his arms across his chest and tapped the floor with his foot.

'As far as my recollection goes, we went as far as we could with the investigation. Why now, suddenly, do you want it revisited?'

She was losing his attention, fast.

'Lacey's fostered by my aunt, and I've got to know her

well over the last year. She's a lovely little girl and is coming along nicely.'

Sarge checked his watch. 'Skip to the important bit, Birdie.'

'Right. Well, we were in town on Saturday, and she witnessed something that sent her into a severe state of shock. I've no idea what it was, but she's never behaved like that before. I reckon it's related to something that's happened in her past. I mean, what else could it be?'

'This sounds like a job for a counsellor, and I really need to go.'

'You don't get what I mean. I want us to look into the case again to see if we can discover anything that might help us identify her? She might need to see someone, but for now we need to know who she is.'

He frowned. Was that a good sign?

'Birdie, I commend your concern, but we spent enough hours on the case before, with little success. I really can't see how that's going to change, or what good it will do for the child if, as you maintain, she's settled and doing okay.'

'Yes, but, Sarge …'

'It's best left alone. We're already stretched too thin with Rambo out of action, as you well know, and I can't afford to shell out for any more overtime. The budget for this year has almost been spent.' His face was set hard. She knew from experience it would be pointless pushing him further, but that didn't stop her from offering another suggestion.

'Can I look into it myself? I don't mind working overtime and not claiming for it.'

'No. I want your full attention on the carjackings case. We've been investigating it for a couple of months now and still no closer to apprehending the culprits.'

'But, Sarge—'

'Sorry, Birdie. Lacey's case was investigated before, and all avenues were exhausted. Leave it.'

Her fists clenched by her side. 'But, Sarge …'

'Don't *but Sarge* me again. I've decided, and that's it.'

He glared at her, and then turned and marched out of the room. She scowled at his retreating back, then returned to her desk and plonked herself down on her chair.

Spinning to face Twiggy, Birdie said, 'It's so not fair. Why can't he see Lacey deserves our attention?'

'It's not that, and you know it. If he says no, it's no. Don't you get it?' Twiggy asked.

'I do, but you didn't see Lacey and how upset she was. It was gut-wrenching to witness. Something must have happened. Kids don't do that for no reason at all. We need to investigate. We *have to* investigate.'

Why was she the only one to see the importance of this?

'And don't think about doing it on the side, either. You'll end up in the shit if you do,' Twiggy said.

'Agreed. Listen to your elders. We know what's best for you,' Tiny said, jumping into the conversation.

'Did I say I was?' she replied, an idea forming in her mind. It was definitely an option worth exploring.

'No, but knowing you, that's exactly what you're thinking about doing,' Twiggy said. 'You can't fool me. I'm your partner and know you better than you know yourself.'

'Yeah, right. Of course, you do.'

He didn't. Well, he did, sort of. But he didn't know everything about her.

'I'm glad we see eye to eye. Now we've got that sorted, let's interview this woman before we have Sarge breathing down our necks.'

'Give me a minute. I've got to go to the loo.'

She left and went to the ladies', taking her phone with

her. If the team couldn't do it, she knew just the man to ask. Sebastian Clifford.

Clifford was an ex-DI from London, and when she'd seen him last, he was in between jobs. She'd worked with him on the QT, investigating the suicide verdict of his cousin Sarah's husband, Donald Witherspoon. Sarah wasn't convinced the verdict had been correct and had approached Seb to look into it. He'd intended to investigate on his own, but Birdie had managed to force her way onto the case.

She hadn't been in touch with Seb since then and had no idea where he was or what he was doing. When they'd last spoken, she'd suggested he became a private investigator, but she didn't know if he'd decided to or not. It wasn't like he had to work or would be out on the streets because, unlike the rest of them, he was related to the aristocracy, the son of a viscount. His family would always be there for him as backup. It must be nice to have that security.

She'd call him and ask for his help.

# Chapter 4

Sebastian Clifford was sitting at his desk, researching international drug trafficking. He'd recently set up his own company, *Clifford Investigation Services*, and his first job had been acting as a civilian investigator for his friend and ex-colleague DI Rob Lawson who worked in the Homicide and Serious Crimes Command Unit at the Metropolitan Police force.

His phone rang, and he glanced at the screen.

It was Birdie.

He'd been meaning to contact her, but work had got in the way. It was no excuse. What was she going to say when she found out where he was?

'Hello, Birdie. Good to hear from you.'

'You too. How's it going?'

'Well, thanks. And you? How's CID?'

'Same old, same old. Look, I'm sorry, but I haven't phoned for a chat. Well, I have, but you know what I mean. Where are you and what are you doing?'

'I'm here in East Farndon, at Rendall Hall.'

'You're here? That's awesome. You must have known I

needed you. You can add psychic ability to that crazy *remembering everything* talent of yours.'

He laughed at her description of his highly superior autobiographical memory. It was the bane of his life, as it was incessant. With no let up.

'I'll stick with the HSAM, thanks. That's more than enough for one person to deal with.'

'Are you staying here long?'

How was she going to react when he told her? There was only one way to find out.

'I moved in a few weeks ago to take care of the house while Sarah's travelling around the world. I'm not sure how long she'll be away for. It could be months, if not longer. We've left it open.'

Silence hung in the air.

Had Birdie hung up?

'B-but … why didn't you tell me?' she finally said, sounding dejected.

'I was going to, but I've been really busy.' His words sounded lame. After what they'd been through together, he should've been more considerate. 'Sorry, that's no excuse.'

'What have you been doing?'

'Some investigative work for DI Rob Lawson. My friend at the Met. Remember him?'

'Yeah. How could I forget? It felt like *Land of the Giants* being stuck next to the pair of you.'

He laughed at the description. Rob was one of the few people he knew who was close to his six feet six inches. Birdie was over a foot shorter, if not more.

'That's him.'

'How come you're working for him?'

'I've set up an investigation company and he's my first client.'

'What happened to all the *I don't want to be a PI* crap that you were spouting when we last spoke?'

'That's an exaggeration.'

'Is it? I don't think so. Anyway, I'm very pleased because, guess what? I've got a job for you. For *us* really, because I want to be involved. But it isn't one I can pay you for. I'll explain when I see you.'

'I'd like to know a little more now, if you don't mind?' he asked, his curiosity piqued.

'Okay, but I've gotta be quick. Twiggy's waiting for me to go out with him. I nipped to the loo to call you because Sarge turned me down when I asked about investigating this case.'

He shook his head. 'Some things never change.'

'I'll take that as a compliment, thanks. Anyway, did you see on the news last year the case involving a young girl, of about six or seven, who was found abandoned in Market Harborough town centre?'

'Yes, I recall the incident. The child was found near the Old Grammar School. The investigation was unsuccessful, despite a concerted effort and it being in the media. Tragic circumstances.'

'That's the case. Her identity was never discovered and so she was given the name Lacey. She's currently being fostered by my aunt.'

'How is the child?'

'Until Saturday she was doing really well. We were out in town and Lacey saw something which totally blindsided her. I don't have the foggiest what it was because she didn't say and I couldn't see anything out of the ordinary, either. All I know is, it's got to be connected to her past. Because, what else could it be?'

'And since your sergeant told you no, you want me to look into it for you.'

'There's no one else I'd trust to do it. The fact you've now set up your PI company *and* you're living in the area has gotta be a sign. Surely you agree.'

'Except I'm working with Rob at the moment,' he reminded her.

'I thought you were done with the police so how come you agreed to this job?'

'Rob approached me and I needed cases to work on. Once the company takes off, I can afford to be more choosy.'

'Are you enjoying Rob's work?'

'The money I earn covers my expenses, but I'm stuck behind the computer and it's not fieldwork, which I much prefer,' he admitted.

'Is the case taking up all your time?'

'Probably about fifty per cent, give or take.'

'So, what else are you doing? And don't say walking Elsa because I know that at her age, she's happy with one walk a day. How is she, by the way?'

'Loving it here. She enjoys playing in the woods surrounding the house.'

Birdie and Elsa, his nine-year-old yellow Labrador, had developed a strong attachment when he was last there.

'You haven't answered my question. How are you filling your time?'

He could see which way this was going and, knowing Birdie, she wouldn't give up until she had the answer she wanted.

'I'm devising a marketing strategy for the business. It's no good having a company if I don't have any cases to work on.'

'That's not going to happen overnight, which means you'll have time to devote to Lacey. We'll work on it together. What do you say?'

'It's so tempting considering there's *no* payment.'

'As I helped you on Sarah's case, we'll view it as quid pro quo.'

'What? You refused to give me the information I requested unless I *let you* help,' he spluttered.

Their very first conversation, when she'd demanded to be included in the case was firmly etched on his mind. He had no choice. Though, with hindsight, it was a smart move on her part. It had taken the pair of them to solve the case.

'There was that I suppose.'

'Not to mention our success got you out of trouble with your sergeant, and you ended up being praised for your efforts. I'd have said that was more than enough compensation. Don't you agree?'

'Okay, I accept that it was. But I've really got to go, or Twiggy will be sending out a search party to find me. Let's meet this evening and we'll discuss it some more. You can buy me dinner.'

He burst out laughing. 'That makes a change.'

'You know my situation. I'm saving up for a deposit on a house and all my spare cash goes towards that. We can just go for a drink, if you'd rather. Although I expect you're feeling guilty for having been here for so long and not letting me know. Buying me a meal is one way you can redeem yourself. You know, I could've been really upset at being forgotten so easily.'

She was right. He felt guilty.

'Okay, you win. Meet me at the pub in Great Oxendon at seven. And that's my seven and not yours.'

~

'Okay, let's go. We'll take your car, as mine was playing up a bit this morning,' Birdie said to Twiggy when she returned to the office.

They drove to Harvest Road, a recent development to the west of the town centre. Twiggy was moaning, as usual, about his lack of food, but she only had half an ear on what he was saying.

She'd made a joke of it, but why hadn't Seb told her he was back and that he'd started his own PI company? Or was she being supersensitive? It wasn't like they had a history that went back years. They'd only known each other a few weeks. Okay, they'd clicked and solved the case together, but that didn't mean they were going to repeat the process regularly. Apart from Lacey's case, obviously.

'Birdie.'

She jumped at the sharp tone in Twiggy's voice. 'What?'

'I've asked you the same thing twice. Are you ignoring me?'

'No.'

'Answer my question then?'

'Okay, I had tuned out when you were going on about diets and stuff. What did you ask?'

'It doesn't matter, we're here now,' he said, pulling up outside a red-brick detached house.

'Suit yourself.' She unclipped her seat belt and got out of the car.

There was no garden and the front door backed onto the pavement. Birdie knocked and it was answered by a woman in her late forties, wearing a grey trouser suit, pink shirt and black pumps.

'Hello?'

'Mrs Dennis?'

'Yes.'

'I'm DC Bird and this is DC Branch from Market Harborough CID, we're here to talk about the incident you reported which happened at the weekend.'

'I was expecting you. Come on through to the lounge.'

They followed her into a large square room with modern furnishings and sat on the light grey sofa. Birdie pulled out her notebook and pen.

'Please could you tell us exactly what happened.'

'Yes. It was really scary. It was Saturday night. I'd been out with a friend shopping in Leicester for the day and didn't arrive home until late. I couldn't face cooking. The kids were out, and my husband wasn't feeling well, so I went out for a takeaway. It was around eight o'clock, I think. There wasn't much traffic, and I drew up to the lights on Welland Road when a man ran over and jumped in front of my car and banged on the windscreen. At the same time someone tugged at the door handle.' She shuddered.

'What happened next?' Birdie asked, while scribbling down her notes.

'Well ... thank God I'd locked myself in. The man standing in front of the car banged the windscreen again and adrenaline must have kicked in because I rammed the car into reverse and hit the accelerator until I was away from them.'

'What did they do?' Twiggy asked.

'Ran off down Farndon Road.'

'What did *you* do?'

'Pulled into the side of the road and called my husband. He stayed on the phone while I turned around and drove home. I was going to contact the police, but it was late and it wasn't like they'd done anything, so I waited.'

'Can you describe these men to me?' Birdie asked.

'One was tall, looked at least six feet, and the other short. Around five feet five. He wasn't much taller than my car. They were wearing balaclavas and hoodies. From their build and the way they were jumping about, it made me think they were young men. Maybe late teens, early twenties.'

The same as the other victims. But, again, nothing to properly identify them.

'When you say *jumping about*, do you mean agitated, as if they'd taken drugs?'

'Sort of. It's difficult to tell.'

'Were they wearing gloves?'

'Yes.'

No fingerprints. Same as before.

'Is there anything else you can tell us that might help catch them?'

'The taller of the two had a limp. It was his left leg. I noticed it when they ran away.'

'Was he the man who tried to open the door, or the one in front of the car?'

'He was the one who came up to the front.'

'Is there anything else you noticed that might be of help to us?'

'No. It all happened so quickly. I'm sorry if I've wasted your time.'

'You haven't. If anything else springs to mind, here's my card. Call me anytime.' Birdie handed it to the woman.

They left the house and returned to the car.

'If she'd have told us when it happened, we might have found them wandering the streets. Now, we're still no closer to identifying them. Apart from the limp which could've been done if he'd jumped awkwardly in front of her.' Twiggy banged his fist on the steering wheel.

'Are you kidding me?' Birdie stared at him.

Hadn't he realised?

'What?'

'This is the best lead we've had, so far. They ran off down Farndon Road. There are cameras there, unlike any other place they've carjacked. Drive us back to the station so we can get hold of the CCTV footage.'

## Chapter 5

Seb settled himself at a table in the corner of the pub and picked up the menu he'd brought over. He quite fancied the beer and game pie, which he'd ordered when he was last there.

Despite his life changing so much since he'd seen Birdie, he was already feeling at home in his new surroundings. Living in the country and being away from the hustle and bustle of London was enjoyable. After Birdie and he had solved the case, and Sarah had asked him to move in, he'd returned to London to sort everything out with his flat in Notting Hill. He'd decided not to rent it out but instead arranged for his neighbour to monitor it for him, so he could use it anytime he came to the city for a visit. He'd also been to see his parents and explained to them he'd left the police force after his special squad had been disbanded. His mother already knew what had happened and, much to his surprise, she'd kept his secret so he could explain to his father, Viscount Worthington, in person.

His father's reaction had been predictable. He'd been

delighted that Seb was no longer in the force, not considering it to be a suitable profession for him, but he wasn't so pleased when Seb had refused to work on the family estate in Winchester alongside his older brother, Hubert. He hadn't mentioned his new company to his parents or his work with Rob. They wouldn't approve because it was too close to police work.

Seb would be eternally grateful that it was Hubert who was in line to inherit the family title, as it left him free to follow his own path. Although the last time he'd spoken to his brother, he'd sounded a little strange and distracted. Most unlike the normally positive and outgoing person he was. Next time Seb was in Winchester, he'd have a chat with him. But it might not be until Christmas when they all got together for their traditional family celebrations.

Seb's father had been surprised that he'd moved into Sarah's house, and even more taken aback that his niece had gone traveling around the world. He'd kept away from her during the scandal relating to her dead husband, and Seb suspected he was feeling guilty. He wasn't a mean man but was cognisant of how his behaviour could affect his charity work and the public's perception of the aristocracy.

As soon as Seb moved into Rendall Hall, four weeks ago, Sarah immediately left for South America and was currently exploring in Machu Picchu. Her twin sons didn't mind him being there and had visited him once, so far, and they'd talked. Despite their shock at finding out what their father had done, they'd pumped Seb for as much information as they could regarding the case and what was going to happen when it reached court.

Sarah had kept in touch regularly, asking for an update on how everything was going. Rendall Hall, her home, was large, and Seb mainly confined himself to the kitchen and the drawing room. He'd also taken over the study, which was a lovely room with a beautiful outlook and a perfect place to work.

'Oh, here you are.' Birdie's voice interrupted his thoughts, and he glanced up to see her standing beside the table, smiling, a drink in her hand.

He glanced at his watch. 'Not bad. You're only fifteen minutes late.'

'I knew you'd be impressed. I tried extra hard to be here at a reasonable time. It's great to see you.' She placed her drink on the table and walked around to where he sat, giving him a tight hug. Birdie didn't do handshakes. She then sat opposite him. 'I'm glad to see you dressed for the occasion.'

'What do you mean?' he said, frowning.

'Don't you possess any jeans, or T-shirts, or sweatshirts? I thought you were always so smart when you were here before because you'd brought no casual clothes with you, as you weren't expecting to stay long. What's your excuse now, when I assume you have most of your wardrobe with you?'

He had on a pair of trousers and an open-necked shirt. It seemed casual enough to him.

'I have jeans,' he said, realising that his voice sounding a little defensive. 'I wear them when taking Elsa for a walk, but not for going out in the evening.'

'You know I'm only joking, don't you? You look fine.' She smirked. 'You're so easy to wind up.'

'Only by you.' He picked up his pint and took a swallow.

'That's because you usually hang out with the oldies and not young people like me.'

'I'd like to remind you there's only twelve years

between us, and yet you talk like I've got one foot in the grave.'

'I'm mid-twenties and you're knocking on forty ... work it out for yourself. For me it's having a good time and for you it's cocoa, slippers and a good book in front of the fire.'

He wouldn't mention that she'd almost got it right, or he'd never live it down.

'From your perspective, twenty-six is mid-twenties, yet thirty-eight is knocking on forty. How did you work that out? And I take exception to the cocoa and slippers. The rest I can live with.'

'So easy ... So easy.' She leant forward and gave him a playful punch on the arm.

'Why don't you tell me what's been happening in your life since we last saw each other.'

'Not a lot, really. Cricket's going well and we won our last two matches. Thanks to me making a century both times. You should've seen me. I was on fire.' She gave a pretend cricket swing in mid-air.

'Tell me when your next match is, and I'll come and watch.'

'Two weeks on Sunday, we're playing at the leisure centre on the A508.'

'I'll be there. Are you any further with the hunt for your birth mother?'

The smile on her face disappeared. Should he not have asked?

'No. The Adoption Contact Register wouldn't even tell me the date she got in touch with them to say she wasn't to be contacted. I've decided not to rush it and will keep digging away when I can. Work's crazy busy because Rambo's broken his leg, so we're getting loads of overtime, hence why

Sarge wouldn't let me reopen Lacey's case.' She shook her head, clearly frustrated. 'Now it's your turn. Tell me everything, including the real reason you haven't been in touch with me, considering you've been here for a month already.'

The *real* reason. He wasn't sure himself, although he had suspicions.

'The time got away with me. I've been working hard on Rob's investigation.'

'Lame excuse,' Birdie said, rolling her eyes. 'Do you want to know what I think?'

'I'm assuming that's a rhetorical question because you're going to tell me whatever I say.' He sat back in his chair and waited for her response.

'I'll say one thing for you. You're a quick learner.' She took a sip of her drink. 'You didn't tell me you'd moved up here because you were worried that I'd try to force you into letting me help with your PI work and you like to work alone. Am I right? Or am I right?'

She was right.

'It didn't work, though, did it? As you contacted me with a case for *us* to consider despite not even knowing I was here.'

'Touché,' she said. 'Anyway, before we discuss Lacey, tell me more about what you're doing for Rob. Is it secret government stuff? I promise not to blab.'

'It wouldn't be secret then, would it?' he said, laughing. 'I've already told you, it's research, and very similar to the work I was doing before my squad got disbanded, except I don't go out anywhere. There's nothing else to say about it.'

'Sounds really boring,' she said, doing a fake yawn and patting her mouth.

'It's not too bad.'

'Really?'

'Okay, it's boring. But it's *Clifford Investigation Services'* first paid job and I need the money.'

'Since when was that an issue for you?'

'Contrary to what you believe, I can't live on fresh air, and the supermarket doesn't take IOUs.'

'You'll need to keep working for Rob while helping me on this case, then. There's no payment.'

She was acting as if he'd already agreed to help. Was she right? Or was he going to turn her down? A moot point. Not only could he not see himself turning her down, because if it was something she was concerned about he trusted that it needed investigating, but he was itching to do something more exciting.

'Tell me more about it.'

'As you know, the investigation went nowhere. It came to a dead end, other than a few creeps who came forward, as they usually do, claiming that she was theirs. But we soon sifted them out.'

'How did you do that?' He leant forward slightly.

'By not revealing everything. When Lacey was found she had a cardboard sign hanging around her neck with the words, *Speak No Evil* written on it in felt-tip pen. We deliberately kept it hidden from the media so we could flush out anyone who pretended to know her.'

He nodded slowly. 'That's interesting. Do you know where the saying comes from?'

'I'd assumed the Bible. Is that wrong?'

'It's a common assumption to make but, yes, it is incorrect.'

'And I'm guessing you know the truth.'

'Originally it was a Japanese saying, and it was part of *see no evil, hear no evil, speak no evil*. It meant that a person should avoid anything evil. In the West, it's been given a different interpretation. It means turning a blind eye to something that's legally or morally wrong. See what I'm getting at?'

'You think Lacey might have witnessed something that's legally and morally wrong? And the sign was a reminder for her to ignore it?'

'It's a possibility. Although the person who placed the sign around her neck might have believed it had a religious connotation and that Lacey shouldn't do anything bad. Whatever the interpretation, it's certainly important to consider.'

'Lacey's silent for much of the time, could that be related?'

'Do you mean now, after what she witnessed, or has she always been like that?'

'She's quiet but since the incident even more so.'

'Is she still affected by it?'

'She's calmed down a lot, but she's not totally back to how she was. Anyone who doesn't know her might not tell there's any difference because she's always so quiet and seldom speaks. But I can, even though she doesn't articulate her feelings.'

He shook his head. 'The poor child.'

'So, now you know why I need your help. We worked well together last time. This will be no different. Trust me.'

It certainly wouldn't be boring, that was one thing he was sure of.

'I'd like to meet Lacey before making my decision. Is that possible?'

'Yes, but it's too late now because she'll be in bed. Plus, we haven't eaten yet. How about we go around to my aunt's house tomorrow? I finish work at five and will go straight there. I'll give you the address and you can come around a bit later, at six, to give me time to talk to Lacey and prepare her. Is that okay?'

'Perfect. And now I'm going to do my mind-reading act.' He picked up the menu and stared at it. 'Medium rare steak and chips, hold the salad for you.'

'Got it in one,' she said, her lips turning up into an enormous smile.

## Chapter 6

Birdie sat next to Lacey and took hold of her tiny hand. 'I'd like to talk to you about something, is that okay?'

'Yes,' the little girl answered, her voice so quiet Birdie had to strain to hear.

'A friend of mine is coming round soon, and he'd like to meet you.' Birdie looked into the pale blue saucer-shaped eyes which seemed far too large for Lacey's tiny face. 'His name is Seb, and he's a kind man. I'm going to be with you all the time. You can sit next to me while he's here. Is that all right with you?'

'Yes.'

'I have to warn you he's very tall, and you might not have seen anyone so big before. But you remember the book we've read about the Big Friendly Giant?' Lacey nodded. 'Well, he's like that and he's also very kind, too. I've told him what a lovely little girl you are, and that's why he asked to meet you.'

Lacey gave a tentative smile and looked over at Catherine, who was smiling back at her. When Birdie had first mentioned to her aunt about Seb coming over, so they could look into Lacey's background again, she hadn't been sure in case it turned out to be detrimental. Birdie had convinced her they wouldn't do anything to harm Lacey, they only had her interests at heart.

'Do you need the toilet before Mr Clifford arrives?' Auntie Catherine asked Lacey.

The girl nodded, jumped off the sofa and ran out of the room, heading towards the downstairs cloakroom.

'Don't worry, Auntie Catherine,' Birdie said, witnessing the look of anguish on her face.

'I hope we're doing the right thing.'

'We are. You saw how Lacey was on Saturday when she was shocked by whatever she'd seen. How's she ever going to move forward in life with this hanging over her? Part of that means trying to discover where she came from.'

'You're right.'

'Seb's a good guy but I must warn you, he's not like us.' She hadn't intended telling her aunt too much about him in advance in case it put her off letting him come round to meet Lacey.

'What do you mean *he's not like us*?' she asked, frowning.

'Several reasons. First, he's an aristocrat. His father's a viscount. So he speaks really posh.'

'And you've only just told me this now? For goodness' sake, Birdie. What's he going to think when I give him a cup of tea in one of our mugs? I know they're china, but they're only ordinary. I should've got out the best cups and saucers but it's too late now because it will all need washing. It hasn't been used in ages. I don't believe it. He—'

'Don't be daft, Auntie,' Birdie said, interrupting, before her aunt got herself into a state. 'He's not going to expect special treatment. He used to be a police officer, remember, so you don't have to be on your best behaviour or act any different from how you always do.'

Her aunt expelled a breath. 'Okay, I feel a little better now. You said *several* reasons. What else haven't you told me?'

'This will blow your mind. He's got this weird memory thing going on. He remembers every single thing he's ever seen, and everything that's ever happened to him in the whole of his life. It's ridiculous.'

'Like a photographic memory.'

'No, that's what people think. Me too, until he explained it. It's HSAM, which stands for highly superior something or other. You probably won't see it in action while he's here, but I thought I'd tell you because it makes him special and very interesting.'

'You're clearly very fond of him.' Her aunt tilted her head to one side, a tiny smile on her lips.

'Yes, but not in that way, if that's what you mean. He's so different from anyone else I've worked with. And, knowing Seb, he'd say the same about me, too. We made an excellent team the last time, and I'm sure we will again.'

'I'm looking forward to meeting him but if I'm not convinced he's going to help, then we're not going through with it.'

'I get it. After you've met him, if you don't want us to investigate, then we won't. Having said that, I know you'll like him. You'll see that between us we'll do our best and won't do anything to upset Lacey.'

'Are you planning to interview her?'

'No. It wouldn't be fair to her. There's no need …'

She stopped mid-sentence as Lacey ran back into the lounge.

'Okay, love?' Catherine said. 'Sit yourself down next to Birdie. Mr Clifford will be here in five minutes.'

At six on the dot the doorbell rang.

'A man after my own heart who realises the importance of punctuality, I'm liking him already,' her aunt said, staring directly at her.

Like Birdie's parents, her Auntie Catherine had that mad *gotta be on time* vibe going on. Hardly surprising as she was Birdie's mum's sister and their parents had been the same. It was certainly a trait that travelled down the generations.

'You'll be pleased to know that he's nothing like me in that respect and is always on time, if not early.' She turned to Lacey who was sitting ramrod straight next to her, hands tightly clutched together in her lap. 'I'm going to let Seb in now. You stay here with Auntie Catherine, and don't worry. Remember what I told you. He's very nice. Okay?'

'Yes,' she said.

Birdie left the room and opened the front door. Seb was standing on the doorstep, peering down at her. 'Come in. Before we go into the lounge, I want to warn you that Lacey's a little worried. Auntie Catherine as well. But I've told them you're a nice person, despite some of your strange little ways.'

'My what?'

'Only joking. Let's go inside.' She led him into the lounge and closed the door behind them. 'Lacey, Auntie Catherine, this is my friend Sebastian Clifford. Known as Seb.'

Seb took a single step towards Lacey so he was at least ten feet away from her. Birdie approved. He clearly realised getting too close would scare her.

'Hello, Lacey, it's very nice to meet you.' He turned immediately to her aunt. 'Nice to meet you, too, Mrs Cooper.' He held out a hand and her aunt stood and shook it.

'Please, call me Catherine. Take a seat.' She gestured to the other easy chair beside the sofa, where Birdie and Lacey were sitting.

'Thank you.' He smiled at Catherine and Birdie could see her immediately relax. Seb had that way about him. Not only was he a good-looking man, but he had a disarming way about him which seemed to put people at their ease. Unless you were Twiggy. But he hadn't got to know Seb properly.

'Birdie tells me you're living in Harborough. Where about?' Catherine asked.

'I'm staying on the outskirts of East Farndon in a house belonging to my cousin while she's travelling overseas. She's currently in South America. I don't know where she's planning to go next.'

'I've always wanted to travel, but life got in the way, and we never got around to it. Maybe when we retire, we will. I've heard parts of South America are breathtaking. Have you been?'

'Yes, in my gap year I travelled there and also to Asia and the Pacific Islands. I loved it.'

'I didn't know you'd gone to all those places,' Birdie said. 'Then again, you don't know everything about me. Which is probably good, isn't it?'

Birdie glanced down at Lacey who was sitting as still as a statue, and she took hold of her hand. 'Maybe we should go travelling overseas together when you're older. What do you think? We'd have a great time exploring and visiting all those historic places.'

Lacey nodded.

'Who'd like some tea?' Catherine said.

'That would be lovely, thank you,' Seb replied.

'Would you like to help me get everything ready, Lacey? I can't manage it all on my own.'

'Okay,' Lacey said, following Birdie's aunt out of the room.

'What do you think?' Birdie said to Seb once she'd heard them in the kitchen and knew they were out of earshot.

'She's obviously wary of what's going on around her. My niece and nephew couldn't be more different. But, that aside, she has a dignity about her. I could tell by the way she looked at you and your aunt for reassurance that she trusts you both. I understand now, having met her, why you're determined to discover what upset her so much the other day. I also agree that it's important to find out her history because then you can assist in her moving past whatever happened and develop to her full potential.'

Birdie nodded in agreement. He'd got it in one. Not that she'd doubted he would for a second.

'Does that mean you're agreeing to help?'

'It looks like it,' he said shrugging.

She refrained from punching the air, as they had to get Catherine's approval first.

'That's fantastic, now all we need is my aunt's consent. Let's hope you passed the test.'

'Test?'

'Yeah, you didn't think it was all one way, and you had the final decision, did you? If Auntie Catherine objects, then it's a no go.'

'I can live with that,' he said, smiling. 'Will I hear the verdict today, or do I have to wait?'

'I expect it's already being discussed in the kitchen, so with a bit of luck you'll learn shortly. Probably for the best, as I don't want you to lose any sleep worrying over it. You need to be fighting fit so we can begin work tomorrow.'

'You're telling Lacey what you want to do?' He frowned.

'No. That's a stupid idea. But Auntie Catherine will find out her opinion of you.'

'Are you confident I'll pass?'

'Lacey's a really intelligent child and I'm already sure she likes you. I could tell by her reactions while you were talking.'

'Assuming your aunt approves, I'd like to know more about Lacey and how she reacts to situations.'

'That makes sense.'

'What are you doing tomorrow?'

'Working. What else would I be doing?'

'Why don't you come over to the hall when you've finished. I'll make dinner. I know you were desperate to look around when you were there before.'

He wasn't wrong about that. She'd fallen in love with the old hall he was staying at and would love to see more of it.

'Sounds perfect.'

'Can you get hold of the CCTV footage from Saturday around the time around Lacey witnessed something? If we could work out what, or who, she saw that would help.'

'Leave it with me. Expect me around five-thirty tomorrow. You won't regret it. You know you love working with me.'

# Chapter 7

'I want someone on the phones at all times today. DI Curtis is giving a press conference in an hour regarding the carjackings, using the images Twiggy and Birdie found of our culprits. Surely someone will recognise them, even if all we have is a rear view. You can take it in turns,' Sarge said.

'I'll do it,' Birdie said, scanning the room and seeing all eyes were suddenly focused on her. 'What? I don't mind sitting behind the desk sometimes answering the phone.'

'It's unnecessary. You can take it in turns. It's a shame Rambo's not back yet, as he could've done it,' Sarge said.

'Really, I mean it. I'll do it. I'm sure Twiggy won't miss me being with him for one day. It means he won't have me nagging when he wants to make a detour to the nearest bakery.'

'I resent that,' Twiggy said.

'Even if it is true.' She smirked in his direction.

'If that's what you want, then fine. Birdie, you can stay on the phones. I don't have time to debate this.' Sarge frowned, before turning and leaving the office.

'What are you up to?' Twiggy said, once the coast was clear. 'No way would you ever offer to sit on the phones without there being an ulterior motive.'

'I don't know what you mean.' She'd have to tell him eventually but didn't intend to yet, not while there were others around. Not that she didn't trust Sparkle and Tiny because she did. It was more she was worried it would get back to Sarge. Even though he wasn't in the room, she'd have sworn sometimes that he'd bugged the office. How else would he know what they were up to without being told?

'What about when you were on permanent desk duty the other month? You moaned about it non-stop.'

'Because I was being punished for something that wasn't my fault.'

'Oh. Did someone else write-off the police car after driving into a skip?'

'You know what I mean. Anyway, it turned out okay because I ended up working with Clifford on his case and we all know how that ended.'

'That's beside the point. In all the time I've known you, you've never offered to sit on the phones. I know we all have to take our turn, but you hate it and you've always made sure we all know your feelings. So, come on. Spill. I repeat, what are you up to?'

She loved the closeness of being part of a small team, except at times like this, when she wanted to be discreet about what she intended to do. Hiding under the radar was all but impossible in these instances.

After checking whether the others were listening, she leant in towards him and lowered her voice. 'I've got things I want to do today, and it's best you don't know what they are. I don't want you to be incriminated, which you might be if I told you, and then you'd lose your spot as Sarge's favourite.'

Although their boss did like Twiggy, in truth she wasn't sure about him being the favourite, as he treated them all fairly equally. Twiggy was the longest serving on the team, so he often had Sarge's ear. But he wasn't really thought of any differently from the rest of them. Not that she'd tell Twiggy that. She loved winding him up about it because he usually took the bait.

'You drive me mad, sometimes. You're like a child going on about who's favourite. And if Sarge has a favourite, it's not me. If anyone, it's Tiny.' He folded his arms across his chest and glared at her.

'Yeah. No. It's you. Most definitely. I don't know why you don't accept it. I bet you buy him birthday and Christmas presents, don't you? No point in denying it.'

'Give it a rest, Birdie.'

'Whatever. But we can agree on one thing. It's not me. I'm way down the pecking order in this place.'

'Could it be your dislike of rules and your poor time-keeping, do you think?'

'Maybe.' She shrugged.

'You and Sarge have a different type of relationship than the rest of us. You somehow get away with stuff that we don't. Though, it's probably because you do things that none of us would. '

'You're talking rubbish. You do know that, don't you?'

'We're going around in circles. What are you getting yourself involved in now? There's got to be a reason for wanting to stay in the office today.'

'If I tell you, then you've got to swear not to say anything to anyone.'

'Cross my heart,' he replied, doing the sign of a cross with his forefinger against his chest.

'I'm preparing my application for the Sergeants' exam,' she whispered.

Twiggy's jaw dropped. 'Why didn't you tell me? Are you sure you're ready, because not wanting to put you down … but … I …'

'Oh my God, Twiggy. Look at your face. Do you really think I'd be applying? You're such a pillock.'

'I knew you didn't mean it. Anyway, I'm over your secrecy. If you don't want to tell me, then don't. I'm going.'

She'd upset him. It was written all over his face.

'Okay. This really is the truth. I'm working with Seb on Lacey's case. I'm doing it on the side and I thought I'd use my time today to check out what happened last Saturday when she had that shock. The one I told you about.'

'Clifford. I should've guessed.' He turned up his nose.

'I don't know why you have a problem with him.'

'I think he's trouble, that's all. How come he's back here, anyway?'

'He's moved down to East Farndon for a while. I couldn't believe my luck when I found out. So now you know. Okay?'

'No, it's not okay, but you won't listen to anything I have to say. Be careful and don't let Sarge find out what you're up to, or you'll end up on desk duty for your entire career.'

'I know what I'm doing. I'm not stupid, you know.'

'Stupid, no. Headstrong, yes. I hope you find something. I feel sorry for the kid.'

'Thanks, Twig. I'll see you later.'

He pulled on his jacket and left the office, closely followed by Sparkle and Tiny.

With Sarge in a meeting and the rest of them out she was free to do whatever she wanted. She glanced at her watch, it was only a few minutes after nine, and the press conference wasn't until ten, so that gave her plenty of time before the phones rang.

She opened her email and sent a request to the Leicestershire secure control room, which operated twenty-four-seven, for the CCTV footage from Saturday around the time when Lacey went into shock from what she'd witnessed. If they could identify what it was the child had seen, it would make their job so much easier.

She clicked send and then sat back in her chair. What should she do next? There was always the never-ending stack of paperwork relating to cases they were working on. Except she might not have much time, as the phone would ring following the press conference.

Or ... she could use the time to do some research into her birth mother. All she had from her birth certificate was a name. *Kim Bakirtzis.* She'd been living in Leicester when Birdie had been born, twenty-six years ago. If only she could use the PNC database, her search would be so much easier, but she could be fired for using it without good reason. And as much as she wanted to know about her mother, there was no criminal offence involved and so she couldn't justify it. Fortunately, there were the online electoral registers which were available to everyone.

Bakirtzis was an unusual surname and after looking it up on the register she came up with a list of four people with that name who lived in the Leicester area. All she had to do was contact them to find out if any of them knew of her mother. She couldn't believe her luck when she managed to find phone numbers for all of them using both the landline and mobile phone directories.

Her excitement was short-lived, because the first three she called had no knowledge of a *Kim*. Despondency washed over here. Was she wasting her time?

She keyed in the number for the last name on the list and a man answered.

'Hello, my name's Lucinda Bird from Market Harborough. I'm trying to trace someone called Kim Bakirtzis, can you help? Is she by any chance a member of your family?'

She cringed at the sound of her real name, which no one was allowed to use, but she couldn't say DC Bird, as it wasn't a police matter, nor could she use the name Birdie, as it seemed too familiar.

'I'm sorry, no, she isn't.'

Birdie's heart sank. 'Thank you—'

'But I do know who you mean because people often asked if we were brother and sister as we went to the same school,' he interrupted.

Birdie grabbed a pen, her heart thumping in her chest. Was this her mother? A few more questions and she might find out.

'What school was this?'

'Why do you want to know? Are you the police?'

'I am actually a police officer, but this isn't official police business.'

She might not be allowed to play the police card, but him knowing that was her occupation couldn't do any harm.

'Okay. The school was St Augustine's. Kim was in the year below me.'

'What dates were you there?'

She didn't know the exact age of her mother, but assuming she'd been a teenager when she'd given birth, would put her at school in the early nineties.

'From 1989 to 1996.'

The dates fit. It could definitely be her mother.

'Did she have red hair, by any chance?'

54

'No, she didn't.'

Damn. But that didn't mean this wasn't the right Kim.

'Do you have her contact details?' She sucked in a breath and held it.

'Not now. The family moved to Canada in the mid-nineties.'

She gripped the edge of her desk. Canada? It would be impossible to find anyone there.

'Do you know where they lived when they were here?'

'Yes. Saffron Lane. Number 981, I think.'

Okay, so her mother might now be abroad, but at least she now had a lead, and knew more now than she had only a few moments ago.

'Thank you very much for your help.'

Someone at their old address, or who lived close by, might remember the family. She called up Google Maps, checked the location, and then went into an online database to find the name and contact details of the people who lived in the house presently, and those from next door.

There was no landline number listed for 981, but there was for next door. It rang for ages, and she was about to hang up when someone answered.

'Hello,' a woman with a thin and breathy voice said. She sounded very old.

'This is Lucinda Bird from Market Harborough. I'm trying to trace the Bakirtzis family, I believe they lived in the house next door to you until the mid-nineties. They had a daughter called Kim. Do you remember them?'

'Oh, yes, I knew them very well. A lovely family. They moved to Canada a long time ago, but they still send me a Christmas card every year.'

Her eyes widened. This woman knew her mum and maybe where she now was.

'Thank you, Mrs ...' She paused.

'Davis. But you can call me Marie, dear.'

'I'd love to come round for a chat about them, if I may, Marie.'

'Um …'

'I understand you might be reluctant as you know nothing about me. But I am a police officer, even though this isn't an official matter. I can show you my police ID when I get there to prove who I am.'

'In that case, I'd be more than happy to talk to you. I've been on my own since my Rodney died and few people visit these days. I'm going away for a couple of days tomorrow to see my son. Is it okay to wait until I come back?'

As much as Birdie would like to rush off to see her straight away, waiting a few more days really wouldn't matter.

'Yes, that's perfect. Do you know the people who live next door now?'

'The Robinsons. They moved in last year. They're friendly people with three teenage children, but I don't see them much because they're always so busy.'

Damn. They won't know anything. But at least this woman does.

'May I see you on Sunday, if you're back from your son's?'

'Yes, I'll be home then. Come round in the morning, and we'll have elevenses together. I might be getting old but, according to my grandchildren, I still make the best chocolate cake.'

'My favourite. I can't wait to try it.'

Birdie had no time to ponder their conversation as after saying goodbye to Marie, her email pinged with the CCTV footage. After taking a quick look, she downloaded it to her phone, not wanting to risk checking it in the office in case Sarge came in and spotted what she was doing. She'd wait until after work when she was with Seb.

## Chapter 8

Birdie drove through East Farndon until reaching the edge of the village where Rendall Hall, the place Seb now lived, was situated. She turned up the long winding drive which led to the main house. Either side of her were well-maintained fields with sheep in them. She'd visited and fallen in love with the hall when they were working for Seb's cousin, Sarah, investigating the death of her husband, Donald.

She parked on the gravel at the front of the 17$^{th}$ century stone house and knocked on the door, using the large brass knocker. After a couple of minutes, Seb answered. His dog Elsa bounded up behind him and poked her nose around his legs. On seeing Birdie, she got very excited and pushed in front of Seb.

Birdie crouched down to Elsa's level and rubbed behind her ears. 'Hello beautiful, I bet you're loving it here. This is such an amazing place.' She stood and looked at Seb. 'I hope you're still going to give me a tour. All I saw before was the kitchen and the drawing room.' She stepped inside into the large rectangular hall, admiring its vastness.

'Later,' Seb said, as he closed the front door behind her.

'I assumed you'd want to eat straight away. I've made us a chilli.'

'Perfect. I haven't had time to eat since breakfast, it's been so busy.'

'Aren't you busy every day?'

'Well, yes. But today I volunteered to stay in and answer the phones, which were ringing off the hook all day after a press conference about a spate of carjackings we're investigating. We finally have some CCTV images of the culprits which we put out there.'

'You volunteered to answer the phones?'

'Don't you start. Yes, I did. But that was because of our work. I got hold of the CCTV footage from when I was out with Lacey.'

'Was there anything of use on there?'

'I haven't had a proper look yet, in case I got caught. I downloaded it to my phone and also brought the case file with me, which I sneaked out of the office.'

'That's a splendid start, well done. We'll look after dinner.'

'I've also got a lead in the hunt for my birth mother,' she said, dying to share it with someone. The *someone* having to be him as he was the only person who knew about her search.

'That's excellent.'

'I spoke with an elderly neighbour who remembers the family. It turns out that the family moved to Canada a long time ago and she keeps in touch with them. I'm going to see her on Sunday morning, after she gets back from visiting her son, to find out more about them.'

'That was most fortuitous.'

'I know, right? I'm hoping she'll have an address and some photos for me to see.'

'So, you're definitely not giving up?'

'No way. Why did you ask me that? You know why I need to find out about my mother. And you never know, she might have come back after being overseas. Anything could have happened. All I know is I'm not giving up searching.'

'Good for you. I'm here anytime you wish to talk it through.'

'Thanks. I want to find out if my real mother had time-keeping issues like me.'

'You believe it's genetic?' He frowned.

'You don't?'

'I don't know.'

'Well, think about this. My mum and dad are obsessive about timekeeping, and my brothers are, too.'

'But you're not.'

'Exactly.'

'Have you ever thought that you deliberately engage in poor timekeeping at a subconscious level because you're trying to distance yourself from them.'

She had. But had dismissed it.

'Why would I do that? I love my parents. They're the best. And so are my brothers.'

'Because you know you're different.'

'Well, maybe. But I'd never want to hurt my parents. It was bad enough when I told them about searching for my birth mother. They said nothing, but I know they were unhappy.'

'Are you keeping them abreast of your findings?'

'No. If they ask I'll tell them, if they don't, I won't. Is dinner ready, yet?' she asked, not wanting to dwell on her parents or her subconscious any longer.

'Yes. Follow me through to the kitchen.'

The table had been set, and she sat at one end

watching as Seb dished up the meal and placed it in front of her.

'Mmm. Smells delicious,' she said, picking up her fork and having a mouthful.

'I bought some cider. Would you like a bottle?'

'Please. I'll have to come round more often with this sort of service. It's lovely, by the way.'

'I'll give you the recipe, if you like. It's very easy.'

'Thanks, but no thanks. It would be wasted on me with my total lack of culinary skill. The most I can do is bake fairy cakes.'

'You could always learn. I'm more than happy to teach you,' he offered.

'One day, maybe. In the meantime, I'll let you continue cooking for me.'

After they'd eaten, she picked up the plates and headed for the sink.

'Leave that. We'll look at the CCTV footage,' Seb said.

'Where's your laptop? I'll forward it to you.'

'It's in the study.'

She followed him, with Elsa leading the way. How did she know where they were going?

The study was huge and there were more bookcases than she'd ever seen in a single room. They were filled with books. A large desk was in the middle with a view of the garden from out of the French windows. On the desk was an open laptop, a photo in a frame of Sarah, Donald and their children, and what looked like an inkstand.

'I could work in here. It's so much better than the station with our basic, no-frills, offices.'

'I agree. It's a lovely environment.'

'Even if what you're doing is boring?'

'It helps to take the edge off,' he said smiling.

'Has the email come through yet?'

SALLY RIGBY

'Yes.' He uploaded the footage to the laptop and pulled over a second chair so they could look at the screen together.

'Where was this taken?' he asked, as the pair of them peered at the activity in front of them.

'These are the cameras in High Street, and we came out of this shop here.' She pointed to herself and Lacey. 'There we are standing on the pavement outside.'

'Oh, yes, I can see you now. It was a busy day, which won't make it easy for us to find out what it was she saw.'

'Look at Lacey now. She's peering diagonally opposite and down the road a bit. What has she seen?' She squinted, but still wasn't able to work it out.

'A person?'

'If it was then did they see her?'

'Not necessarily.'

'You're right. And if they had, they might have reacted, which we should be able to see on screen.'

'There are no people looking in your direction, only cars going up and down the street.'

'So, let's assume that if it was a person they didn't notice Lacey. But what if it was a car, she was looking at? It would have been moving very slowly for her to spot it.'

'The cars aren't going fast because of the amount of traffic. Would she have recognised a number plate?'

'I don't know. She can read, but that's different from remembering a registration plate number. I think it's more likely that she recognised a person. But who?'

'Don't dismiss it being a car, yet. Rewind the footage so we can see which cars were around and check them.'

'If only we could ask her, it would make this so much easier. But we can't.'

Birdie rewound the footage, and they stared at all the cars going past in both directions.

'It would be a good idea to record them. It's a shame we can't see the registration plates from this angle. Are there other cameras we can look at which might give us a better view?'

'There's one on the opposite side of the road but it might not help because it doesn't capture everything. The joys of living in a small town. We don't have cameras like you get in London where no one can hide from them.'

'There are still ways of avoiding them, if you know what you're doing. Note down the make, model and colour of these cars and ask your aunt if she's noticed any of them hanging around before. In case they were being followed.'

'Do you think that's likely?'

'Anything is likely.'

'Yes, but if that was the case then why hasn't Lacey reacted before?' She clenched her fists. 'This is so frustrating.'

'It's a needle in a haystack so we shouldn't exclude anything. Talk me through the investigation.'

Birdie picked up the thick file and opened it. 'There was a case conference and Lacey was placed into temporary foster care while they were trying to trace her family. Copies of reports from the various agencies involved are in here.'

'I remember the national appeal. It was on TV, on social media, in the papers. You couldn't have done more.'

'I know. But it all came to nothing. Officers went into the shops in the area to see if anyone had spotted anything. But no. Loads of interviews were taken with people in the area, but they all came up blank. Missing persons databases were checked, and international agencies involved, but it's almost as if Lacey appeared out of nowhere. Which we know is nonsense.'

'Was Lacey's DNA taken and checked against the PNC?'

'No, it wasn't. It couldn't be done without a judge for the Family Court signing off on it, and we didn't go down that route because of the cost implications. You know how expensive DNA testing is. Budgets are stretched enough as it is.'

'It's the same in all forces. Were there any other leads?'

'As I've already told you, people came forward pretending to be her parents, the sick bastards, but we knew straight away they were lying because of the sign around her neck.'

'I assume that was dusted for prints.'

'Yes, and there were no forensics we could use.'

'I'd like to speak to Catherine, away from her home and any distractions. Will she come here, do you think, so we can have an undisturbed in-depth conversation?'

'Why can't you do this at her house?'

'I'd rather do it without Lacey being there.'

'Okay, that makes sense. It's easier to get my aunt to come to you, than take Lacey out somewhere because she's much better in her own surroundings. I'll offer to look after her in case my uncle won't be around.'

'We should also interview some of those involved in the original case conference. I'm assuming names and contact details are in the file.'

'Yes, I'll leave them with you.'

'Perfect. You make the arrangements with Catherine and we'll go from there.'

## Chapter 9

'Lacey, I'm going out for a while and Birdie's going to look after you. Is that okay?' Catherine crouched down beside the child, who was sitting quietly reading.

The little girl looked at her and smiled. 'Yes.'

Catherine stood and turned to Birdie. 'I might be gone for a couple of hours.'

'We'll be fine. I've got lots planned for us to do. To start, we'll do some baking. We'll make those little cakes with sultanas in them which we both love. What do you think, Lacey? Would you like that?'

'Yes, please.' Lacey's eyes lit up. Birdie was the only person to elicit such a response from her. Catherine had no idea what magic her niece possessed, but she'd love to bottle it.

'You know where everything is. Don't forget to clean up after you've finished,' she said, knowing that her words would fall on deaf ears. She didn't mind, if it kept Lacey entertained and took her mind off whatever had happened.

'You know me too well,' Birdie said, laughing.

'You've been the same your whole life,' Catherine said.

'After we've made the cakes, we'll read or watch the telly, so take as long as you like. I'll make Lacey some tea if you're not back.'

'I don't imagine Mr Clifford will want to spend much time with me, as I won't have a lot to tell him.'

She had to admit, and this was only to herself, she was a little nervous going to visit him.

'That's what you think. Seb will have plenty to ask you. He's very thorough.'

'We'll see. Take care, the pair of you. I'll be back later.' She grabbed her coat from the peg by the front door and left the house.

While driving to Rendall Hall, she thought about the strange relationship Birdie had with Sebastian Clifford. Despite only meeting him once, it was obvious how different they were from one another. Being an aristocrat she'd have expected him to be more aloof and uncaring than he clearly was. He must have been the exception. Either that or she was stereotyping. Considering she hadn't met one before, it wouldn't be beyond the realm of possibility. That said, she agreed with Birdie, that he seemed a genuine person, and the fact they were going to reopen Lacey's case and hopefully discover her past, had to be a good thing.

She hoped.

Catherine turned onto the drive that led to the house and when it came into view, she let out a low whistle. The grounds. The house. Everything was spectacular. Birdie hadn't been wrong.

After parking, she walked up the steps and knocked on the door. She waited a while and was about to knock again, when Seb opened it.

Despite having seen him the other day, his presence still

took her breath way. He was huge. And commanding. A very handsome man. Would Birdie and he … no. There was nothing like that between them.

He looked down and smiled.

'Good to see you, Catherine.' He held out his hand, which she shook. She didn't have small hands, but his enveloped hers.

'You, too.'

'Thank you for agreeing to see me. I thought it would be better if we could talk freely away from your home and Lacey.'

'That was a good idea. Even if she was in another room, she might have overheard.'

'I also want to show you some CCTV footage that Birdie has accessed, to see if there's anything of note on there from your perspective. Would you like some coffee, I've made a fresh pot. And then we'll go through to the study and talk.'

'Thank you, that would be lovely.'

She followed him through to the kitchen, admiring everything on the way. It really was a lovely house. Although awful circumstances for him to be there. She'd read about the Donald Witherspoon case and had felt sorry for his family. According to Birdie, they knew nothing about him swindling so many people out of their money.

He poured them both a mug of coffee and passed hers over. Then they headed to the study, where he gestured for her to sit on one of the easy chairs which looked out onto the garden.

'How's Lacey holding up following the incident?' He placed his mug on a coaster on the low coffee table and she did the same.

'She's okay. Still a little more reserved and withdrawn but we're getting there.'

'It's obvious you care for her a great deal. Could you give me some background, if you don't mind, on how you came to be fostering Lacey?' He sat back in the chair, steepled his fingers, and looked directly at her, his whole demeanour relaxed.

Was this his interview technique when in the police? Make someone feel comfortable so they'd tell him exactly what he wanted to know? Or was she overanalysing? It wouldn't be the first time.

'My husband and I couldn't have children, so we fostered. And have done for many years. It was fortunate when Lacey was abandoned that we had space for her.'

'I imagine it was a tough time for everyone as Lacey wasn't communicating.'

'Yes, it definitely was. We'd successfully fostered challenging children in the past, but Lacey was very different. We hadn't encountered a child so uncommunicative before.'

'Birdie is full of praise regarding your success with her.'

She felt the warmth rush up her cheeks. For goodness' sake. She was a grown woman and nearly old enough to be his mother, so why was she blushing at the compliment? She coughed and raised her hand to her mouth trying to hide the colour in her face.

So embarrassing.

'From the beginning I established a rapport with her, even though it wasn't much, so they asked if we'd carry on taking care of her. We did so for six months until the second case conference. We then agreed to foster her permanently.'

'How is Lacey with your husband?'

'She was uncertain about Pete at first. The same as she is with everyone. She accepts him now, but won't interact in the same way she does with me. Or Birdie. Lacey idolises my niece. There's a connection between them that is quite extraordinary.'

'How long did it take for the bond between them to be formed?'

'When we first had Lacey, Birdie visited most days and was very patient with her. It developed from there. It took a little over two months for them to become very close.'

'Perhaps being adopted, Birdie felt she could relate to her,' Seb said.

'Yes, that could be a reason.'

They must be close if Birdie had confided in him. She tended to keep details regarding her adoption private.

'Has Lacey's future been discussed?'

'For the time being she'll remain fostered by us as she needs the stability. There are no plans for her to be put up for adoption, it's far too early for that.'

'What can you tell me about her schooling?'

'She's not at school yet, but I'm a qualified primary school teacher, so I've been teaching her. Her reading's very good and so is her maths. Way above what you'd expect for someone of that age. Wherever she came from, someone taught her well.'

'Does she enjoy learning?'

'That's an interesting question. It's difficult to know, to be honest. One thing I've noticed, is that if she gets anything wrong, she tenses as if expecting to be punished. I always reassure her that making mistakes is a part of learning, but ... whatever happened in her life to silence her like that, we don't know.'

'What else can you tell me about her? Anything which might give us a clue as to where she came from.'

Catherine paused for a moment, thinking through everything about Lacey. 'She likes her routine and gets upset if things are out of sync and not as she expects them to be.'

'Her previous life was likely to have been ordered, and disciplined, I suspect.'

'Yes, I agree.'

'Do you stick to routines outside of the house as well?'

'We go to the library on Thursday. Swimming at the leisure centre on a Sunday morning. And do the food shopping on Tuesday. Any other bits we'll usually buy on a Saturday. So, yes, we do.'

What was he getting at?

'Have you noticed recently anybody following you?'

Now she knew.

'No, not at all. But, I haven't been looking. When we're out my eyes are on Lacey. Not that I think she'll run away, because she always keeps very close to me.'

'With your routine it would be easy for someone to discover what you do regularly.'

'Yes, you're right. The thought hadn't even crossed my mind. Should I have been varying our activities?'

'We don't know if you've been followed, but after what happened last Saturday, it's something to consider. We'll look at the CCTV footage that Birdie accessed and you can see if there's anything, or anyone, familiar to you.'

He walked over to the desk and opened the laptop. He then pulled up another chair, and they both sat and stared at the screen.

'There's Birdie and Lacey,' she said pointing to the screen.

'Yes. Look at the direction Lacey is facing. Can you see anything familiar? A car. Or a person.'

She stared at the footage, but nothing stood out. 'I don't recall seeing any of those cars before. Or any of the people caught on camera, either.'

'Have you asked Lacey what she saw that was so upsetting?'

'I mentioned it to her, but she tuned out and wouldn't answer. I told her that I knew she was very upset and asked if she wanted to talk about it. She shook her head. There was no point pushing it. I knew she wouldn't say anything and it would only end up upsetting her even more.'

'I understand. It sounds like you did the right thing. I've seen the reports from all the participants in the case conference. How successful did you view their interaction with Lacey?'

'Not very, to be honest. They weren't to blame. Lacey wouldn't respond. It made it very difficult for them to assess her properly.'

'I'm planning for Birdie and me to speak to the psychologist and the social worker. It might help gain further insight into the case from a more professional viewpoint.'

'That's a good idea. The more information you can glean the better. Dr Miranda Watkins is the psychologist and I've taken Lacey to her a few times. Stephen Shaw is the social worker, and he's very nice, too.'

'Going back to Lacey, is there anything that you can think of, any routine that she goes through herself, that might give us any clues about her history?'

'I've often thought there was something religious in her past because of the way she sometimes mumbles in her sleep.'

'In what way is this religious?'

'It's the sounds she makes, rhythmic and very much like she's praying, although the words are indecipherable.'

'Have any children you've fostered in the past done this?'

'No. Never. That's why it stood out.'

'Is there anything else about her that comes to mind?'

'Lacey always places her cutlery in a certain way and acts fearful if she does it wrong, or forgets to do it. I would definitely say that wherever she was brought up, she had a strict routine. She wasn't undernourished when we found her, but she wasn't overweight either. Initially, she wouldn't eat sweets or biscuits. Nor did she understand what we meant by having a treat. If anything she feared them. She's much better now, but she doesn't get excited about sweets or chocolate in the way most children do. Make of that what you will.'

'It all adds to the picture of what happened to the child before she was abandoned. Thank you, Catherine, your input has been invaluable.'

'I'm glad to have helped. Let's hope by doing this we're not going to unearth something that will set the child back.'

## Chapter 10

The following day, Seb contacted both the psychologist and the social worker, both of whom were prepared to meet with him to discuss Lacey and her progress. Once appointments were arranged, he called Birdie.

'Morning,' she said.

'Are you at work?'

'Yeah, I've been here since eight-thirty. How did it go yesterday with Auntie Catherine? We couldn't speak when she came home because Lacey was still up.'

'It was a very informative and useful meeting. She gave me some interesting background to the case. She didn't recognise any of the cars in the vicinity and didn't think that they'd been followed, but it was worth having a look.'

'Just because my aunt didn't think they'd been followed doesn't mean they hadn't been. Lacey saw something, or someone, that she knew or she wouldn't have been affected so badly.'

'Yes, there most definitely had to have been something to trigger the response.'

'What's next?'

'I've arranged an appointment with the psychologist for later this morning. Are you able to come with me, by any chance?'

He'd like her there, if possible, because she'd spent a lot of time with the child.

'Yeah, I should be able to. I'll take an early lunch. What time?'

'Eleven-thirty, Roman Way. Dr Watkins is part of a group practice offering psychological and counselling services. I've looked it up on Google Maps and it's easy to find.'

'I'll meet you outside. It'll be interesting to see the psychologist and get her input. According to my aunt, Lacey was always quieter than usual when they had their fortnightly meetings, which must have made it very hard for them to make any progress. But, every little helps, I suppose.'

'Meet me outside at eleven twenty-five.'

'Gotcha. Better go, I've got a lot on today.'

He still had an hour and a half to kill before having to drive into town, so he did some research into children who had been kept in captivity, and what the psychological implications were for them after they'd been discovered.

The number of cases appearing on his screen shocked him. They were from all over the world. According to what he read, what had happened to these children in the past stayed with them for much of their lives, in varying degrees. Some children suffered irreparable damage right into adulthood, whereas others had learnt to deal with it, even though it never totally left them. At present, they didn't know whether Lacey had been kept captive, or what her circumstances were, but if she had been held, he hoped that she'd end up being able to deal with her situation.

At least the young girl was in the right place with Catherine. He'd been exceptionally impressed by the woman's caring attitude but, that aside, there was going to be a long road ahead of them if Lacey was ever to cope in the wider world.

At eleven o'clock, he left Rendall Hall and drove into Market Harborough. The practice was in a 1940s brick and pebble-dashed detached house that had been turned into offices for several counsellors and therapists. Houses either side of it had also been turned into commercial premises.

He stood outside the building and waited beside the low brick wall in front of the entrance. Their appointment wasn't until eleven forty-five, but he'd told Birdie twenty minutes earlier knowing she'd most likely be late.

At eleven thirty-five, feeling vindicated for the decision he'd made, he caught sight of Birdie running down the street. As she reached him, she bent forward and rested her hands on her thighs, gasping for air.

'Say nothing,' she said between breaths. 'I know I'm late. I got stuck on a phone call, and the woman I was talking to went on and on. I couldn't be rude and hang up on her as she potentially had some evidence that would help the case Twiggy and I are working on.'

'These things happen.' He waved his hand dismissively.

'My car's in the supermarket car park as I didn't want to risk there being nothing free around here. I ran non-stop all the way from there.'

'It will keep you fit.'

'I am fit. That's why I play cricket and train.'

'Really?' he said, arching an eyebrow. 'Why are you out of breath now, then?'

'Oh, shut up, and let me recover.' She stood upright

with her hands in her hips, her words sounding less laboured.

'Don't worry, you've got plenty of time to get your breath back as we've still got ten minutes. Our appointment with Dr Watkins isn't until eleven forty-five.'

'You what?' she said, her eyes wide and blazing. 'Why the hell did you tell me eleven-thirty, then?'

'Why do you think?' he said, unable to resist a chuckle.

'I'm glad you find it funny. Because I don't. I nearly killed myself trying to get here and now you say there's another ten minutes. You knew I'd be on time. I'm only late first thing in the morning ... And sometimes in the evening.' She glanced away, her cheeks tinged pink. Whether that was from exertion or embarrassment he wasn't sure.

'You're late for everything, Birdie, which is why I wanted to limit the chance of us not being there on time, considering Dr Watkins had agreed to see us, and we'd be taking time out of her appointment schedule. Appointments that people pay for. Which we're not, as you're no doubt aware.'

'Okay, make me feel guilty, why don't you?' she said narrowing her eyes.

'Not my intention, I can assure you.'

'So you say,' she said, appearing to have recovered from her run. 'Anyway, I'm here now, so let's go in and talk to her.'

He looked at his watch. 'We've still got five minutes. We can wait out here, or go inside and sit in the waiting room. Your choice.'

'We'll stay here and I'll update you on what I'm doing on Sunday. Although ... after how you've just been to me I'm not sure whether I want to share.'

'You know why, and I was vindicated. You were late.'

'Details,' she said, waving her hand. 'Well? Do you want to know, or what?'

'It's entirely up to you. If you wish to tell me what you have planned then I'd be delighted to hear, although I thought you were seeing the woman who lived next door to your birth mother on Sunday morning.'

'How do you know?'

'You told me the other day when you came over to the house. Don't you remember?'

'Bloody hell. I must be losing it. I'd totally forgotten that I'd filled you in on what was happening. I blame you for this.'

'How is it my fault?'

'I didn't forget things before. It's hanging out with older people like you that's done it.'

'I fail to see how you can blame me—'

'I'm joking, you twit. I can't believe you thought I meant it. I must have forgotten we'd talked about it before because of being so wrapped up Lacey's case. Come on. Let's go inside and see the psychologist.'

## Chapter 11

Birdie pushed open the white door to the building and walked into the reception area and up to the desk situated in the centre. Seb followed close behind.

'We have an appointment with Dr Watkins,' she said to the receptionist, a woman of around Birdie's age, who was staring at a computer screen.

'Miranda's office is down the corridor on the right-hand side. You'll see the sign on her door. If you'd like to sit outside in the waiting area, she'll call you in when she's ready.'

They headed down the corridor and into a small room with chairs around the edge. In the centre was an oak coffee table, with magazines on top, and in the far corner was a play area, with two boxes of toys and a play mat on the floor. On the walls were photos of psychologists. She recognised Freud and Carl Jung, and there were also Erikson and Adler, who had their names displayed underneath them.

'Her photographs are of psychoanalytic psychologists. I'm assuming, therefore, that Dr Watkins uses psychodynamic theory when working with children,' Seb said.

'I have no idea, but wouldn't be surprised, as that's a common perspective. Well, from my limited knowledge, which is A level psychology.'

'I studied criminology at university, which included psychology.'

'So, something we have in common, at last,' she said, grinning in his direction.

'We are not totally dissimilar. We ...' He paused and stared at her. 'Another joke?'

'You got it,' she replied, smirking. 'I hope she's not going to be too much longer, in case Sarge starts wondering where I am. As far as he's concerned, most of today I was going to be in the office. Then again, I could always say something came up.'

'As this is meant to be your lunchtime, I'm sure it will be fine.'

'That depends on how long we are.'

The door to the doctor's office opened, and a woman walked out keeping her head bowed. She didn't even look at them, instead kept heading down the corridor.

'It shouldn't be much longer, now,' Seb said.

They sat there for a further five minutes and still weren't called into the office.

Birdie strummed her fingers impatiently on her legs. 'Come on.'

'Be patient.'

'Easy for you to say. I'm—'

Before she could finish her sentence, the door to the office was opened by a tall woman of about fifty, who was wearing a calf-length floral skirt, which was gathered in at the waist, and a long-sleeved cream blouse that was tucked in. 'Mr. Clifford?' she asked, looking directly at Seb.

Seb and Birdie both stood.

'Yes. I'm Sebastian Clifford and this is DC Bird who has accompanied me today.'

'I didn't know the police were reopening the case.'

'I'm not here officially. Lacey is fostered by my aunt, Catherine Cooper,' Birdie said.

'Oh. I see. Come on through to my office.'

They entered the large square room which had a desk in the far corner and in the middle a low table with three chairs around it. Under the window, there were three small beanbags and some toys.

'No couch for your patients to lie on, then?' She cringed at her flippant tone, and didn't dare look at Seb, as she could imagine the expression on his face. She hadn't intended to sound rude.

'No. That's not the way I work. I'm a child psychologist, and we sit and talk. Please take a seat. You said you wanted to discuss Lacey. What would you like to know?'

Birdie glanced at Seb. How much should they tell her?

'As I explained, we're trying to discover where Lacey came from and thought you might be able to give us some help, from a theoretical standpoint, as to what might have happened to her in the past. How many times have you met with Lacey?' Seb asked.

'I saw her when she first came in with social services, a few days after she'd been found, and she was extremely uncommunicative.'

'Could you explain what you mean by this?' Seb asked.

'Lacey didn't look at me once. She kept her head bowed, and her face remained expressionless, no matter what I asked her. It was like she'd gone into her own little world.'

'Would you say she did that as a safety mechanism, and that it was a type of behaviour she'd engaged in before?'

'I would, most definitely, attribute it to protecting herself. Whether she'd done so in the past? I suspect yes, but can't be one hundred per cent sure. I would need Lacey to tell me this herself.'

'How often did you see Lacey after this?'

'Following on from this initial meeting, I saw the child fortnightly. Mrs Cooper would accompany her. This continued for six months. During this time Lacey didn't communicate, but she appeared more relaxed than when I first saw her.'

'Please, can you be more specific?' Seb asked.

'She no longer kept her head lowered, although didn't make eye contact with me. She wouldn't move from Mrs Cooper's side, or play with any toys when I suggested she might like to. But I could tell she was listening when I spoke and she was paying attention to what was going on around her.'

'Did you witness her going into her own little world at all, after that first time?' Seb asked.

'Only once, when I asked Mrs Cooper to go out into the waiting room so I could speak to Lacey alone. It didn't work, and I only tried it that one time. I was concerned that she might revert back to her previous state if I did it again.'

'You said these meetings went on for six months. What happened after that?'

'At that time we had a case conference, and it was decided to make the foster arrangement with Mrs Cooper permanent. To have taken Lacey away at that point would have been disastrous.'

'Have you seen Lacey since?'

'No, I haven't. A decision was made to leave it in the hands of Mrs Cooper and the social worker to decide when to bring her to see me again. DC Bird, you mentioned Mrs Cooper is your aunt. From your perspective, how would you say Lacey is doing now?'

'She has made good progress in some areas. My aunt and I think she's a very gifted child. Her reading age is way above her actual age, assuming she's around seven. My aunt didn't teach her to read, she already knew how. She'd pick up books we read to her and then start reading to herself, saying the words so quietly, we could hardly hear.'

'So she's speaking now?' Dr Watkins said, leaning forward in her chair and giving Birdie her full attention.

'Not really. She doesn't chat and when she does speak she gives mainly one-word answers, but she certainly understands everything.'

'This is good progress, indeed. It might be time for me to resume sessions with Lacey. I'll contact Stephen Shaw, her social worker. Does she play with toys?'

'Not particularly. She colours and draws pictures. She also loves baking, which I do with her sometimes.'

In her peripheral vision, she could see Seb frowning. He was no doubt wondering how she was able to bake, considering how inept she was in the kitchen.

'Some children don't enjoy playing with toys, so that's not necessarily an indicator of any underlying problems. Gifted children would much rather seek out the company of adults and engage with them in a more mature way.'

'That definitely fits in with our view of her ability. But the fact she hardly talks does concern us.'

'What can you tell us about abandoned children in general?' Seb asked. 'Have you worked with any in the past?'

'Except for Lacey, none directly. My knowledge is mainly through research and reading articles. Children who have been abandoned often struggle to form healthy relationships and this can lead to emotional and behavioural problems and also to long-term mental health issues.'

'In what way is this manifested?'

'Abandonment as a child can lead an adult to being unable to trust others and this in turn can lead to a lack of self-esteem. Which brings a raft of consequences.'

'When children have been subjected to abuse, do they still suffer from these issues?' Seb asked.

'From my experience, I've found that children from abusive situations don't always know anything else, so even if Lacey came from a harmful background she would still suffer from abandonment problems as she would undoubtedly have formed an attachment with whomever was bringing her up, whether they abused her or not. May I ask if anything specific has happened to prompt you to look into her case again after all this time?'

Birdie glanced at Seb, and he nodded. She'd tell the psychologist as she'd been with Lacey at the time of the incident.

'We believe she saw something recently which we suspect might be related to her past,' Birdie said.

'Could you be more explicit?' Dr Watkins said.

'We were in town the other day, and Lacey was visibly affected by something she'd seen. It was so bad that she had an accident and wet herself. She'd never done that before.'

'Did you question her about it?'

'Not in any detail, as she was so upset. My aunt tried later, but she clammed up and refused to speak. We didn't want to push her. But it persuaded us to take another look.'

'In your professional opinion, Dr Watkins, if we located Lacey's parents, would this be a good thing?' Seb asked.

'I'd love to have a definitive answer, but it's difficult to know, as we have no knowledge of how Lacey lived before she was left. I do believe that once we have an idea, it will help in her treatment.'

'That's why we have to look for them,' Birdie said, nodding.

'Good luck with your investigation. Before you go, how is Lacey's schooling going? Is she still being taught at home by Mrs Cooper?'

'Yes, because she's not ready to go to school yet.'

'I'll speak to Lacey's social worker and suggest that she should see me again, and will also contact Mrs Cooper. Is there anything else you wish to discuss? My next appointment will be arriving shortly.'

'No, that's all. Thank you for your time, it's much appreciated,' Seb said.

'If you need to speak further, then give me a call and we will make another appointment.'

They stood, and the psychologist held open the door for them. As they walked through the waiting room, there was a woman sitting with two young children.

'Have you made an appointment with the social worker yet?' Birdie asked once they'd left the building and were standing outside on the path.

'Yes, for Monday. Are you able to come with me?'

'Sorry, I'm on a training course all day. Can we meet after I finish so you can tell me about it?'

'I'll meet you from the course and we can go out for a drink.'

'Perfect. Do you have anything planned for the weekend?'

'I'm going to work on my research for Rob, to free up time for working on Lacey's case during next week. You?'

'Work tomorrow and then Sunday it's Leicester to see Marie Davis. I can't wait. It's so exciting now I'm actually getting somewhere.'

## Chapter 12

When Seb arrived home, Elsa came charging towards him, as usual, excited to see him. He leant down and gave her a rub.

'Hello, girl. Give me a couple of minutes to change and we'll go out for a long walk. We might as well take advantage of the weather, as according to the forecast it's going to rain later.'

He took off his coat, hung it on one of the pegs in the lobby and went upstairs. As he was opening the bedroom door, his phone began to ring. He pulled it out of his jacket pocket and glanced at the screen. It was his mother. Why was she phoning? They'd only spoken a few days ago. Was something wrong?

He pressed the key and accepted the call. 'Hello, Mother.'

'I'm glad to have caught you. What are you doing?' she said, dispensing with any pleasantries.

'Working on a couple of cases. Why?' he asked, frowning.

She'd never shown much interest in his activities in the

past. If anything, his parents buried their heads in the sand when it came to his work. It was the only way they could deal with it not being appropriate. Their opinion, not his.

'We're at the house in London and need you here. We have a problem with Hubert.'

What had his brother been doing that was bad enough for him to be called? Hubert had never stepped foot out of line. He was an impeccable heir to the Worthington estate and title.

'What sort of problem?'

'He's not his usual self and refuses to do anything other than stay in his room. He won't even come out for meals, choosing to eat alone. We are at a loss as to what to do? I'm extremely worried.'

Was Hubert depressed? It certainly pointed to that, although Seb didn't want to jump to any conclusions without knowing more about the situation.

'Has he been to see the doctor?'

'I thought maybe he should, but when I mentioned it to him, he refused. Your father thinks Hubert should simply pull himself together and stop being so ridiculous, which isn't helping matters.'

'Have you spoken to Virginia?' he asked, referring to his brother's wife.

'No. She's down in Winchester with the children, and when I asked Hubert whether he wanted to see her, he refused, saying it wasn't necessary. This situation is very difficult and we need you here.'

'What do you expect me to do? I'm not a doctor or a therapist. It sounds like he needs professional help, and I'm not qualified in that field.'

'You're misunderstanding. We don't wish you to make Hubert better. We realise you couldn't do that,' his mother replied, sounding puzzled.

'Sorry, Mother. You'll have to explain as I have no idea what you're asking of me.'

'Your presence is required to assist your father in his duties. He has an event to attend, and he'd planned to take Hubert, but he's now refusing to go. Your father insists that you take Hubert's place.'

'Why didn't he ask me himself?'

'He's snowed under with his work and requested that I contact you instead.'

Seb sat on the edge of the bed. He had no desire to attend events with his father. One of the reasons he'd moved away from the family was because he found it repressing. But if his brother Hubert was unwell, then he should do what he could to help. Except, if he wasn't prepared to seek treatment, then how long would he remain in this state?

'I understand that, Mother, but it's extremely difficult for me to leave everything. I'm in the middle of two cases, both of which need my attention and I can't simply drop them.'

'But you've left the police. What are these cases?'

He had informed his parents about becoming a private investigator, but she must have forgotten.

'My company has been employed by the police, in a research capacity, and I've also taken on another case.' She didn't need to know all the details.

'Sebastian, we're not asking you to move back here on a permanent basis. We understand that you have your own life to lead, even if we don't approve of what you do. All we're asking is that you make the time to attend some of these events with your father. Until Hubert is back to his old self.'

He breathed a sigh of relief. At least they realised he

wasn't returning to the nest. But he needed to be clear that it was a temporary measure.

'I understand now. I'll be here if you need me, but we can't simply leave Hubert to his own devices. Something has to be done.'

It would be easier for him to speak to his brother in person. If his parents weren't going to insist that he sought some help, then it would be up to him to do so.

'Thank you. We'll definitely look into helping your brother, if he'll accept it. In the meantime, your father will be grateful for your company.'

'We'll take it one event at a time. Tell me about the first one.'

'It's a black-tie charity auction being held at The Savoy Hotel on Thursday of next week. Your father is on the board, so it's important the family is well represented. Unfortunately, I have another engagement that evening so won't be able to attend.'

'That should be fine, but I'll confirm with you later, once I've checked my diary.'

As much as he was prepared to assist, especially as Hubert wasn't well, he also realised that if his mother believed it was easy for him to leave what he was doing to be there with them, then she would expect it all the time and that would only lead to him being drawn further and further back into the family life that he'd rejected.

'You can stay overnight at the house with us, rather than your flat, then you and your father can discuss the event and leave together.'

'That will be fine. I'll return here, to East Farndon, the following day.'

'Do you have the correct attire?'

'Not with me, but I'll call in at my place on the way to collect everything.'

He'd contact his neighbour, Jill, and ask if she'd take his suit to the dry-cleaner. It had been a long time since he'd last worn it. He hadn't bothered to bring any formal clothes with him to Market Harborough, not envisaging he'd be attending any events which called for them.

'Marvellous. Assuming Hubert is still here when you arrive, then perhaps you will talk to him. He might open up a bit more with you, although I'm hoping by then he will have gone back to the estate to be with Virginia and the children.'

'Does he know that you're asking me to come back to assist?'

'No, we didn't tell him.'

'So, he might still be planning to attend the Savoy event with father, in which case you won't need me.'

'He's not leaving his room and has already missed one function. When we asked him about future events, he said he wasn't prepared to commit to anything.'

'You should mention to him that I'll be attending in his place, because he may still decide he wants to go. I don't want him to feel pushed out at a time like this, when he's unwell.'

'I'll talk to him before you arrive. Thank you for agreeing to go with your father, we do appreciate it.'

His mother ended the call, and Seb remained seated on the bed. His priority was to make sure his brother got back to doing what he did best. Being the heir.

## Chapter 13

Birdie had tossed and turned all night, her mind constantly on the visit to Leicester she was going to make. Even when she did fall asleep for a couple of hours, she had the weirdest of dreams, during which she went to meet her birth mother, but as soon as she got to the place, there was a note sending her to somewhere else.

She never did get to meet her. It went on and on.

Finally, at seven o'clock, having been fully awake for over an hour, she decided to get up and go downstairs for some breakfast.

The kitchen was empty, as usual for that time on a Sunday morning. It was the one day when everyone stayed in bed until at least nine. It was a family tradition. It meant that she could eat her breakfast in peace and not have to talk. All she wanted to do was decide what she was going to ask Marie Davis and hope that she'd be giving her some useful information.

She'd planned on leaving at ten to make sure she arrived in Leicester with plenty of time to spare. But that still left her with well over an hour to fill before she had to get ready. She'd go back to bed and check out her social media accounts. That way, she wouldn't be disturbed.

She took herself upstairs, picked up her phone from the bedside table, and spent some time looking at all the posts her friends had put up. They cracked her up. But it still only took her half an hour. She couldn't stand waiting a moment longer. She'd go early and that would give her time to check out the area her birth mum had lived in. She ran to the shower and was soon dressed, made-up, and ready to go.

On her way out, she popped into the kitchen for a glass of water. She opened the door, and an intoxicating smell invaded her nostrils. Her mum was standing by the hob cooking the usual Sunday breakfast of bacon, eggs, sausages, and hash browns. Her stomach rumbled, even though she'd just eaten.

'As much as I hate to say this, nothing for me, thanks. I'm on my way out.'

'I wished you'd told me before I'd put all this bacon on.'

'Sorry, but I'm sure Dad, or one of the boys, will eat it.'

Both of her brothers were at Leicester Uni, Arthur in his second year, and Thomas had just started. They lived at home, neither of them wanting to move out.

'I'm sure they will,' her mum said, chuckling. 'Where are you going so early on a Sunday?'

'I've arranged to meet a friend in Leicester. We're going to look around the shops and then go for lunch. I should be back early afternoon.'

'Okay. You have fun. We might be out when you get back, as your dad wants to visit some of the garden centres to get an idea for the water feature he's planning to build out the back. I take it you'll be in for dinner tonight?'

'Totally. No chance of me missing roast beef and York-shire pudding. I'll see you later.'

The roads were clear and the drive to Leicester didn't take her as long as she'd anticipated. She was in Aylestone by ten-thirty and she drove straight to Saffron Lane, the street where her mum used to live.

It was a typical working-class area with rows of terraced houses, some of which looked as if they'd been well taken care of and others which were more rundown. She got out of her car and walked along the other side of the road to the house that she was going to be visiting so she could check it out without being spotted. Marie Davis's house was neat and tidy, and had a small patch of grass in front with flowers all around the edges. To the left, the house had paint which was peeling, the windows were dirty and the grass overgrown. The house to the right was the one where Birdie's birth mother had lived. That looked to be well looked-after.

She glanced at her watch. There were still twenty minutes to go, so she returned to her car and took a drive around the area to familiarise herself, and to see the local school. No wonder she was never early. The waiting was doing her head in. At least with being late, as she invariably was, it meant that she didn't have to hang around twiddling her thumbs.

Eventually, five minutes before she was due at Marie's house, she headed back and parked outside.

She knocked at the front door and a man answered. Marie said she'd be alone. Who was he?

'I'm Lucinda Bird from Market Harborough. I had an appointment with Mrs Davis this morning.'

'Oh, yes, she mentioned to me that you were coming to see her. She was worried about letting you down by not being here. I'm her son, Craig. You'd better come in.' He opened the door fully, and she stepped inside into a narrow hallway which was nicely decorated, in a very traditional manner, with floral wallpaper and a beige carpet. He led her into the front room, which had a dark brown sofa and one easy chair, both facing the television in the corner. Where was Marie?

'Is everything okay?' she asked, sensing the tension in the air.

'Please sit down and I'll fill you in on what has happened.' He gestured to the sofa, and he sat on the chair. 'I'm sorry to have to tell you, my mum had a stroke on Friday while she was staying with one of my brothers in Nottingham.'

Birdie's hand shot up to her mouth. 'Oh no. That's awful. How's she doing?'

'She's still in the hospital near my brother. The doctors are assessing her and she's doing as well as can be expected. Fortunately, she can talk, although she's slurring a little. She managed to give me a list of things to pick up, so I stopped by. She has no feeling down her left side but the medical staff told us that it will hopefully improve as time goes on. It could have been so much worse.' His face paled, and his eyes were glassy with tears.

'She's in the best place possible,' Birdie said, to try to reassure him.

'We know.' He nodded.

'What's going to happen to her when she's discharged?' hoping her question wasn't too intrusive.

'That's what the family has to decide. She can't come back here and live on her own because she'll need assistance. It doesn't help that we're all scattered around the country and none of us live very close.'

'Please send her my best wishes when you see her.'

As sorry as she felt for Marie, she also felt sorry for

herself, too. It meant that she'd hit a dead end in the search for her birth mother. Well, for a while, at least.

'Certainly. Now, I understand you wanted to speak to my mum about the family who used to live next door to us. The Bakirtzis. Would you mind telling me what interest you have in them?'

She sat up straight. Was she going to find out about them after all? That would be amazing if she did. But she wasn't prepared to tell him the truth. Instead she'd tell him what she'd planned to tell his mother.

'I'm asking for a friend who has been trying to contact Kim. Did you know her at all?'

She hoped he believed her. She hadn't thought beyond saying that it was for a friend. If he asked why the friend wanted to know, she'd have to make up something on the spot.

'Oh, yes. We all knew the family. We were quite close. My mum was friends with Kim's mother and missed them a lot when they moved.'

'According to your mother, they moved to Canada. Do you remember exactly when they went?'

'I don't, but it's got to be over twenty-five years ago. Mum would know. Obviously, you can't ask her today but maybe when she's a bit better you can organise another visit to wherever she ends up living.'

'I don't want to bother her while she's unwell. She mentioned that she received a Christmas card from the family each year. Do you happen to know their address, by any chance?'

'I'm sorry, I don't.'

Damn. This was getting her nowhere. But she could hardly push him to go searching for his mother's address book to see if she had it. She'd have to try to find the family herself.

'Before I go, is there anything else can you tell me about the family, that I can pass onto my friend?'

'From memory, I think there were four children, but I can't remember their names. They were all a lot younger than me. I think Kim was the eldest, but I could be wrong.'

'How old would Kim be now, do you think?'

Would he think that an odd question to ask, considering she was meant to asking for a friend?

'I'd say, she'd be around fortyish.' He paused. 'Maybe forty-one or forty-two. I can't be sure though.'

Clearly, he didn't think her question odd. Or if he did, he didn't mention it.

She wanted to ask what her mum looked like, but didn't dare.

'We might have a photograph of them somewhere, if that helps?'

Had he read her mind?

Her heart thumped wildly in her chest. Was she about to see what her birth mum looked like?

'Yes, please.' She could hardly get the words out and hoped he didn't notice her excitement. She drew in some calming breaths.

'Let me see if I can find the right photo album. Mum keeps them in one of the sideboard cupboards. Bear with me for a minute as there are loads here to look through.'

'Thank you for taking the time to do this.'

He headed over to the old light-wood sideboard that ran alongside the far wall. He opened a cupboard and rummaged in there for a few minutes, while Birdie anxiously drummed her fingers on her leg.

'Right. It looks like I might have found one. I remember a party we held for my dad, and they all came round.' He flipped through some of the pages and nodded. 'I was right,' he said, walking towards her with the album in his hand. He sat beside her, the open album on his lap. 'Here's a photo with all of them from next door.'

Birdie stared at the smiling family in front of her. *Her family.*

'Which one is Kim?'

'That's her on the end, with the dark blonde hair.' He pointed to a teenage girl with long hair who wasn't very tall and who was smiling. A broad, inviting smile.

She looked happy. Was she pregnant then? It was impossible to tell how old she was.

'Who's that boy?' she asked of the boy with red hair standing next to her.

*Red hair. Her father?*

'That might have been her boyfriend at the time. I don't remember his name.'

'Was it a long-term relationship?'

He frowned. 'I've no idea. Mum would probably know, as she knew plenty about them. Is it important?'

'Oh, no. I just wondered, that's all.'

She didn't want to drop herself in it.

'Do you mind if I take a picture of this with my phone? To show my friend. She'd love to see all of them together.'

'Of course not.' She pulled out her phone and took a photo. 'Actually, why don't you take the photo with you, I'm sure my mum wouldn't mind,' he suggested.

'Thank you. That's very kind. And thank you for all your help. Please send your mum all my best. I hope she makes a full recovery. It was good of you to take the time to talk to me.'

'This isn't a police matter, then? Mum mentioned that you were in the police.'

'No, it's something I'm doing for a friend. I did explain

everything to your mum when I spoke to her. Do you mind if I keep in touch to see how she's doing?'

'Not at all.' He gave her his number, which she keyed into her phone.

'Thanks. I'll see myself out.'

## Chapter 14

The pub Birdie had chosen for them to meet was fairly busy, full of locals. It was a typical country pub with low beams, wooden furniture, and an open fireplace. As he glanced up, he saw her walk in. Only twenty minutes late. Not bad.

She stopped at the bar, ordered a drink and came over, holding it in one hand and the menus in another.

'Sorry,' she said, dropping down on the chair opposite him.

'You don't need to apologise every time you're late to meet me. I always expect it. Don't worry.'

'I bet you always arrive on time, though. Just in case. No need to answer, I can tell by your face.'

'One of us has to be punctual.'

'You're so funny.'

'And yet you still continue rolling your eyes. Surely I warrant a different expression every now and again?'

'That depends.'

'On what?'

'You, of course.'

He reached for his glass and took a large swallow. Sparring with Birdie was most enjoyable.

'How was the training course?'

'Interesting. It was about crime scene management and forensic awareness. Obviously, it didn't go into a huge amount of detail, but there's a course at the uni which I'm thinking of taking part-time. Unless I go for one on cyber-crime. I can't decide which one as they're equally fascinating.'

'Why not do both?'

'I don't have that much free time, what with cricket and working with you.'

'I didn't mean concurrently. Do one this year, and another one next year.'

'Maybe. I'll see how everything else I'm involved in goes.'

'How did the visit to Leicester go yesterday?' He was surprised she hadn't told him already.

'Not as I imagined, but it was good. Sort of.' An unreadable expression crossed her face. He couldn't tell whether it went well or not.

'Would you like to talk about it?'

'Sure. I went there as planned but the woman I'd arranged to see, Marie Davis, had a stroke last Friday so she wasn't able to speak to me because she was still in hospital.'

'Goodness, that's dreadful. How did you find this out?'

'Lucky for me, her son, Craig, happened to be there collecting some of her belongings when I arrived. If he hadn't been, I'd be back to square one with no further leads. He was kind enough to ask me into the house and we had a chat about their old neighbours. He didn't remember much, but at least he knew them.'

'Did he ask why you were interested in them?'

'Yes, and I told him it was for a friend. He accepted that. It helped that his mum had told him I was a police officer.'

'Did you tell him it was a police investigation?' His jaw tightened. That could get Birdie in a lot of trouble if it was reported to her superiors.

'What do you take me for? I didn't say that to him. I'm not stupid. Anyway he had more important things on his mind to worry about, like what was going to happen to his mum once she was discharged from hospital. It's going to be a problem for the whole family.'

'Yes, those things can be a worry. What did he tell you?'

She filled him in with everything she'd now learnt.

'He gave me a photo of my mum to keep.'

'Do you have it with you?'

'Yes, I also copied it to my mobile.' She pulled out her phone and slid it over to him. 'She's the blonde girl with long hair, on the far right.'

He stared at the screen. 'Who's the boy standing next to her?'

'He thought maybe her boyfriend, but he couldn't remember his name or anything about him. Are you thinking the same as me?'

'Which is?' he asked, wanting to check before saying anything.

'Hello. The red hair. The same as mine. And it's curly.' She grabbed hold of her ponytail and waved it in front of her face. 'Do you think he's my dad?'

'It's possible. If one parent has red hair and the other doesn't, there's about a fifty per cent chance their child will be red-haired.' He didn't like to add that the boy's eyes and face were the same shape as Birdie's, too, because she'd never shown any interest in finding out about him and it would only complicate matters for her.

'That's what I thought. Definitely possible. But I don't know his name, and possibly the only person to tell me is Marie and I can't speak to her until she's better. That's if she does recover enough to speak to me. If I could trace him, he might be able to tell me more about Kim.'

'I didn't realise you were interested in him.'

'I've been focused on finding my mother, but I'm not dismissing learning about my father. It does feel like I've come to a dead end though.'

'How can you say that? You now have a photograph of your mother and you know the approximate date she left the country. That information is going to be very useful.'

'Yes, but Canada? How the hell will I find her there?'

'You could try tracking down someone from her school who might be able to tell you more about her and the boyfriend. Knowing his name would be extremely helpful.'

She sighed, picked up her drink and took a sip. 'You're right. That's what I'll do. But not yet. I'll wait until after we've finished with Lacey's case. Tell me about your interview with Stephen Shaw.'

'He was a pleasant enough chap, and concerned with Lacey's well-being, but I didn't get any more out of him than what we already knew. He visits her on a regular basis and said that social services are happy with how she's progressing, and your aunt's input into her care and development. Legally, he wouldn't be allowed to tell me anything else, but it was good to ascertain his overall view of Lacey's situation.'

'What we need to do now is speak to people who were around when Lacey was found. Even though it's over a year later, we might learn something that isn't in the police files. Often people remember things after the fact. Although anything important, they should have contacted the police about it.'

'Maybe. Maybe not. Sometimes people add in new information without even realising when they're talking about a situation at a later date.' That had happened to him on a number of occasions in the past.

'True. And there may well be some witnesses who didn't come forward at the time, if they didn't want others to know they'd been in the vicinity. But we won't be able to reach any of them unless we have a press conference or put out a media alert. Which we can't, as the case isn't official.'

'We've got the name of the person who found Lacey so we'll contact her first. Also, we should visit the shops and cafes in the area to see if they remember anything more than when they were spoken to initially.'

'Okay. That sounds like a plan. I'm off on Wednesday, so why don't we spend that time visiting places?'

'Wednesday's good for me, too. We'll see if June Charles, the woman who found Lacey, is available. I'll call her now, and then we can make our arrangements for the other visits around the time she can see us.' He picked up his phone from the table.

'I don't have her number with me, do you? No you don't, because you remember it. I keep forgetting about your crazy SHAM thing.'

'It's HSAM,' he said, as he keyed in the number.

'Well, you know what I mean.'

'Mrs Charles,' he said when his call was answered.

'Yes?'

'This is Sebastian Clifford. We're reinvestigating the case involving the little girl you found abandoned in Market Harborough a year ago. May I come along with a colleague of mine to go over it again with you? We have additional information which we'd like to check, if you don't mind.'

'Not at all. I'd been wondering recently how the little girl was. I'd be happy to help.'

'Are you available on Wednesday morning around ten?'

'Sorry, I work mornings, but I can do the afternoon at two. I collect my granddaughter from school at three, so will need to leave by a quarter to. Will that give you enough time?'

'Yes, that would be perfect. Thank you, we appreciate your cooperation.'

'Do you know where I live?'

'We have your address on file, unless you've moved since the incident?'

'I'm still here. I probably will be until they put me six feet under.' She laughed. 'I'll see you, then.'

He ended the call. 'She can't do the morning but will be available in the afternoon at two. Let's go into town on Wednesday morning and visit the shops and cafes that have a view of where Lacey was found, and later we'll interview Mrs Charles. Before then, I'd like to look at the CCTV footage from around the time Lacey was abandoned. We haven't checked that yet.'

'A copy should be in the digital file. I'll download it so we can watch first thing Wednesday morning before we leave. Shall I come out to you at eight-thirty, and we can check the footage and then go into town?' Birdie suggested.

'Yes, that works. Now, let's order something to eat.'

# Chapter 15

'You're not going to believe this. The computers were down most of yesterday so I couldn't download the CCTV footage,' Birdie said as she followed Seb into the house on Wednesday morning. She shivered. It was as cold in the house as it was outside. According to the weather forecast it was going to be a warm day. It certainly wasn't yet.

'That's a shame,' Seb said, as he led her through to the kitchen, where he got two mugs from the dresser and filled them with coffee from the machine. He poured milk into hers and handed it over.

'I even went in early first thing this morning, but Sarge was hanging around and wouldn't leave me alone. I pretended I'd gone in to collect something as it was my day off. Honestly, what is it with that man always being there at the *wrong* time? Let's hope he doesn't suspect what I'm doing about Lacey, or he'll go off on one big time. I'm going to pop back in later and download it then.'

'Won't he still be around? You've always told me he's always at the station and that you wouldn't be surprised if he lives there.'

'Not this afternoon because he was moaning about having to go to the dentist. Luckily, one of his teeth has fallen out. Well, I don't mean it's lucky because it can't be nice for him. But that's the trouble when you get old, you start losing your teeth. My dad's the same. The other day, all he did was bite into a piece of toast and one of his teeth cracked and fell out. He almost swallowed it.'

'The joys of getting old. No comment from you necessary, thank you.'

'I don't know what you mean,' she said, smirking.

'Yes, you do. Let's not worry about the CCTV footage. We have other things to occupy us until we do have it.'

'What's the plan, now? Have you had breakfast?'

'Of course.'

'In that case, let's go to the place where Lacey was found, on one of the seats in front of the Old Grammar School.'

'I know it well. It's near the street where I was attacked.'

She was still haunted by thoughts of when Seb got beaten up really badly with a baseball bat while they were investigating Donald Witherspoon's death. He was lucky not to have been killed. A smaller man might not have survived such a beating.

'Don't remind me. I can still, so clearly, see your face after the attack. Have you completely recovered?'

She'd forgotten to ask him up until now. And she called herself a friend.

'My ribs still hurt occasionally, but they can take a long time to recover after being broken. Other than that, all my bruises have gone.'

'And your face is back to its former glory.'

'Meaning?'

Did he really not know how attractive he was?

'You know what I mean. Anyway, back to Lacey. After we've seen where she was left we'll visit the shops and cafes. We have copies of their statements, but it's still good to go over them again.'

'Providing the staff haven't changed, which they might have as it's a year later. Although their contact details should be on file.' Seb said.

'We can follow up with anyone who isn't still there. We'll take both cars so it saves me from having to come back here. I can go straight to work after and download the footage. I'll meet you at the grammar school.'

She followed him down the track and back through the village. After that she couldn't keep up with him as her Mini was no match for his BMW. She didn't want to push her car as it was already living on borrowed time. She'd love a new one, but as all her money went into her house deposit fund, she had to make do with what she'd got. It was a little temperamental, but she'd got it sussed.

Once she arrived in town, she parked in Roman Way and headed to the Old Grammar School. Seb still wasn't there, so she walked around the outside of the building and then under it. The peculiar looking building had always fascinated Birdie. It had been built on stilts, so that local farmers' wives could use the covered area for their weekly butter market instead of having to move it away from the high street. She scanned the area from all angles and as she arrived back at the front, she could see him marching up High Street towards her.

'You got here before me. Where's your car?' Seb said.

'Roman Way, over there,' she said, pointing down the street.

'I'm in Symington.'

'That's a bit of a walk. Still, the exercise will do you good.'

'It didn't take long. Show me exactly where Lacey was found.'

She led him over to the bench facing the road. It was slightly in front of the building. 'We don't know if she was walked to the bench or whether she was sent to it by someone in the shadows who watched until she sat down. No one saw anything, and the cameras didn't pick it up either.'

'Lacey could have come from behind the building and walked underneath until she reached the bench. That way she wouldn't have been seen until she got there,' Seb said.

'Maybe whoever she was with told her exactly where to go so that they wouldn't be spotted dropping her off.'

Birdie sat on the bench, to get the same view that Lacey would have when she was there, and Seb sat beside her.

'It would be someone who knew the area, if that was the case,' he said.

'Knew it, or had spent time checking it out. But I agree with you, it would most likely be someone familiar with the town. It's not like people pass through the centre on their way to other locations. You have to detour off the main road to get here.'

'Okay, so we now suspect that whoever left Lacey knew exactly the best place to drop her off where they wouldn't be caught on camera and, de facto, had knowledge of the surroundings. If the child was seated where we are now. Who can see her?'

'People in the Olive Tree Café over there have a perfect view.' Birdie pointed across the road.

'There's also the newsagent, and the shop next to it, Crystal Haven. I can't work out what they sell.' His brow furrowed.

'The name should give it away. They do crystals,

incense and oils, and tarot cards. I often go in there. But let's go to the Olive Tree first as they have the best view.'

'Okay.'

They headed over to the café, and the smell of baking hit her immediately as she pushed open the door. They headed up to the counter and stood behind the person being served. Soon it was their turn.

'I'm hoping you might be able to help us. Do you remember the case a year ago when the little girl was found by the Old Grammar School?' Birdie asked the woman behind the counter.

The assistant shook her head. 'I don't know, sorry. I only moved to town six months ago.'

'Is there anyone else who might?'

'The manager has been here for years. I'll get her.'

They left the queue and stood a little to the side. After a few minutes a woman came over to them. She was wearing the same maroon coloured uniform as the rest of the staff.

'Hello, I'm Tina Webb, the manager.'

'We're looking again at the case of the little girl who was found on the other side of the street last year. Were you working that day?' Birdie asked.

'Are you from the police?'

'I am a police officer, but this is a private investigation,' Birdie said.

'I see. Yes, I was working that day. The police came in and spoke to me, but I didn't actually see anything. It all happened during a very busy time and it wasn't until two police cars turned up and parked opposite that I paid any attention.'

'Did you notice *anything* strange on that day, or days either side?' Seb asked.

'Not that I remember. How is the little girl? I followed

the case on the news, but after a while nothing was reported. Did you find out who left her?'

'She's doing very well, but we still don't know how she came to be there. We'll leave you to it, as I can see you're busy. Thanks for your help.' Birdie said.

'You're welcome,' the woman said.

They left the café and Birdie turned to Seb. 'Well, that was a waste of time,'

'If you're running a busy café, you're not going to see a little girl sitting quietly on a bench over the way. There would have been people milling around and going in and out of the café all the time, so we can hardly blame her.'

'I'm not, it's frustrating, that's all. Come on, let's go to the newsagent, we might have better luck there.'

The shop was empty and towards the back there was a man stocking shelves. He looked at them as they approached. 'Good morning. Do you need any assistance?'

'We're revisiting the case of the little girl who was found over the road by the Old Grammar School, last year. Do you remember the incident?'

'Yes, I do. It was shocking. I was working that day and when the police came to see me, I told them that I'd noticed her sitting on the bench, but didn't really think anything of it as there were lots of people around. I assumed she was with one of them. If only I'd have known the truth, I might have spotted something.'

'So, you only saw her when she was sitting, not before then?'

'That's correct. I did explain all this twelve months ago.'

'Yes, we know, but we're going over it again to make sure we haven't missed anything. Thank you for your time.'

'You're welcome. I wish I could've helped you further.'

After they'd left the shop, she grimaced. 'I think we're

clutching at straws. I expect everyone we speak to will say the same.'

'Don't dismiss it straight away. We'll go to the crystal shop, now, and then call it a day until we visit June Charles this afternoon,' Seb said.

A wind chime jangled as Birdie pushed open the door and they stepped inside. She could smell sandalwood incense and breathed it in. It was one of her favourites. There was no one around and she headed over to the glass cabinet in the centre, displaying a variety of crystals.

'Look at that fuchsite, isn't it beautiful?' She pointed at the piece of green sparkling crystal and then glanced at the price. 'Whoa, it's expensive.'

'The green colour is because there are small amounts of chromium in there.'

'You know about crystals? Forget that question. What you *don't* know is what I should be asking.' She grinned in his direction.

'It's named after a German mineralogist named Johann Fuchs and it's the stone of rejuvenation and renewal. It will help you achieve balance in your life, emotionally, mentally and spiritually.'

'Impressive,' a voice came from behind them.

Birdie recognised the woman from when she'd been in the shop previously. 'You get used to his knowledge once you've known him for a while. We're looking into the case involving the little girl who was found over by the grammar school a year ago.'

'Oh, yes, I remember it very well. The police came to see me on the day it happened and I told them that I hadn't seen anything.'

'Have you remembered anything since?'

'If you look out of the window, you'll note that it's not

easy to see anything from this angle. Nothing has changed, for me, from that day—'

'But,' Birdie said, pre-empting what the woman was about to say.

In her peripheral vision she noticed Seb giving her a funny look. She shouldn't have interrupted. It was questioning 101.

'But ... my next-door neighbour's daughter, Ruby, was working here on work experience at the time the child was found, and we happened to be discussing the case a few months ago when I was at her house having coffee with her mother. We were wondering what had happened to her. It was then that Ruby mentioned seeing a car driving around a few times.'

Birdie's skin prickled. 'Did she mention the colour or the make?'

'No, sorry.'

'Did she say whether she'd recognised the car as belonging to anyone she knew, or that it had been hanging around at all?'

The woman shook her head. 'No.'

'This isn't in the files. Did she tell the police?'

'She'd already gone home when they came, so maybe not. I also think she would've told me if she had when we were talking about it.'

'Did you give the police her contact details?'

'Um ... from memory, no, I didn't. It's a long time ago. I remember a police officer in uniform came in and asked me if *I'd* seen anything that morning and I said no.'

'Is that all he asked?'

'Yes. He was only here for a couple of minutes, if that, because he got called away.'

Which is why he didn't ask whether there was anyone

else working in the shop. Birdie bit back a frustrated sigh. How bloody annoying was that?

'Please could we have Ruby's details?'

'I can let you have the address and her mother's phone number. Ruby will be at school now … you are the police, aren't you?'

'I am an officer, but this is a private investigation,' Birdie said.

'That's okay then.'

After taking down the details they left.

'How annoying that the original officer got called away and didn't remember to go back to the shop. But at least we're now getting somewhere. I'll call the girl's mum.' She pulled out her phone and keyed in the number she'd been given.

'Ava Weatherall, speaking,' the woman answered.

'This is Lucinda Bird. I've been speaking to your neighbour at Crystal Haven, because we're looking into the case of the little girl who was found in the town centre twelve months ago. We understand that at the time your daughter, Ruby, was doing some work experience at the shop. We'd like to have a chat with her after school, if that's okay with you.'

'Um … I suppose so. But I don't know how she'll be able to help.'

'We have some routine questions. Nothing to worry about.'

'Okay. We'll be home after three-thirty.'

'Thank you. We'll see you then.'

## Chapter 16

June Charles lived in a Victorian terraced house in Clarence Street. Seb knocked on the dark red painted door which fronted onto the road, and a woman in her fifties, wearing a uniform from one of the large supermarket chains, answered.

'Hello, Mrs Charles, I'm Sebastian Clifford. We spoke on the phone on Monday. This is my colleague, Birdie.'

'Come on in. I was about to put the kettle on. Would you like a tea or coffee?'

'Tea with a splash of milk would be lovely, please,' Seb said.

'Same for me,' Birdie added.

'We'll talk in the kitchen, this way,' Mrs Charles said.

Seb gestured for Birdie to go first, and they headed, single file, down the narrow hallway, which had the stairs going up the right-hand side, and into the galley kitchen. They stood in the doorway, as it wasn't large enough for them all to be in there, while the woman put tea bags into a stainless-steel teapot, took out three china cups and saucers from the cupboard and placed them next to the kettle. She then leant against the kitchen cupboards and faced them.

'Thank you for agreeing to see us,' Seb said.

'I must admit, I was surprised when you phoned. I didn't realise the police were still looking into the matter.'

'The case has remained open the whole time, but lack of evidence had meant it wasn't able to progress. Until recently, when the little girl saw something which we suspect could be linked to her past. We're investigating, unofficially, to see if there was anything missed at the time, or not reported if it wasn't viewed as relevant by the person who witnessed it,' Birdie said.

'I see. How is the little girl? Wasn't she called Lacey?'

'Yes, that's the name she was given by social services. She's still in foster care and progressing very well under the circumstances.'

'Poor little thing. Who would abandon a child of that age? It sickens me what some people do. Thank goodness it was me who found her and not some paedophile. You hear all sorts of stories about what goes on. And right under your nose, too.' The kettle pinged, and she filled the teapot with water.

'She was indeed lucky that you were the person who found her,' Seb said, leaning against the doorway, his arms folded. The woman was right. It could have been so much worse for Lacey if the wrong person had got hold of her.

'Please could you run through exactly what happened that morning. In as much detail as you remember.' Birdie pulled her notebook and pen from her jacket pocket.

'It's ingrained in my mind like it happened yesterday. It was a few minutes before nine o'clock in the morning. I wasn't working that day and I'd gone into town early to do a few bits and pieces. I wanted to drop off my coat at the dry-cleaner because I'd spilt beer on it, and then I had planned to buy some wool from the shop in St Mary's Place. My niece had announced she was pregnant, and I wanted to knit something for the baby. People don't seem to do that nowadays, do they? When I had my children, I was inundated with cardigans, matinee jackets, and blankets that had been knitted specially for me.' She poured the tea into cups, added the milk and passed one each to Birdie and Seb, while continuing to talk.

Ten minutes later she reached the moment when she'd come across Lacey.

'I was walking down High Street and noticed a small child sitting on her own, wearing a thin, cotton short-sleeved dress. It wasn't a very cold day, but it still appeared strange so early in the morning. That's what caught my attention. She was staring ahead, her hands clutched together in her lap. There were people around but from where I was standing it didn't look like any of them were *with* her, so I went over to see if she was okay. I thought that maybe she was sitting on her own while her parent or carer had popped into one of the shops. Then I saw the … you know … hanging round her neck. I was asked by the policewoman who interviewed me not to mention it to anyone. Which I haven't. *Literally* to no one because I knew how important it was for identifying her. It would stop anyone from saying she was theirs when she wasn't.'

'Thank you for complying with the officer's request, it was extremely important that you did, for Lacey's safety. What happened after you went over to see how she was?' Seb asked.

'I didn't want to scare her, so I crouched down to her level and asked where her mummy was, but she didn't respond. Instead, she stared at her knees. Her legs were like little white sticks. It was as if she hardly got any fresh air, she was so pale, and there wasn't an ounce of fat on her.'

Seb coughed. He'd asked for detail, but the woman kept going off at a tangent. At this rate, she wouldn't have finished before she was due to leave to collect her grand-daughter.

The woman gave a wry smile. 'Sorry, I do have a habit of *chuntering on* as my Eddie always says. He's my other half, in case you wondered.'

'I thought he might be,' Seb said, giving an encouraging nod. 'You were saying?'

'I asked her again if she was with anyone but she still didn't answer. There were two women standing fairly close having a chat, and I interrupted and asked if Lacey was with them but they said no. So, I phoned the police and stayed there until they arrived with social services. I sat next to the child on the bench and talked the whole time wanting to reassure her that everything was going to be okay, and also to make sure that she didn't run away. In all the time we were waiting she didn't say a single word. At first, I thought she might not understand me, but there was the occasional look in her eye that made me realise she probably did. Anyway, that's everything that happened and it's exactly what I told the police when they asked me at the time it all happened.'

'We're very grateful for what you did. It was very kind of you,' Birdie said.

'It was nothing. I did what any other decent person would have in the situation.' The woman's chest puffed out, clearly appreciating the praise.

'Did you notice whether there was anybody watching you while you were with Lacey? Maybe from a distance,' Birdie asked.

The women chewed on her bottom lip. 'Um … I don't think so. But other than trying to work out if anyone recognised her, I wasn't looking around. It didn't even

Speak No Evil

enter my head that someone might be watching us. I'm sorry.'

'There's no need to apologise, you did a great job. The fact that you went over to her, instead of carrying on with your shopping, and that you phoned the police and waited, meant she didn't come to any harm.'

'And you say that she's doing very well now.'

'Well, considering what had happened to her, she's improving in many areas. In particular with her school-work,' Birdie said.

'That's so good to hear.'

'Back to when you were sitting with Lacey, did she look anywhere in particular or show any indication that she recognised anyone or anything?'

'She looked at me when I first sat next to her, and a couple of other times, but other than that she didn't look anywhere other than at her knees. When the two women from social services arrived, she didn't try to run. After they told her who they were, and one of them offered her hand, she went with them. She was compliant and didn't cry or get upset. She didn't look back at me at all.'

'What happened after they took her away? Did you notice anyone paying particular attention to what was going on?' Seb asked.

'I have no idea. Once she'd gone, the police came over and I gave a statement. That took about twenty minutes and then I left and carried on with my jobs. Obviously, I followed the story on the news and waited to see if anyone had come forward, but after a few days the story seemed to disappear, so I had no idea what happened to the child. I did think about phoning the police to ask but didn't want to waste their time.'

'We wouldn't have minded,' Birdie said.

'So, you say she's still in foster care. Doesn't anyone want to adopt her?'

'She's happy with her foster carers, as she's been with them since she was found.'

Seb was pleased that Birdie didn't mention the child was with her aunt. It wasn't relevant, and he didn't want the woman attempting to contact the child.

'That's good. The main thing is that she's settled and healthy.'

'She's very healthy and we have high hopes for her future. That's all we need from you. Thank you for taking the time to speak to us.'

'Actually, before we go, I'd like to return to the sign around Lacey's neck,' Seb said.

'Yeah, that was really weird, wasn't it? I've never seen anything like it before.'

'Did she touch it at all?'

'No. She took no notice of it which made me wonder if it was something that she always wore. *Speak No Evil* is something from the Bible, isn't it? She might have come from a religious house. Not that I've heard of children wearing signs like that around their necks.'

'It doesn't originate from the Bible, but that's a common misconception,' Seb said.

'Oh. I didn't know. Is it something more sinister and creepy? Was she in a cult or something, do you think?' The woman's eyes darted from him to Birdie.

'We don't know, but nothing is off limits during our investigation.'

# Chapter 17

'After we've interviewed Ruby Weatherall, I'll go back to work and download the CCTV footage from when Lacey was left. I've got cricket practice tonight so can't get out to you later, but I can do tomorrow after work, if that's okay?' Birdie said, after they'd left June Charles's house and were standing beside her car.

'I'm afraid not. I'm returning to London to go to a charity event at The Savoy Hotel with my father. While there, I'm going to schedule a catch-up meeting with Rob to discuss the case we're investigating.'

'The Savoy. Wow. That sounds fun,' she said, unable to hide the envious tone in her voice. Why didn't she ever get invited to go to places like that?

'I'm not there for pleasure. My father needs me for support.'

'I thought your older brother, the future Viscount Thingy ... sorry, I can't remember the name ... doesn't he do all of these posh affairs?'

'Worthington. It's Worthington. Hubert's not too well, so I'm stepping in to help.'

'Is it serious?'

'I don't know yet. I'll find out more when I'm in London.'

'I'm sorry to hear that. I hope he gets better soon. And remember, I'm always available to accompany you, if you want to make it more bearable,' she said with a grin.

'Tempting. But no thank you. I'm not sure my father would be able to cope with your little idiosyncrasies, as you're definitely an acquired taste.'

'I'll take that as a compliment … I think. Say hi to Rob for me. Tell him …' she hesitated. 'Actually, never mind. He's a superior officer so I better not risk saying anything out of order in case it jeopardises my future in the force.'

Seb laughed. 'I'm sure he won't hold anything against you, as he knows what you're like having already met you.'

'Well, I don't want to risk it just in case. When will you be available for us to get together? I know we're missing something. It got to be in the files. Or in the old footage we haven't yet looked at. We'll have to go through everything again.'

'I'll be returning sometime Friday afternoon at the latest. Come over to the hall after work and I'll cook again.'

'That works for me. What are we going to have?'

'I have no idea. Do you really need to know now?'

'No. I just wanted to know what to expect, so I can get the taste for it during the day. Come on, let's go and visit this girl and see what it is she saw. Follow me, I know a shortcut.'

She waited for Seb to fetch his car and then drove to Douglass Drive, with him keeping his distance the whole journey. The houses were 1970s semi-detached, brick and tile properties and the one belonging to the Weatheralls had gravel instead of a front lawn, like several houses in the street, designed to provide extra parking. There was a red Toyota Corolla on the drive and Birdie parked on the street close by. Seb pulled up behind her.

A woman in her forties, with short blonde hair, dressed in jeans and a pink V-necked jumper, answered the door.

'Mrs Weatherall?' Birdie asked.

'Yes.'

'I'm Lucinda Bird, we spoke on the phone earlier, and this is Sebastian Clifford who's assisting me with our enquiries.'

'Ruby's just got back from school. She panicked when I said you were coming to see her, but when I told her she wasn't in any trouble, she calmed down. That's right, isn't it? She's done nothing wrong, has she?' The woman pressed her lips together.

'She's absolutely not in trouble. We'd like her help, that's all,' Birdie said, hoping to reassure her.

'Good. Come in and we'll sit in the lounge. Ruby asked if I was allowed to stay with her while she's being interviewed. Is that okay?'

'Of course, it is. We expected that you would want to. This is all very informal,' Birdie said, smiling.

They walked through the tiny square entrance which had coats hanging on pegs and went directly into a large open-plan lounge with stairs leading up from it, and a dining area at the end with a chrome and glass circular table. The rest of the furnishings were modern and there was a massive telly on the wall, blaring away. Birdie could hardly take her eyes off it. She'd seen them that big in the department stores but had never come across anyone who owned one. It was possible to see every single blemish on the skin of the chat show host.

'Take a seat and I'll get Ruby. She's in her bedroom.'

They sat on one of the oatmeal-coloured sofas while

Mrs Weatherall jogged up the stairs. Birdie could hear her tapping on a door and calling her daughter.

She turned back to look at the telly until Mrs Weatherall and Ruby joined them in the lounge. Ruby was still wearing her school uniform.

Birdie and Seb stood to greet her.

'Hello, Ruby. I'm Lucinda Bird and this is Sebastian Clifford, we'd like to have a quick word with you about the time the little girl was found in High Street, when you were on work experience at Crystal Haven in town.'

'Yeah, Mum told me.' She plonked herself down on the other sofa, and tucked her feet under her, not appearing at all fazed by them being there, which was different from the impression her mother had given them.

'Please will you turn off the television, Mrs Weatherall,' Seb asked.

'Oh. Sorry. Yes. I don't usually have it on during the day. But I wanted to see an interview with—'

'Mum,' Ruby said, glaring at her.

'Sorry.' She picked up the remote and turned the telly off.

'Ruby, I'd like you to go through exactly what you saw on that day,' Seb said.

'I didn't see the little girl because it's hard from the angle of the shop. But when I was doing some of the window display for Mrs Green, I noticed the same car kept driving past.'

Birdie exchanged a glance with Seb. This could be exactly the lead they were waiting for.

'Can you describe the car?'

'It was silver and not very big.' She hesitated. 'About the same size as our car, I think.'

'Do you mean my car, or your dad's?' Mrs Weatherall asked.

'Yours.'

'I've got a red Toyota Corolla, it's out the front.'

'I saw it when we arrived. Do you think it was actually the same make, Ruby?' Birdie asked.

The young girl wrinkled her nose. 'I'm not sure. I don't know much about cars.'

'That's okay. Do you remember what time you saw the car going past?'

'Not really. But it was definitely before the police arrived because I remember them stopping outside the shop with their lights flashing.'

'How many times did this car drive past?'

'Three. But it could've been more. I remember seeing it once. Then when I saw it again, I thought, oh, they just went past. And then it went past again.'

'Could you see who was driving?'

'No, it wasn't that close or going that slow.'

'Did you notice how many people were in the car?'

'Not really. I think maybe one, but I can't be sure. And I don't know whether it was a man or a woman. The first time I noticed it again it was a glance. And when I saw it a third time I remember thinking it was weird but didn't have time to look at the driver properly.'

'Do you remember the exact time this all happened?'

'Maybe about a quarter to nine. It was before we opened the shop. Mrs Green had told me to do the window display before then. So that's a definite. Yep.'

'Do you remember how much time elapsed between each of your sightings?'

'Um … maybe five minutes. I'm not sure. Not very long.'

'Do you think the driver could've been looking for a parking space and that's why you saw them several times?' Seb asked.

'Ohhh. Yes. That could have been it. It didn't enter my head at the time.' She glanced at her mother and pulled a face. 'Sorry.'

'No need to apologise. Did you tell the police everything you'd seen?' Birdie asked.

'Nope. I wasn't there when they came in. I only worked part of the morning to make up my work experience hours because I'd been off during the week to go to the doctor. I left at eleven and didn't go back again because it was all finished. We only had to do a week.'

'Did you follow the story in the news?'

'I don't watch it.'

'I can never get her off her phone, that's why,' Mrs Weatherall said.

'Did *you* discuss it with Ruby?' Birdie asked, turning to face the girl's mother.

'I don't remember. If she'd have told me about the car, I might have contacted the police. But if it was someone looking for a parking space … you know … it wouldn't have seemed important.' The woman blushed. 'I didn't think. I'm sorry.'

'Me, too,' Ruby said.

'Neither of you did anything wrong. It was down to the police to find out who was in the shop at the time. It's not your fault at all. We can look into it now. I'm assuming that you didn't take a note of the number plate, Ruby?'

'No. I didn't see it.'

Birdie stood, and Seb did the same. 'Thank you for your time, Ruby, you've been very helpful. We may wish to speak to you again in the future. We'll call your mum if we do.'

'Okay.'

'This is so frustrating,' Birdie said when they'd got

outside. 'If which ever officer went into Crystal Haven hadn't been called away, we'd have known all about this.'

'We know now, and there's no point in going over what might have happened.'

'You're right. And at least it's given us something to work with. I'm going back for the CCTV footage to check for this car and find out what the driver was doing.'

'Okay. I'm going back to East Farndon. Elsa will wonder where I've got to. I'll see you Friday evening. Dinner at seven-thirty.'

'Enjoy your time in London.'

'Thanks, but it's not my idea of fun having to dress up in black tie.'

'I've already offered to go with you. Maybe I should go in your place.'

'You know the answer to that.'

## Chapter 18

Birdie parked in a side street and not the station car park, in case Sarge drove past after he'd been to the dentist and spotted her car. She'd assumed he wouldn't be coming back to work after, but with him anything was possible.

Or was she being paranoid? Maybe, but she'd come up against him so many times it was better to be safe than sorry.

When she reached the office, there was no one around, which surprised her as Twiggy had mentioned tackling his mountain of admin during the day. Though, knowing him, he'd got fed up with it and wandered into town to the bakery to pick up a snack or three.

She strolled over to the desk, hung her jacket and handbag on the back of the chair and then opened the online file relating to Lacey's case. She found the CCTV recording and clicked on it, but it wouldn't open. She clicked again.

'What's going on?' she muttered to herself.

She tried several more times, but still with no joy.

Damn. She'd have to ask for another copy. She picked up the phone to call the secure control room.

'Rogers.'

Just the person she was hoping would answer. She wouldn't have a problem now.

'Hi, Len, I'm after some Market Harborough footage from twelve months ago. We have a copy here but I think it's corrupted as it won't open. Any chance you could send it to me again? The only thing is, I need you to keep this request between us.' She'd helped him out with an address a while back when he was trying to track someone down, so she could rely on him to keep it to himself.

'What's the exact date and which cameras?'

'15 May. I'm interested in the cameras capturing High Street and The Square between say eight and ten-thirty in the morning.' That should give enough time to spot the car Ruby had mentioned, and anything else of interest.

'Hang on a minute and I'll see what I can do. It might take a while. Shall I put you on hold? This month's offering is Handel's *Water Music*.'

'I'll wait, but without the music thanks, mate.'

'You've got something against the classics?'

'Not at all, but I'm happy to sit in silence.'

She drummed her fingers on the desk, staring absent-mindedly into space, her mind wandering, while listening to the rhythmic sound of Len striking the computer keys. After five minutes, she was about to hang up and call back a bit later when it went quiet.

'I've got it all,' Len said.

'Oh, that's amazing. You're a lifesaver.'

'How shall I record it in the log?'

'Could you say I requested it, but don't put a case number against it for the moment. I know you could get in trouble, but I wouldn't ask if it wasn't really important. If anything transpires, I'll update you so the records can be amended.'

He sighed loudly, which she took as a sign he was going to agree.

'You do know I wouldn't do this for anyone else, don't you?'

'That's because you like me. And I'm the only person who laughs at all of your cringeworthy dad jokes.'

'I hate to admit it, but you're right. So, answer me this. What do you call a shoe made out of a banana?'

She rested her head in her hand. She'd set him off without even trying. 'I give up, what *do* you call a shoe made out of a banana?'

'A slipper. Get it?' A loud belly laugh echoed in her ear.

'Yes, I get it. That is *so* bad. Don't tell me any more … my head can't stand it.'

'Ouch. You know how to hurt a man. Right, your footage is on its way over to you, now. Anything else you want while I'm here?'

'That's all for now, thanks. I owe you one.'

'Yeah. Right. I'll add it to the list,' he said, still laughing as he ended the call.

Birdie stared at her computer screen until the email pinged and a link to the footage arrived in her inbox. She downloaded it and began to watch, working her way backwards from the time when the police were with Lacey. She hoped to be able to see how Lacey had ended up on the bench in front of the Old Grammar School, but she couldn't. It was like one minute she wasn't there and the next she was. It was impossible to see the direction she came from. Which meant, as she'd discussed with Seb, that the child didn't arrive from the pavement side, but from underneath the old building. So, if she was dropped off in a car then whoever left her would have parked around the back where there were no cameras.

Coincidence?

No such thing.

If only Lacey would tell them what had happened that day their job would be so much easier. Did she even remember? She could've blocked out everything from her mind.

Birdie checked the cars and saw the one Ruby had mentioned going around the block several times until the last time when it was driven into an empty parking space someone had vacated. It was a silver Volkswagen Golf.

The driver, a woman wearing a long-sleeved dress, who looked to be in her thirties, although the grainy footage made it difficult to tell exactly, got out of the car and headed across the road to the Olive Tree Café. Birdie continued watching until thirty minutes after the time the police arrived and Lacey was taken away and the woman still hadn't left. It seemed unlikely she was connected to Lacey, but Birdie took down the number plate details, which she could see thanks to the slightly angled position in which the woman had parked.

Birdie rewound the footage to watch again around the time when Lacey was left but still nothing stood out as being suspicious. She jotted down all the number plates she could see, intending to run them through the database hoping to find something worth pursuing. Sometimes luck was on their side, although she doubted it would be in this case. The scene was so normal it wasn't funny. There was nothing out of the ordinary going on.

From footage between eight-thirty and nine she had a list of fifty plates to check. Without any help, it would take her hours and it had to be done straight away in case she didn't get another opportunity. She'd be lucky to make cricket practice that evening.

Twiggy walked back into the office clutching a brown paper bag in one hand and a cup of coffee in the other, hoping to be alone to enjoy his treats. But his luck wasn't in, as Birdie was there, staring intently at her computer screen.

He plonked himself down on his chair and placed the bag and cup on his desk which was next to hers.

'What are you doing here on your day off?'

'Nothing,' she said, clicking her mouse and minimising the screen.

'If you say so. Then why are you hiding it?'

'Are you okay? You're acting even grumpier than usual.'

'Stop changing the subject.'

'Okay. I'll tell you what I'm doing, if you tell me what's up with you.'

'If you must know, I'm knackered, fed up and starving.'

Birdie frowned. 'Okay, let's take this one at a time. Why knackered?'

'I spent most of last night trying to find Alex who'd told us she was staying at a friend's house, but it turned out the pair of them had gone to some club,' he said, referring to his eldest daughter.

'How did you find out?'

'Her friend's mum phoned to speak to her, and we discovered we'd both been given the same story. Said they were staying at each other's house.'

'Where had they planned on sleeping?'

'With another friend whose mum is a single parent and works nights.'

'Were they okay when you found them?'

'Yes, but that's beside the point. They're underage and had been drinking.'

He'd never been so scared in his whole life. Anyone who'd been in the job as long as he had would've felt the same. Alex would be lucky if she was allowed out of the house again, other than school, until she reached the age of thirty and could show some more common sense.

'Don't worry, Twig. We've all done it. Is that why you're fed up?'

'No. Well, yes, in part. But it's mainly because Evie's decided to drop the Paleo diet and she's now got me on some regimen where I can only eat between certain hours and nothing after dinner at all, not even a tiny snack and no more than a thousand calories a day. Do you know what that means? I'll tell you. I'm spending the whole time starving and I'm going to evaporate into nothing.'

'What's in there?' Birdie pointed at the bag.

'Nothing,' he said sliding it across the desk away from him.

'It doesn't smell like nothing.'

He glanced at the bag, the smell from the hot snack invading his senses. 'Okay, it's a Cornish pasty and a vanilla slice. But in my defence—'

'There is no defence. You cheat on your diets all the time and I'm guessing that what you're about to eat now will be your entire day's calories, and some, in a couple of bites.'

'Don't tell Evie, for God's sake.'

'I think she'll be able to work that out for herself. Do yourself a favour and stick to it for a few weeks, and then you can go back to normal eating.'

'Easy for you to say, but you should try it sometime. It does my head in.'

'Whatever. I'm only making a suggestion. But if you do want me to keep your secret then you can give me a hand here,' Birdie said, smirking.

He had no choice, and she knew it. He didn't mind. It beat continuing with his paperwork.

'I thought you weren't doing anything,' he reminded her.

'I'm checking cars that were in the area around the time Lacey was found.'

'You're still looking into the case, then?'

'I'm hardly going to change my mind, am I? It's not interfering with my other work and Seb has plenty of time when I'm not available.'

Twiggy tensed at the mention of that man. He couldn't help it. Who wouldn't when comparing themselves to someone who was intimidatingly tall, in great shape and good-looking? Everything Twiggy wasn't. To top it all, and most importantly, Birdie seemed to prefer working with Clifford than him. Why?

'I would've helped if you'd asked instead of going straight to him.'

'Don't go all stupid on me. I didn't want to put you on the spot and make you feel like you had to get involved in case it got you in trouble. Look, I've got fifty number plates to check. Are you going to lend a hand?'

'What if Sarge comes in after his visit to the dentist?'

'I'm hoping he won't. Do you think he will?' She twisted some loose strands of hair around her fingers.

'Probably not. When he left earlier, he said he'd see me in the morning. So, you should be in the clear. But you never know with him, so we'd better get a move on.'

'Does that mean you'll help?'

'It does.'

'Thanks, Twig. You're a lifesaver.'

'But we'll keep it between ourselves.'

'As we always do. Because we're partners,' she said, smiling at him.

Why did he allow himself to be jealous of Clifford when there was no need for it? He was an idiot.

'Okay, let me have something to eat, first.' He grabbed the paper bag and pulled out the pasty and took a couple of bites before replacing it. 'I'm all yours,' he said, his mouth still full.

'Right. We'll take half the cars each and see how quickly we can run them through the system.'

'Am I looking for anything specific?'

'Something out of the ordinary that catches your eye,' Birdie said.

They sat in companionable silence keying number plates into the database.

'I've got nothing, so far. Are you sure this is the best thing to do?' Twiggy asked, frustrated by their lack of progress.

'Yes … Actually, no. Stop for a moment, I need to check something.'

He leant in towards her and watched as she called up some CCTV footage on her screen.

'What are you looking at?'

'You see this silver Golf being parked and the woman crossing the road and heading into the café? She'd driven around three times before pulling into a space. Nothing to cause alarm. But … look at the car, there's a dent in the back wing.'

'Yeah, I see it. So …'

'Wait a minute,' Birdie interrupted as she called up some other footage. 'This is from the day that Lacey saw something, and it upset her. We were standing outside on the street. Look over the road. What do you see?'

'He peered at the screen. A silver Golf with a dent in the back.'

'It's the same car. Except the plates are different. I'll look them both up. *Now* we're getting somewhere.'

Twiggy sat back in his chair, finishing his pasty, which was now cold, and then eating his cake, while Birdie peered at her screen. After a few minutes she turned and grinned, her eyes shining.

'The plate from when Lacey was abandoned is registered to a Laura Kingston who lives in Creaton, a village in Northamptonshire on the A50. You probably know it, as it's only twenty minutes away. Her car was reported stolen that weekend. Very convenient, don't you think?'

'Except … why leave a plate on a stolen car if it's going to be involved in an incident? The police would've been on the lookout for it.'

'I don't know. But I'm going to find out.'

'What about this second sighting?'

'The car now has fake plates. It's the same car. It has to be. I'll take screenshots of both vehicles. I can't believe it. We've finally got a break. Yes.' She punched the air in typical Birdie fashion. 'And I still have time to get to cricket practice.'

'Now what? Are you going to involve Sarge?'

'No, definitely not. This is a lead, but it's not enough. It's only the start. I'll let Seb know, and we'll decide our next steps. I'm not seeing him until Friday evening because he's going back to London for a day or two. I'll take everything I've got, to discuss with him.'

He bristled. Bloody Clifford. Again.

'In that case, if we've finished up, I'm going home to

see what culinary delights I'm being served tonight. Knowing my luck, it will be a plate of cabbage.'

'Enjoy,' Birdie said, smirking.

'You wait until you're older and can't eat and drink whatever you want. Then it will be my turn to laugh.'

'If you say so. I think I'll stop for a pizza after cricket practice. Mmm … I can already smell the melted cheese.'

'Button it. I'll see you in the morning.' He glared at her then picked up his things and left.

## Chapter 19

'Over here.' Seb glanced in the direction of the voice, as he walked into the pub in central London, and saw Rob standing at the bar, beckoning. 'A pint?' his friend asked when he got there.

'Make it a half, I've got a long day and night ahead of me.'

'Good to see you again. We could have done this over the phone to save you the trouble of coming here,' Rob said, once they'd got their drinks and had sat down at a table under the window.

'It's no trouble. I'm attending a charity event at the Savoy this evening with my father and staying the night at my parents' London home.'

'Sounds like fun.' Rob knew how intense his family could be, so he didn't need to hide it.

'Nothing could beat it. That's why I wanted to meet up with you, to get a taste of normality. What's happening in your life? Anything interesting?'

'Nah. Same old, same old. I'm overworked and underpaid. Nothing changes. How's my research coming along? Made any inroads, yet?'

'I'm making progress, although it's not fast. There's an intricate network of people involved in the shipments of drugs, which go via a number of different countries, on a variety of vessels. I should have a report for you within the next couple of weeks.'

'Thanks, mate. How's the new company going? Got any work yet, other than mine?'

'It's early days, but I do have one other case. I'll tell you what it is, but this is to go no further.'

'My lips are sealed.'

'I'm working on a case with Birdie, the DC from Market Harborough. Do you remember her?'

'How could I forget? Send her my best the next time you see her.'

'She actually asked me to pass on her regards, too.'

'I liked her, very much. She was a refreshing change from some of the DCs around here. Why is it all *hush-hush*?'

'We're looking into a case from over a year ago that came to a standstill. Birdie came to me as she couldn't convince her sergeant to reopen it. Hence the need for discretion, as he doesn't know what we're doing.' Seb took a sip of his beer.

'Tell me about it?' Rob asked.

'A little girl was found alone in Market Harborough, and they were unable to trace where she came from. Birdie knows the child as she's being fostered by her aunt. There was an incident, witnessed by Birdie, when the child saw something and was badly shaken. Birdie believed it was linked to her past. I trust her instincts and have agreed to help.'

'Who's paying for this?'

'I'm not being paid. It's pro bono.'

'You won't make your fortune that way.'

'According to Birdie, I owe her from the last case when she worked for free.'

'And you agreed?'

'Not exactly.'

'She's got you wrapped around her little finger. You should ask her to join your company. That way you might actually make some money, because I bet she won't support work being done for nothing.'

'You're probably right. But I'm not in the position to take on any staff yet.'

'Fair enough. Tell me, what's it like living in the sticks now you've been there a while?' Rob turned up his nose. He hated anything other than city life.

'I'm enjoying it and not missing London one bit.'

'And Annabelle?' he asked, referring to Seb's ex-girlfriend.

'I haven't heard from her since we split. I believe she might be seeing someone else, but I don't know, nor am I interested in finding out.'

They'd been in a relationship for almost ten years, but after he'd left the force, she'd sided with his family about going to work for them and he'd realised they were on different pages. Annabelle came from a perfectly suitable family, according to his parents, and it had turned out that they'd been conspiring behind his back to persuade him to return to the family fold.

'Have *you* met anyone else?'

'No, I'm happy being single and spending time with Elsa. She loves being away from the city and living in the country. It's given her a new lease of life. Less about my mundane existence, tell me what's going on with you?'

'The big news is Maddie and I are expecting a baby in August.'

'And you waited until now to tell me? Congratulations, I'm thrilled for you.' He lifted his glass and clinked it against Rob's.

'Thanks. We'll celebrate when she's born.'

'You know it's a girl?'

'Yes, we asked at the scan. Maddie's delighted. We both are.'

They discussed the work Rob was doing for a while longer and then Seb glanced at the time.

'I should leave as my parents are expecting me. It's been great catching up and congratulations again on your news. Send my love to Maddie. We'll meet up again soon.'

He left the pub and hailed a taxi to Ovington Square in Knightsbridge, where his parents had their London residence. He didn't have a key, so when he arrived, he rang the bell.

'Good afternoon, sir,' the family butler said when he answered.

'Hello, Bates. Good to see you again. How are you?'

'Very well, thank you, sir. Your parents are in the drawing room awaiting your arrival.'

'I'll go and see them now. Is my room ready as I'll be staying overnight?'

'Yes, sir. Everything's in order.'

Seb headed through to the drawing room which was situated on the ground floor of the four-storey home. His father was reading a newspaper and his mother a book, when he entered the room.

'Mother. Father.'

'Sebastian, you're here,' his mother, Charlotte, said as she walked over to greet him.

He bent down and kissed her on both cheeks. His father, Phillip, joined them and they shook hands.

'Good to see you, Sebastian,' he said.

'Sit down and I'll organise some tea.' His mother rang the bell and a young woman, whom Seb didn't recognise, hurried in. 'Tea for three, please, Angie.'

'Tell me more about Hubert,' Seb said, once they were alone again.

'He's staying here with us and spending most of the time in his room. It's most disconcerting,' his mother said.

'You can't leave him like that. It sounds like he needs professional help.'

'You know my view on outsiders being involved in family affairs. I'm sure he'll get over it,' his father said, waving his arm dismissively.

Seb gave a frustrated sigh. 'He might not, though, Father. We can't ignore this. He should go to the doctor and get some counselling and medication, if it's needed.'

'He's going through a bad patch. It happens to all of us at some point during our lives. I know it did to me, and I forced myself to carry on. Eventually, I was fine.'

'That doesn't make it the right course of action to take. Virginia should be with him,' Seb said, not wanting to condone his father's view.

'She's with the children. They have school.'

'Is she aware of Hubert's mental state?'

'We don't know. We haven't discussed it with her,' his mother said.

'Why not? If you talk to her, she might come to London to help. I'm sure the staff could take care of the children for a few days. I'll speak to Hubert. He simply can't be allowed to remain like this without any support being offered.'

'Cliffords are made of strong stuff. I have every confidence he'll work it out. But until that time, I need you to be available whenever you're needed,' his father said.

How could he be so naïve?

'I'm happy to go with you tonight, as I was able to rearrange my work commitments, but it's not always going to be possible. You can't rely on me.'

'It's your own company, so surely that means you can make yourself available.' His father exchanged a glance with his mother and frowned.

'I have clients, and they can't be let down. One of them being the Metropolitan Police.'

'Didn't you tell me that you'd cut all ties with the police force?' his mother asked, tilting her head to one side.

'The work came up, and I took it. It's my company's first official case.'

'I'm not surprised they want to employ you, with your *Super Memory*,' she said using the term she always did when referring to his HSAM.

'What time are you wanting to leave this evening, Father?' he asked, not wishing to discuss his employment any longer.

'I've arranged for the car to collect us at six. The reception commences at six-thirty, followed by the meal at eight.'

'Is there anyone in particular you wish me to speak to?'

'No, it's only your presence that's needed. We're representing the family. You do know it's black tie?'

'Yes, I have everything that's required with me.'

'I'll make sure your attire is pressed and ready for when you change,' his mother said.

'Thank you. I'm going upstairs to talk with Hubert. I'd like to see for myself how he is. Save me some cake, when it arrives.'

'You might be able to cheer him up and bring him out of his doldrums,' his mother said, hopefully.

Seb shook his head. It was no use, they would never understand. 'I'll be suggesting to Hubert that he seeks some professional help. What's happening with his work? Is he doing any at all?'

'The estate is being run by the manager and I'm over-seeing everything else. Which isn't what I expected to be doing at my age,' his father said.

Seb left the room and headed up to the third floor, where his brother had some rooms. He knocked on the door.

'Who is it?' Hubert called out.

'Sebastian.'

'I'm not receiving visitors.'

'I'd like to talk to you, please may I come in?'

'I'm in no mood for a chat.'

'I haven't seen you for a while. I won't stay long. Promise.'

There was silence for a long time.

Should he knock or leave him?

'I'll speak to you but only for a few minutes,' Hubert said, before he had time to decide.

Seb walked in and swallowed hard. Hubert was seated beside a small round table, overlooking the rear of the property. He'd lost an awful lot of weight and his face was pale and drawn.

Seb marched over and shook his brother's hand. He pulled out the chair opposite and sat.

'I can already see from looking at you that you're struggling. Why don't you tell me about it?'

'There's no point.' Hubert turned his head and stared out of the window.

'There's *every* point. Surely you don't enjoy being like this.'

'What's enjoyment got to do with it?'

'Hubert, listen to me. I'm no expert but it's obvious you're not well. I don't mean physically sick. This is a mental health issue. There's nothing to be ashamed of, it happens to one in five people at some time in their lives.'

'How do you know?' his brother asked, for the first time actually looking directly at Seb.

'I read it. Speak to me. Help me understand what you're going through.'

'Okay, I'll tell you. Day-to-day living is hard. Too hard. I can't be bothered doing anything at all. All I want to do is sit and stare out of the window. At times, even that's too much effort.'

Hubert talking like this to Seb was a complete role reversal of how their relationship had been in the past. His older brother had always taken the lead, and Seb had allowed him to. But now …

'Is Virginia concerned by your condition?'

'We haven't discussed it. She doesn't realise the extent of how I feel. It's not something I wish to share. Some days are better than others and I manage to be more active. At least, I do when I'm at home. Being here is easier, as I don't have to do a thing.'

'But she must have noticed your weight loss.'

'She was aware that I'd been trying to lose a few pounds.'

'This is more than a few pounds.'

Hubert shrugged. 'Yes, I suppose it is.'

'If you've managed to talk to me about it, you can speak to Virginia. It will help.'

'No. I don't wish to. I don't know until I wake up in the morning what the day's going to be like. Today isn't a good one.'

'Hubert, you need to visit the doctor and explain what's happening.'

'And admit that I can't cope? No. That's not the way we do things in this family.'

'Now you sound like Father and his outdated ways. Times have changed, there's no need to be embarrassed and hide your feelings. There's no stigma attached to mental illness. You're not unusual. It's something that can be dealt with, by medication, counselling, or both. Please seek some help.'

'It's easy for you to say. I can't be viewed as weak, not with the weight of being the future Viscount Worthington on my shoulders. You don't have that to worry about.'

Thank goodness.

'No, I don't. But I have other pressures. Everyone does. And sometimes these pressures get to the point where people find it's necessary to seek outside help.'

'You make it sound easy, but it isn't.'

'Take it one step at a time. Why don't you go back home to the Estate and speak to Virginia? Make an appointment with the family GP. Or find another one if you don't wish to speak to them, and they can refer you on to someone who can help.'

Hubert clenched and unclenched his fists, as they rested on the table.

Would he agree?

'I can't leave because I'm meant to be going to the Savoy with Father tonight,' he finally said.

'Why do you think I'm here? Mother and Father asked me here to go to the event instead of you. Didn't they say?'

Hubert turned away from Seb, instead staring out of the window. 'I don't know, they may have done. I can't remember. I block out much of what they say to me. In particular, Father. I don't want to hear him trying to persuade me to keep a stiff upper lip and be stoical. I'm happier being left alone, where no one can bother me. Do you understand?' He turned back and Seb grimaced at the pain he witnessed in his brother's eyes.

'I do,' he said gently, resting a hand on Hubert's arm. 'But I also know that being left to languish alone won't be of any benefit to you, at all. You have to make the decision to deal with what's happening, if not for you, for your wife and children. It can be fixed. I promise you.'

'How do you know?'

'I know people who have been in the exact same situation and I've witnessed them get better and come through their depression.'

'You think what I've got is depression?'

'I believe so. Hasn't that crossed your mind?'

Hubert shrugged. 'Maybe. I'm not sure.'

'You're depressed, and it's curable. How long have you been staying in London?'

'I drove up here a week ago, wanting some time to myself, forgetting that Mother and Father were going to be here.'

'Have you spoken to Virginia during this time?'

'She messaged two days ago and asked how I was.'

'To which you replied?'

'I didn't.'

'What did she say when you told her that you were going to stay here for a while?'

'Nothing. You have to understand, we're not in each other's pockets. It's not unusual for me to be away.'

'Answer me this. Do you wish to get back to normal mental health? By that, I mean, to be feeling in control of your life and your feelings.'

His brother nodded. 'Yes.'

'Then return to Winchester, explain everything to Virginia and book a doctor's appointment immediately. There's nothing wrong with admitting that you need help. Your wife will understand.'

'And I look like a weak person, not up to following in my father's footsteps.'

'You believe that now because of your condition. Trust me, you will get better.'

Hubert audibly sucked in a long breath. 'Okay, Sebastian, you've convinced me. I'll go back this afternoon.'

'Why don't you wait until tomorrow, so you avoid the rush hour traffic?'

Was his brother in the right frame of mind to undertake the journey?

'No. I'm going now, before I have time to change my mind.' Hubert stood and walked over to the wardrobe. He took some clothes out and dropped them on the bed.

'You're doing the best thing.'

'I'll contact Virginia and let her know to expect me.'

'Good, call,' Seb said patting his brother on the back. 'You'll get through this and be back to how you used to be.'

'We'll see. I'm not so convinced as you are, but I'll try. For my family's sake,' Hubert said, giving a pained smile.

'I'm going to have tea with Mother and Father. Remember to keep in touch and let me know how you're progressing.'

Seb left and headed downstairs to his parents. Despite the positive attitude he'd displayed in front of Hubert, he was shocked at the change in him. His brother had always been the loud, outgoing one. Now he was a shadow of his former self. Seb hoped this was only a blip.

# Chapter 20

'I fail to understand why Sebastian can't return from Market Harborough to assist me, even if it's only for a short time while things are difficult,' Phillip Clifford said to his wife as he stared at himself in the mirror while tying a full Windsor knot in his navy tie. They'd arrived home later than he would have liked from the Savoy last night, and his tetchiness was in part because of being tired.

He had a meeting with the chair of a large charity later. They were intent on persuading him to sit on the board of directors, but he was unsure whether he'd have the time now he couldn't rely on Hubert to pull his weight. All the more reason for his younger son to step up.

'He has his own life to live, and we've always encouraged that,' Charlotte said.

'Only because I believed that eventually he'd see sense and return home to us. Family comes first, and now that Hubert isn't contributing, Sebastian should feel duty-bound to take his place until his brother is back working at full strength. Whenever that will be.'

'Hubert is planning to see someone for his problem,

and he'll soon return to work. Sebastian spoke to him yesterday and achieved more than we have been able to since this problem first took hold. I can't tell you what a relief that is.'

'I know what you're going to say, but in my day one had to get on with things oneself, with no outside interference.'

'This is no longer *your day*,' Charlotte said gently, standing behind him so he could see her reflection in the mirror. 'I realise now that there's no shame in Hubert seeking expert advice. He'll soon be back in the saddle, you'll see. We're lucky that Sebastian visited and could help his brother, as well as stepping in at such short notice to go with you to the Savoy. Talking of which, how did it go last night?'

'Sebastian was very good, but he's not in the same league as Hubert, who, when on form, is a natural at these events. Sebastian's a little more reserved, but he certainly was an asset. The event was a success, and they raised a substantial amount of money.'

'I'm pleased to hear it. But you can't expect Sebastian to be there whenever you need him. He's got his own career to pursue now as an investigator.'

'I had hoped he'd have nothing more to do with the police force, but it appears he's still working with them. Surely he could find something more suitable to engage in.' He gave a frustrated sigh.

'He'll forge his own path, even if we don't approve. He always has done.'

'Yes, you're right. He's been like that for his whole life, so it's futile to expect him to be any different. But one can hope. It disappointed me when his relationship with Annabelle ended. I'd hoped she could make him see sense and do something more fitting with his life.'

'They weren't destined to be.'

'She was eminently suitable and would have been an excellent addition to the family.'

'But she wasn't the one for Sebastian. I believe she might have met someone else. There was a photograph of her at the races in this month's *Tatler*. I'll find the copy and show you.'

'I hope Sebastian finds someone soon. He's not getting any younger. He'll be forty before he knows it.'

'People don't marry as early as they did in our time.'

'Hubert did.'

'Hubert was lucky to have known Virginia for most of his life. Her mother and I had planned on them marrying from when they were children, if you remember. He'll make a fine viscount as long as you're patient with him while he gets through this minor hiccup.'

'I'll speak to him after breakfast if he graces us with his presence.'

'That won't be possible. He returned home yesterday afternoon.'

Phillip frowned. 'Why didn't I know that?'

'You were busy getting ready, and I didn't want to bother you.'

'I would have liked to speak to him before he went.'

'He told me he was going to make an appointment to see someone as soon as he arrived home. He was worried about what your reaction would be and I explained we would support him in whatever he did. Was I correct in saying that?'

'Yes, you were. He's my son. If he thinks speaking about it to a stranger will be of benefit, then so be it. I'll telephone him later.'

'I'm sure he'll be his usual self in next to no time.'

'I hope you're right. Let's go down for breakfast. I have

149

a busy day ahead and will need to leave early as I want to pay a visit to my tailor before my appointment later.'

Seb picked up his overnight bag from beside the bedroom door and was on the way out when his phone rang. It was Birdie.

'Can you talk?' she said.

'Yes, is there a problem?' He returned to his room and closed the door behind him.

'I didn't want to call yesterday because you were going out. I wanted to let you know what I found in the CCTV footage.'

'We have a break in the case?' He dropped onto the bottom of the bed.

'Yes. I was working with Twiggy and—'

'DC Branch has been assisting? Is that wise?' He didn't mean for that to sound as it did. The man was Birdie's partner, and they trusted one another. But he wasn't comfortable in the older officer's company. He knew that the feeling was mutual.

'He won't tell Sarge, if that's what you think. I couldn't have done it without him. I had fifty cars to check, and I'd still be there now without his help. What is it with you two? Why can't you get along?'

'I don't know why you think there's an issue,' he lied.

'Anyway, as I was saying. I was looking at the cars on the footage when I noticed that the car being driven around several times when Lacey was left, the one Ruby mentioned, was also there the other day when she had her shock. It's a silver Volkswagen Golf. The number plates are different, but it's got an identical dent in the back. I discovered the car had been stolen just over twelve months ago.

The owner, Laura Kingston, lives in Creaton, a village twenty minutes from Harborough.'

'Well done. You've made excellent progress.'

'We have the image of the woman going into the café twelve months ago, so we should go back there and see if the manager recognises her. Then we can interview the owner of the stolen car. Are you free on Saturday? I'm not working.'

'Yes, I am.'

'But you're still cooking for me tonight though, aren't you?'

'Yes. I was planning to make a curry, if that meets with your approval.'

'Perfect. And I'll bring the wine. By the way, the spicier the better for me.'

'I'd have expected nothing less.'

'Are you having a good time?'

'I'm not here to enjoy myself.'

'That tells me everything. But surely the food was good at the Savoy?'

'There is more to life than food, although yes, the meal was very good.'

'So, not all bad, then. I'll let you go. See you later.'

He ended the call and headed downstairs to the dining room, leaving his luggage in the hall by the front door. He intended on having a quick breakfast before calling a taxi to take him to the station. Providing there were no hold-ups, he should be back in East Farndon before lunch. Fred, the man who mowed Sarah's lawns once a fortnight, was looking after Elsa for him. Fred was used to having dogs around, so he was sure there wouldn't have been a problem, but he wanted to get back to see her as soon as possible. He missed her when they weren't together, and judging by her response when he returned from being away, the feeling was mutual.

He arrived at the dining room at the same time as his parents.

'Good morning, Father. Mother.' He followed them in, glad he had the chance to speak to them over breakfast and not have to find them afterwards, which would delay his departure.

They sat at the long Edwardian dining table and gave their breakfast orders to one of the staff, Seb's being cereal, scrambled eggs and two slices of toast. What would Birdie say about breakfast being served in this manner? He stifled a grin, as he doubted his parents would appreciate his thoughts.

'Did you enjoy yourself last night?' his mother asked once they were alone.

He wasn't going to tell the truth, that it was extremely tedious, and he couldn't believe four hours could go so slowly.

'It went very well. A substantial amount of money was raised for the charity, which was the prime objective. There was no holding back on the bidding during the auction. It astonished me how much people would bid for a meal out with a celebrity. A rapper who I hadn't even heard of. I must be getting old.'

'My sentiments exactly, Sebastian. You need to find yourself a wife. Have some children.'

'Phillip,' Seb's mother scolded.

'It's fine, Mother. It's nothing I haven't already heard from Father many times, including last night. I will repeat what I told you then. If it happens, it happens. I'm perfectly happy with my life as it is.'

'Que sera, sera. Whatever will be, will be,' his mother

sung. 'Doris Day has always been one of my favourite singers.'

Seb smiled to himself. 'I'm glad you understand.'

Their breakfasts were delivered, and they sat in silence while eating.

'Have you decided when you're returning to Sarah's house, Sebastian?' his mother asked.

'I'm leaving immediately after breakfast, as I have a lot of work to do.' He glanced at his watch. He should be away within the next thirty minutes, all being well.

His mother's face fell. 'Oh. I was hoping you were going to stay a bit longer, considering we haven't seen you for a while. I cancelled my weekly facial thinking we were going to be together today.'

He stiffened. This wasn't the way his mother usually behaved. He'd never known her cancel appointments to spend time with him. Had Hubert's illness affected her more than she was letting on? 'I'm sorry, it's not possible. Another time, I promise.'

'Surely you can spare some time to be with your parents. You're disappointing your mother,' his father said.

'I explained that I could only stay a short time. Long enough to step in for Hubert last night. How did *your* evening go, Mother?' he asked, wanting to change the subject.

'Most pleasant, thank you. I was sorry to have missed your father's charity event, but there wasn't much I could do as I'd committed myself to attending the Renaissance art exhibition.'

He breathed a sigh of relief that she seemed back to her usual self.

'I'd have liked to have seen it, that's one of my favourite periods in art.'

'Stay until tomorrow and we can go together this afternoon,' she suggested, smiling.

'You know I can't, but thank you.'

'Hubert is due to attend a polo tournament with me next month. Will you be able to go in his place?' his father asked.

Watching a polo match was hardly a good enough reason for him to drop everything, although he doubted his father would understand.

'If I have the time, and Hubert isn't available, then I will, but as I've already mentioned, I'm very busy at the moment working on two separate cases and they have to take priority.'

'You mean your family doesn't.'

'Father, I've already explained this to you. I understand you need help with certain things, but last night you didn't really need me. You could have gone on your own.'

It was like going around in circles.

'I disagree. The family has to be represented and as your mother and Hubert weren't able to attend, it meant that you were required.'

'Once Hubert has received some help, he'll return to work in no time. It's been lovely seeing you both, but I can delay leaving no longer.'

'Have you heard recently from Sarah?' his mother asked.

'Yes, she contacts me regularly. She's currently enjoying exploring South America. Going away was the best thing for her and each time we speak she's excited about all the places she's visited.'

'Is she on her own?' His mother frowned.

'She's travelling alone, but there are plenty of people she's met up with who have now become friends.'

'I think that's very brave of her. I would have done nothing like that when I was younger.'

'She's not much younger than you.'

'True, but I still think she should be admired her for her courage. How are the twins getting on at university? Don't they miss their mother?'

'Sarah contacts them regularly, too. They've been back to the hall once, and I spoke to them. They're young students and too wrapped up in university life to worry about their mother travelling overseas. Now Donald's murder case has been settled, they're both doing well. When the court case is heard, it will all be dragged up again, so I'll have to support them then. Although it may not come to court until next year and Sarah might be back.'

'That's all we need,' his father said, shaking his head and tutting. 'It caused a lot of damage to the family's reputation.'

'There's nothing we can do about it, Father. But we should be there for Sarah and the children. It was bad enough that Sarah felt abandoned by her family when she needed us the most.'

His father cleared his throat. 'What else could we do?'

'Put family first.'

'Easy for you to say, my boy. But not so easy when you consider our position in society.'

'Stop,' her mother interjected. 'Sebastian, you're right, but you must understand your father's point of view. When the case comes to court, I will be there for Sarah.'

'Thank you, Mother.'

He finished his breakfast and bade them both farewell, glad to get away. As much as he loved his parents, rehashing Donald's case would not get them anywhere.

## Chapter 21

Birdie ran over to the bedroom window and glanced out at the street. Seb's car was already there. Crap. She hadn't finished doing her make-up. And as for breakfast, she'd have to forgo that. They were going to the Olive Tree Café, so she could buy something to go from there.

It was all his fault that she'd got up late. She'd ended up staying much longer at his place than she'd originally intended and hadn't arrived home until gone one in the morning. The curry he'd made was to die for. She wished she could cook like that. Actually, no, she didn't. She didn't have the time or patience. After dinner, they were so involved in looking at the footage and discussing the case that time flew by. It was so exciting that they were finally getting somewhere.

She finished getting ready and ran down the stairs.

'I'm going out with Seb for the day, as we're working on the case. I don't know when I'll be back,' she said, popping into the kitchen and seeing her mum sitting at the table, her hands wrapped around a mug.

'I saw Lacey yesterday with Catherine. She appears

almost back to how she was before the incident. She was smiling and talked a little. Obviously not to me, but to Catherine. How's the investigation going?'

'We've got a lead. I'll tell you all about it later.'

'That's fantastic. Fingers crossed it amounts to something.'

Birdie ran out of the house, opened the door to Seb's car, and jumped in.

'No need to say anything. I know. I'm sorry.'

He grinned in her direction. 'My lips are sealed. Right, let's go to the café and see if Tina Webb is available.' He pulled out onto the road, heading in the direction of the town centre.

'Who?'

'The manager, we met her, remember?'

'Oh, yeah. While we're there I—'

'Want to buy something for breakfast?'

She turned to him. 'Correct. If I hadn't been so late home last night, I'd have gone to bed earlier and then been up in time to have something to eat.'

'If you had left the house earlier, you'd have more than likely gone to the pub to meet your friends and then gone out clubbing and arrived home even later than you actually did.'

'Maybe. I'm surprised you could stay up so late. It must have been way past your bedtime when I left.'

'Your sense of humour never fails to amuse,' he replied, glancing in her direction.

'That's why you like having me around. You know, I can't stop thinking about why Lacey was left. What are your thoughts?'

'There could be many reasons, depending on who it was that left her. Was it her mother? Was it her father? Was it a friend? I think once we find out these details, our understanding will increase.'

'Or was Lacey in danger? Would a mother leave her child if someone was threatening to hurt them? If sexual abuse was involved, she could've thought leaving her for social services to find was a better option than having to endure that. Especially if she believed she could no longer protect the child.'

'You make a valid point, as it rarely starts until the child gets older, say, around the age Lacey is now.'

'But, if that's the case, then why didn't the mother report the abuser? Unless she feared them.'

'We need to know the whole scenario before we make any assumptions regarding whether abuse was involved.'

Birdie stared out of the window, thoughts circulating through her mind. She turned back to Seb. 'The thing is, we know Lacey had been looked after. She'd been taught manners, she knew how to read, and could take care of herself when it came to dressing, washing and cleaning her teeth. All of which she did without being asked. We've always said that Lacey is very advanced for her years.'

'That, too, could indicate issues. She could've been too scared to misbehave and act like a normal child of her age, because of the consequences.'

'There were no bruises or anything to show physical abuse when she was found.'

'As you know, abuse doesn't have to be physical for it to be damaging. I repeat, we shouldn't be making any assumptions until we discover exactly what circumstances she lived in.'

'Well, let's hope we're on our way to finding all out.'

When they reached the café. Birdie pushed open the door, and the noise hit her. There was a line of people at the counter and most tables were taken.

'A popular place,' Seb said.

'We'll get in the queue and ask for Tina when we get to the front. While we're there, I'll order something to take-away for breakfast. Do you want anything?'

'Coffee to go. Nothing to eat, as I've already eaten.'

Although there were five people in front of them, they soon reached the front.

'Yes?' the girl who served them asked.

'Is Tina here?'

'She's in the kitchen, as a member of staff didn't turn up this morning.'

'I'd like to order some food to go, but also need to speak to Tina regarding a case we're investigating. Can you call her out, or should we go to the kitchen?'

'I'll take your order and then it's best for you to go through.'

Birdie ordered, and then they headed behind the counter and out into the kitchen. It was a large area, almost as big as the seating area in the café. There was a large double oven, a hob, a microwave, dishwasher and sink. A stainless-steel table stood in the middle, behind which there were three people making sandwiches, all wearing white overalls, hairnets and disposable gloves.

Tina was one of them, and when they walked in, she glanced up.

'This is …' she hesitated. 'Oh, I remember you from the other day. Are you here to see me?'

'Sorry to bother you when you're so busy, but we'd like to show you a photo of someone to see if you recognise her.' Birdie took a step towards the woman, her phone in her hand, and the photo app opened.

'Don't get too close, because you're not dressed proper-ly.' Tina removed her gloves, laid them on the table, and joined them.

'This woman came into the café on the same day and time that Lacey was abandoned. It's not a good image but we're hoping you might recognise her?'

Birdie held out her phone, and Tina stared at it. 'Hmm. I'm not sure.' She tapped her lip with her forefinger. 'Actually, I do remember her. Not her, but the bag she was carrying on her shoulder. It was a handmade raffia bag in sapphire blue. When I admired it she said she'd made it herself.'

'Where did she sit?'

'Next to the window at one of the small round tables.'

'Would she have been able to see the Old Grammar School?'

'Yes, if she sat on the right-hand seat. Which she did. Oh my God, I can't believe I didn't think of this before.'

'How long did she stay for?'

'I don't recall. Maybe half an hour, or a little longer. All she had was a coffee.'

'Can you describe her to us?'

'Umm … She was average height. Maybe in her thirties. I don't remember her hair or eye colour, sorry.'

'It's fine, you've given us more than we had before. If you think of anything else, please call me.' Birdie took out a card from her pocket and handed it to her. 'Thanks for your time. We'll leave you to it. It's crazy busy out there.'

'Tell me about it,' Tina said, giving a wry grin.

They left the kitchen, collected their takeaway from the counter, and walked out of the café.

'I knew today was going to be good. We could've identified Lacey's mum,' she said to Seb on their way back to the car.

'One step at a time,' he cautioned.

'And the next step is Creaton. Let's go.'

# Chapter 22

'Laura Kingston lives towards the top of The Jetty, on the left,' Birdie said, as they drove along the Brixworth Road and reached the edge of Creaton. 'It's a cul-de-sac, the second road on the left, opposite the playing field. You can't miss it.'

'You know this area, I take it?' Seb said.

'Yes, I had a friend who lived on The Green. This is definitely an area I'd consider living in, if I ever save up enough money for a house deposit. Or Cottesbrooke, which you can see in the distance. When I was young, Mum and Dad would bring us to the annual church fete held in the grounds of Cottesbrooke Hall.' She pointed over the fields to the next village, where Seb could see the church tower standing proud against the rolling landscape.

'I know of the Hall. It's a Queen Anne house, but has an Arts and Crafts garden, circa 1930.'

'You've been there, too? When?'

'No, I've never visited. I would have read about it.'

He approached The Jetty and turned in, driving to the top as instructed. There were several modern detached houses facing down the road and with views of the open fields.

Birdie rang the bell and a woman in her forties, wearing leggings and a baggy jumper, answered.

'Hello, I'm Lucinda Bird, and this is Sebastian Clifford. We're looking for Laura Kingston?'

'That's me.'

'We'd like to speak to you regarding a stolen car from twelve months ago, as we believe it might link to a case we're investigating. Do you have a few minutes?'

'Are you the police?'

'Private investigators,' Birdie said.

'Don't tell me you've actually found my car after all this time.'

'Not exactly. May we come inside?'

The woman opened the door, and they walked into a square hallway. She ushered them to a modern lounge, which went from front to back of the house.

'Please take a seat. Would you like anything to drink?'

'We're fine, thank you,' Birdie said, as they both sat on the black leather sofa. 'Please, could you go through what happened when your car was stolen?'

Laura Kingston sat on the edge of a single leather chair next to them and leant in towards them. 'I went over all this with the police.'

'We'd like to get a fresh perspective on it.' Birdie pulled out her notebook and pen, her face set.

If the incident had been investigated by the Northamptonshire Police, she most likely wouldn't have seen the file.

'I explained I thought I knew who'd stolen the car, but the police couldn't find her. I'm not even sure how hard they tried. No offence.'

'If you could go through the story, from when you discovered your car was missing,' Birdie said.

'We went to Center Parcs at Sherwood Forest, in Nottingham, and left first thing on Friday morning, the 14$^{th}$. My car was on the drive and the keys were inside the house on the hook in the hall, where they were always kept. Easy to steal.'

Birdie looked up from her notebook. 'So you believe that someone broke into the house and stole the car keys?'

'No. She didn't break in. She didn't need to as she had a front door key.'

'She?'

'The person who stole my car.'

Birdie frowned. 'And the police didn't trace her. Who is she?'

'My cleaner, Tessa Casey. Or, ex-cleaner. I haven't seen her since that weekend. She always came to clean on a Friday morning, and I'd given her a key in case I was ever out when she arrived. When we got home from Center Parcs on the Sunday afternoon, the car had gone and we didn't see Tessa again. According to one neighbour, the car wasn't in the drive after Friday morning, so we assumed she took it then.'

'I accept that it all pointed to Tessa, but did you consider an alternative version? That it might have happened when she was working. Perhaps she'd left the front door open, and an opportunist thief came in and took the keys and car?' Seb asked.

'In this village, at the top of a cul-de-sac? How likely is that? If it wasn't her, she'd have come to work the following Friday, but she didn't. We had to change the lock on the front door because she still had the key.'

'Does she live locally?' Birdie asked.

'Holcot. At least that's what she told me. It turned out that the address she'd given me doesn't exist.'

'Did you take references or do a check when you took her on?' Seb asked.

'No. I placed an ad in the local newsagent and she answered it. She told me she cleaned for several people in the vicinity. I gave her a trial and was happy with her work, so I kept her on. I didn't leave her alone in the house for the first few months. I liked her. I still can't believe how stupid I was. It taught me a valuable lesson. I won't ever employ anyone again without checking references.'

'How long did Tessa work for you?'

'Six months. She was a great cleaner, which made what happened even more devastating. I still haven't been able to bring myself to employ anyone else. We're muddling through doing it ourselves.'

'Did Tessa drive herself to work?' Seb asked.

'No. Either she had a lift, or she caught the bus.'

'Who would bring her?'

'I saw her being dropped off once by a man. It might have been her brother, as she sometimes mentioned him.'

'Did she talk about the rest of her family, in particular, any children?' Birdie asked.

'She gave me the impression that she was single with no other family. She certainly didn't mention having any children. Why?'

'We're trying to get a fuller picture. Is this Tessa?' Birdie took out her phone and showed Laura Kingston the image.

The woman nodded. 'Yep. That's her. Even side-on I can tell because of the way she's bending forward slightly. And that's her blue bag. She always had it with her. I think she made it herself. Or someone made it for her. She told me it was home-made.'

'Thank you. One more question. When you last saw your car, was it damaged in any way?' Birdie asked.

'Yes, there was a dent at the back. I was in the super-market car park and accidentally reversed into one of those small black bollard things. I totally didn't see it. My husband had a hissy fit when it happened but it's easy for someone of his height to see all around the car. I'm barely over five feet two and have so many blind spots in a car that it's not funny. We planned on waiting until the car's next service before getting it fixed. So what happens, now, if you've found the car? The insurance company paid out, so should it go to them?'

'The car we believe might be yours currently has false number plates. If it's recovered and they find ownership to be yours, then you will need to contact your insurance company, as they will deem it theirs and class it as salvage-able,' Seb said.

'When will this happen?'

'Not until we have the car in our possession. All we have at present is CCTV footage, which is where we got Tessa's image from,' Birdie said.

'I thought you actually had it. So, there's nothing for me to do, in that case.'

'No. But if you remember anything else about Tessa, please contact me.' Birdie ripped out a piece of paper from her notebook, wrote her mobile number and handed it to the woman.

They left the house and headed back to the car.

'Do you know Holcot?' Seb asked, as he pulled over his seat belt and clicked it in place.

'Yes, go back the way we came and when we get to Brixworth, we'll take the Holcot Road. It's a village about six miles away from here. It won't take us long.'

'There's a chance we might come across the stolen car.'

'*If* the cleaner actually lives there.'

'It's surprising how many people stick fairly close to the

truth when lying. It makes the lies easier to remember. Even if Tessa gave Laura Kingston a fake address at the time of her employment, she may well have told her the correct area.'

'Plus, we now have her name, so should be able to track her that way. I'll get onto that on Monday. In the meantime, Holcot, here we come.'

# Chapter 23

Birdie stared out of the window as they drove along the winding lanes. Wild flowers dotted the countryside. It was so peaceful. She could understand why people wanted to live in a rural location. Especially somewhere like this, with vibrant cities in easy reach by train or car.

'Do you miss London?' she asked, turning to Seb, who was staring intently, concentrating on the road ahead.

'I don't miss the traffic, although …' He pulled onto the side of the road to move out of the way of an oncoming tractor. 'Driving around here takes a bit of getting used to.'

'Your family lives on an estate that's in the country. Tractors shouldn't be alien to you.'

'I haven't lived there for a lot of years and our estate isn't far off the M3. The roads are much straighter.'

'Have you thought about moving up here on a more permanent basis? Now you've set up your company you could work from anywhere.'

Would she like to have him around all the time? She had to admit to enjoying his company, even though they had nothing in common. Apart from a desire for justice and not giving up until they could solve a case.

'I'm semi-permanent now, with Sarah being away. I'll decide when she returns.'

'Tell me about this marketing strategy you're devising for *CIS*.'

'I don't want to spend my time working on potential divorce proceedings and following people for hours on end. That would not be fulfilling. I'm going to be selective on the cases I accept.'

'They might not come along regularly. Divorce work is like the bread and butter for private investigators. Surely you would need to take some of these cases?'

'That's where working with Rob fits in. I'd rather be a civilian researcher for the Met where I can dictate my own working hours. As my reputation builds, and more cases come my way, then I'll pull back from my work with him.'

'Sounds like a plan. But you still haven't told me how you're going to find these *special cases.*'

'I'm going to utilise my connections. I had an excellent reputation when working at the Met. And also …' he hesitated.

'Your family and society friends?'

'How did you know?'

'It's obvious. They're the ones with the money who can afford your services. I think it's a great idea. I might even leave the force and join you.'

He glanced in her direction. 'Really?'

'No. I'm just messing around. Can you seriously ever see me leaving the police? Turn here.' She pointed to the road on the left.

They drove for a further five minutes, until reaching the Holcot sign, and Seb pulled in.

'Do you know where the village shop is? I'm assuming there is one.'

'I've no idea. Why?'

'If we want to discover where Tessa Casey lives, then the village shop is the place to start. They'll know about everyone who lives here.'

They drove further and came to the shop. As they opened the door, the overhead bell rang. Birdie scanned the area. It was empty. It was a general store and typical of other village shops she'd been in; full of many things, not only food but also games, cleaning products, magazines, books. It was jam-packed.

'How they ever find anything in here, beats me,' she said.

'I'm sure the staff can lay their hands on everything. It's nice to see shops like this still in existence.'

They approached the counter, and a man came out from the back.

'Are you the owner?' Seb asked.

'Yes, I'm Paul Bryson.'

'We're private investigators, and we'd like to ask you a few questions, if you don't mind. Do you recognise this car?' Birdie held out her phone with a recent image of the car with the fake plates.

The man nodded. 'Yes, I do. I think it belongs to a retired priest and his sister who rent a cottage on a farm just out of the village on the Walgrave Road.'

A retired priest with a stolen car. That was weird. She pulled up a photo of Lacey. 'And this little girl, do you recognise her?'

Bryson stared at the phone for quite a while. 'No, I've never seen her.'

Did that mean that everything they'd discovered so far

about their connection to Lacey was a bunch of coincidences?

'What can you tell us about the priest and his sister?' she asked.

'Very little. We don't see them much as they seldom shop here and are rarely seen out walking. But you know what village life is like. Most people know who people are, even if they don't actually speak to them.'

'Do you know their names?'

'His name's Patrick Casey. I know that because of the time a parcel was left here for him.'

'How did you find out he was a priest?'

'He mentioned it to my wife when they first moved in. I have no idea where in the country he worked, though.'

'Is his sister's name Tessa?'

'I couldn't tell you.'

'How long have they lived in the cottage?'

'At least two years. Before then one of the farmhands had it, but he died.'

'Where does the farmer live?'

'On the farm with his family. His land goes as far as Walgrave and they have a large house there.'

'How do we get to this cottage from here?'

'Take a left onto the Walgrave Road, travel two miles out of the village and you'll see a farm track on the right. Drive up there for about half a mile and you should come across it.'

'May I ask why you're looking into these people? They've never caused any trouble around here.'

'Sorry, we're not allowed to disclose anything in case it jeopardises our investigation. We have no idea whether the Caseys are linked to it. It's a line of enquiry we're following.'

She didn't want the village grapevine working overtime. These people might be nothing to do with Lacey's case. But if they were, she didn't want to risk losing the only lead they had because of local gossip.

'Heard and understood,' Bryson said, tapping the side of his nose.

They left the shop and jumped back into the car.

'That was bizarre, don't you think? We know Tessa was in the car on the day Lacey was abandoned, and that the car was around when she got upset last Saturday. But the guy in the shop didn't recognise Lacey. It makes no sense. Could we be wrong? Are we missing something? Or ...' She froze. 'Or was Lacey kept locked up in the cottage and never allowed outside? Oh my God, Seb. Do you think that happened to her?'

Nausea washed over her, and she squeezed her eyes shut, trying to force back images of Lacey being kept a prisoner.

'Let's not jump to any conclusions. I think we should check them out.'

'He's a retired priest. My aunt has heard Lacey sound like she's saying prayers in her sleep. I'm not jumping to conclusions. It's staring us in the face.'

'Birdie, you've got to keep calm and not get emotion-ally involved, or it will hamper our investigation.'

She knew he was right, but it was hard.

They followed Paul Bryson's directions and soon arrived at the track, but there was no sign of the cottage in the distance. They turned in and after a couple of minutes' drive the road ended, and they were in front of an old farmhouse that looked as if it had seen better days. The house was double-fronted and two storeys, but not large. There were barns by the side of it.

She scanned the area. 'There's no car here, unless it's in one of the outbuildings. Or maybe they're out. Even if the car is here, I can't do anything about it as I'm not officially on duty and Sarge isn't aware of what we're doing. Let's knock on the door and if no one answers, we'll have a scout around.'

They headed to the front of the house. Paint on the windows was peeling and Birdie could see around into the back garden, which was planted with vegetables. She could've sworn she saw the net curtains at the window twitch. Were they being watched?

Birdie gave a sharp rap on the door, and after a short while was about to knock again when a woman answered. She looked a little older than Birdie and was very thin with fine blonde hair hanging loosely around her face. The remains of a yellow bruise was noticeable under her eye. Was she the woman in the image?

'Hello?' she said, her voice soft.

'Are you Tessa Casey?'

'Umm … yes.' She nodded.

'I'm DC Bird from Market Harborough police, and this is Sebastian Clifford. We'd like to come in to ask you some questions.'

She shouldn't have played the police card, but she instinctively knew that it would be the only way to get inside. She'd deal with Seb's wrath later.

The woman's grip tightened on the wooden door, and her eyes darted from Birdie to Seb.

'What about?'

'Is it right that you used to clean for Laura Kingston in Creaton?'

'Yes,' the woman whispered.

'Is your brother here?' Seb asked.

'No. He went for a walk.'

Good question from Seb. A black eye. Jumpy and

scared. Did he think the woman was being abused by her brother?

'Please, may we come in?'

'Okay, if it's not for long.'

Tessa stepped to the side, and Birdie and Seb walked into the kitchen. The room was bare, other than a square oak table in the middle with three mismatched chairs placed around it. On one wall was a picture of what looked like the Virgin Mary with a baby in her arms.

Seb pulled out a chair and sat down, and Birdie did the same. Tessa leant against the kitchen sink, staring directly at Birdie.

Was she more comfortable with women than men?

'We'd like to know about the last time you cleaned for Laura Kingston because it was the same day as her car was stolen.'

'I didn't take it. I promise I didn't. Did Mrs Kingston say I did?' Her fingers clutched the green cardigan she was wearing so tightly that her knuckles were white.

'Do you know who stole it?' Birdie asked, deciding not to answer the woman's question.

She shook her head. 'No.'

'So why didn't you return to work after that shift?'

'I'd been called away on a family emergency and didn't know when I'd be back. I was going to leave a note but forgot.'

'What emergency was this?' Seb asked.

She bowed her head. 'I'd rather not say.'

'The car was stolen by someone who had access to the keys, which were left in their usual place. Can you account for this?' Birdie asked.

'I might have forgotten to lock the house when I left. I don't know.'

Birdie didn't want to push it because she wasn't there

officially, but surely the woman didn't expect them to believe her.

'Can you explain to me why you didn't contact Laura Kingston to let her know why you'd suddenly left the job, and to return her house key?'

'I couldn't because I'd lost my phone and then didn't have her details. I didn't know about the car being stolen.'

'The police tried to find you and couldn't because when you started working for Mrs Kingston you gave her a fake address. Why?'

'I was scared. I-in case she came here.'

'Was that likely?'

'I didn't want to risk it because …' She turned her head and stared out of the window; her mouth open.

Birdie glanced to see what had distracted her. Approaching the house was an older man who looked to be in his late forties, early fifties. Was he the brother? He had a similar build, only he was much taller.

The door opened, and he stared at Birdie and Seb. His eyes narrowed.

'Who are you?' His face was set hard.

'DC Bird from Market Harborough police and this is Sebastian Clifford.'

Seb walked towards the man, towering over him.

'What do you want?' the man asked, taking a step backwards.

'Are you Patrick Casey?'

'Yes.' He turned to his sister. 'Are you okay?'

She nodded.

Birdie pulled out her phone and called up the image of the woman who got out of the car on the day Lacey was abandoned. She held it out for Tessa to view.

'Is this you?'

'Let me see,' Patrick said, hurrying over. 'No, that's not my sister. Where was this taken?'

'This is CCTV footage from a Saturday morning twelve months ago. The person in this image was seen coming out of a car parked in High Street. This car had been stolen the day before from the house where Tessa used to clean, in Creaton.'

'I told you, I didn't take the car.'

'Mrs Kingston identified you in this image. She particularly recognised the blue bag that you always carried.'

'It's not me. And that's not my bag. She's wrong.'

'Why are you looking into this now?' Patrick asked.

'We're investigating the abandonment of a young child on the same morning as this footage. We believe the car is connected to it. Do you recognise this girl?'

Birdie pulled up the photo of Lacey and showed it to him.

'No,' he said, giving it a cursory glance.

She then showed it to Tessa. 'Do you?'

The woman shook her head even before taking a proper look. 'No.'

'Do you remember the story of when this little girl disappeared? It was in all the media.'

'We don't have a television and I don't read the papers,' Patrick Casey said.

Birdie pulled out her notebook from her jacket pocket. 'Before we go, I'd like to take down a few details. You are Tessa and Patrick Casey, and you're brother and sister?'

'Half-brother and sister. We had the same father. I don't see why this is relevant,' Patrick said.

'There's a big age difference between you.'

'Twenty-five years. But so what?'

'Do you have a car?' Birdie asked.

'No.'

'With being so isolated, how do you get around?'

'Public transport. We don't go out often. We prefer to stay here.'

'According to our sources, you've been seen driving a silver Volkswagen Golf, the same as the one stolen from Mrs Kingston, only with fake plates on it.'

'Your sources are wrong. I know nothing about this.' Patrick said.

She didn't want to push it until they had more to go on.

'We were also informed that you used to be a priest. Is that correct?'

'Yes. I took early retirement eight years ago.'

'Why did you retire early?' Seb asked.

'Personal reasons. That's it. We're not prepared to answer further questions unless you arrest us and we have a lawyer present. Please leave.'

# Chapter 24

Patrick watched their visitors leave the farm and drive down the track. When they were out of sight, he turned to his sister, exasperation coursing through him. Everything could come crashing down if they weren't careful. They'd lasted this long without their history being known, and he wasn't prepared to let anything alter that.

'What were you doing speaking to the police? You know our situation.'

'I couldn't refuse. They came to ask me about Mrs Kingston's car because I cleaned for her. I don't know how they found out where we lived. They asked why I left the job and I said it was a family emergency. That wasn't a lie. I didn't tell them what it was.'

'We'll have to get rid of the car. At least they didn't ask to search the barn, so they don't know it's there.'

'Are you going to sell it?'

'I know someone at the pub who might take it off my hands. I'll have to risk driving it until then. I can't be without transport. It's bloody annoying.' He thumped the table in frustration, and his sister tensed.

'Can you buy a different number plate for it from the DIY shop?'

'Yes, I will. But what I want to know is why were they asking about Emily? You told me she ran away, so how can this be related to you in the car?'

None of this was stacking up.

'She did, and I couldn't do anything to stop her. I looked for ages, but she'd totally disappeared. You already know that.'

'Yet, according to them, she was found in the town centre and the Golf was connected to it. I'm assuming that meant she was seen running from the car. What aren't you telling me, Tessa?'

'Nothing. I promise. Emily didn't run away from the car when it was in High Street. She'd already gone by then. When we went into Market Harborough, I deliberately parked in a side road because there weren't any cameras. It was from there that Emily disappeared, before I could do anything about it.' She hung her head.

Did his sister miss the child as much as he did?

It couldn't be possible.

'If that was the case, why did you then park on the high street where you *could* be seen on camera? Either you're keeping something from me, or I'm losing the plot. And's not what's going on here.'

'I knew you'd be mad at me for everything I'd done. All I could think of was finding Emily and going back home. I drove around the block several times, hoping to see her, but it was like she'd vanished into thin air. In the end, I parked and went over to the nearest café. I didn't know what to do. I'm sorry. I wanted to call the police but couldn't risk them coming here and finding out the truth about our lives. I had no choice.'

He got it. He did. But then losing Emily had almost

destroyed him. She'd meant everything to him. He'd brought her into the world. The day he'd delivered the child was permanently etched on his mind. It gave them an unbreakable bond. At least her birth hadn't been registered so there was nothing linking her to them.

He rested his head in his hand. He'd thought he was over this, but clearly, he wasn't. The whole thing was one unholy mess.

'I still don't understand why you had to take the car. None of this would have happened if it wasn't for that.' He locked eyes with his sister.

What wasn't she telling him?

He'd get it out of her, eventually. However long it took. He'd spent his life protecting Tessa, and then the child. Everything he'd done was for them.

'What happened hasn't changed since I told you last year. I missed the bus and couldn't get back home for hours. You know how few buses there are on that route. You'd gone away and Emily was on her own. I didn't mind leaving her for a morning, but any longer and she might have harmed herself.'

'What would she have done? The child always behaved herself when left alone.'

'Because she knew what would happen if she didn't.'

'So you could've left her for longer.'

'You're confusing me. I didn't want her to be on her own for too long. Mrs Kingston had gone away for the weekend, so I borrowed the car. I wasn't going to keep it. I'd planned to take it back the next day but when Emily ran away, and I couldn't find her, I was too upset so I came home.'

'Let me get this straight. You'd planned to take Emily out to Market Harborough on Saturday morning and after that return the car to Creaton?'

Why hadn't she told him all this a year ago?

It was his fault. He should've asked, but he'd been so distraught at Emily's disappearance, he wasn't thinking straight.

'Yes.' She gave a vigorous nod.

'And then what? How were you going to get home?'

'We were going to catch the one o'clock bus from along the Brixworth Road.'

'Okay, I understand now. But what I can't get my head around is why she ran away when she'd done nothing like that before.'

'I don't know. Why do you keep asking me? It just happened. One minute she was sitting in the back of the car and the next she'd gone.'

'What were you doing when this happened?'

'I closed my eyes for a moment and must have drifted off to sleep.'

He frowned. This was the first time she'd mentioned this, too.

'You went to sleep? Why didn't you tell me this before?'

She screwed up her face. 'I don't know. I don't know. Maybe it's good for her being somewhere else so she can go to school and have a normal life.'

Had she done it on purpose? Was it a ploy to get the child away from him?

'You were quite capable of teaching her yourself and so was I.'

'Do you think we should go to the police?'

'Don't be stupid. We've got the stolen car and that will get us in trouble. It's now twelve months later, and we've moved on. Emily's no longer part of our family.'

'I wish I hadn't taken her to Market Harborough. I thought it would make a pleasant change for her because she was always stuck at home. It wouldn't have happened if you'd been here instead of going away.' She scowled at him.

He raised his hand, and she flinched. 'That's no excuse for what you did. You're lucky no one saw you take the car, and they weren't able to trace it here.'

'Except they have now.'

'They can't prove anything. If they come back when I'm out, tell them you know nothing. If they find out we're related to the child, we could end up in prison and I, for one, am not going back there.'

He shuddered as memories of his past flooded his mind.

'That was for something different,' Tessa said.

'If all this took place over a year ago, why are they investigating now? What's happened for them to check cars in the area recently and compare it to last year, and work out ours has fake plates?'

'I don't know. We hardly ever go into Market Harborough,' Tessa said.

'It's something to do with Emily.'

'Do you think she saw us last Saturday?'

'I don't know. Did you catch sight of her when we were at the ATM?'

'No, but I wasn't looking. The thing is, she was only in the car that one time, so surely she couldn't have recognised it. I wonder how she's getting on, what she's doing and if someone's looking after her properly.'

'It has nothing to do with us. You lost her, and that's it. We don't have to deal with her any longer. Frankly, it's much easier that way because children aren't cheap. Whoever has her now can pay for food and clothes. We can do what we like.'

He played down his true feelings because he didn't want Tessa to know how often he thought of the child and how much he missed her. She wouldn't be able to deal with the truth.

'Except we never do anything. I spend my time here. I enjoyed it when I was working. Can I get another job?'

'Not now. Not until this has blown over.'

## Chapter 25

'Let's find somewhere to stop for a drink,' Seb said.

He drove them into Brixworth and turned left into the village, rather than right, which would have taken them to the A508. He needed time to process everything they'd witnessed.

They stopped at the first pub they came to and found an out of the way table to sit at with their drinks.

'You've hardly said a word since we left the cottage. What do you make of everything?' Birdie asked.

His body tensed. If there was one thing which caused him to lose his cool, it was signs of abuse. He'd deal with it by drawing inwards until he had his feelings under control. It was imperative for him to remain objective in his occupation. He viewed his response as a major failing, although most times he could rein it in.

'I don't want to make accusations that can't be substantiated, but we witnessed a very strained relationship between Tessa and her brother. Did you notice the bruising under her eye?'

'Yeah, that was an old bruise. I also spotted one on her

arm. She was definitely scared of him. Did you see the fear in her eyes when he arrived at the house?'

'I did. They were both on the defensive and hiding information from us.'

'It was probably the car. I bet it was hidden in one of the barns, or put somewhere out of the way. We should have demanded to look in the outbuildings, to see if we could find it.'

'Without a search warrant? Even a half-decent lawyer would get them off before charges could be made. We have to play everything by the book.'

'You're right, I suppose. However frustrating it is. Do you think Tessa is the woman in the picture?'

'She was certainly the same build, but other than that, it's impossible to tell. It's not a good image as it's only her profile.'

'Laura Kingston thought it was her, and surely she should know as the woman had worked for her.'

'It's possible, but you know how often witnesses are mistaken, particularly if they are fixated on something. Laura Kingston's identification was more to do with the blue bag hanging on the woman's shoulder than actually examining the profile. It would be hard to make a case against Tessa without the bag. Speaking of which, I didn't see any sign of it in the house. Did you?' Seb asked.

'No. Considering she hadn't been expecting us to turn up, if she was as attached to the bag as Laura Kingston said, then where was it? I'd have expected it to be draped on the back of a chair. Or hanging somewhere close by, like a hook or the bannister. But it was nowhere to be seen in the kitchen.'

'She might have placed it in a cupboard or drawer. Or maybe in her bedroom.'

'Don't you think the place was freezing and bare?

There were hardly enough possessions in the kitchen for me to believe that it was lived in.'

'Some priests vow to live a simple life. Patrick might have wanted to remain like that, even though he was no longer one,' Seb suggested.

'Okay, that makes sense. What did you make of their reactions to the mention of Lacey and then when we showed them her photo?'

'Most illuminating. They denied knowing her even before they looked at the image you showed them.'

'That's what I thought, too. They kept their faces blank, almost *too* blank.'

'His face was set hard, as if he was determined not to give anything away. She attempted to be the same, but there was a flicker of recognition in her eyes when she first caught sight of Lacey.'

'Really? I didn't notice,' Birdie said.

'I thought I'd seen it but replayed the conversation in my mind to make sure I wasn't mistaken.'

'Are you ever?'

'I make mistakes, the same as everyone does.'

'If you've got a search engine in your head instead of a normal brain like the rest of us, then how can you be? It can be pretty annoying, actually.'

'I thought you were referring to the poor decisions I've made in the past.'

'Ah … well, that's a conversation for another time. Lacey's our top priority at the moment. Do you think Tessa's her mum?'

'They have identical colouring, and the same shaped face, but we'd need a DNA test to confirm it.'

'Did you spot the likeness with Patrick as well? You know he could be her dad?'

'There's bound to be a family resemblance. He's her

uncle. Assuming he's also Lacey's father is making an unsubstantiated leap. Again, a DNA test should prove his paternity or otherwise. But that's not something we're able to do.'

'I'd stake my life on them being involved. DNA test or no DNA test. He wouldn't have been so aggressive if they had nothing to hide.'

'I agree with you, but it's imperative we tread carefully. We don't want them taking off somewhere.'

'We also need to work quickly, for the same reason.'

'It would appear that they've been living under the radar where they are. It won't be easy to find somewhere similar at short notice. Yes, we should act quickly, but not irresponsibly. Let's get as much information as we can about the pair of them and then decide on how to proceed.'

'Drink up and let's go then. I'll go into work once we get back and do some research into them. I'll call round and see you later.' Birdie picked up her glass, which was still half full of cider, tapped it on the side of his glass and then raised it to her lips and finished it in one go.

'Saturday's your day off, so what are you doing here?' Twiggy asked Birdie as she walked into the office and headed over to her desk.

'I want to do some research, providing Sarge isn't around. His car wasn't in the car park, so I'm hoping he's out. Is he?' She pulled out her chair and sat down in front of the computer screen.

'It's all clear at the moment because he's with Sparkle interviewing witnesses from the drugs raid. They went out about an hour ago, so you've got a bit of time.'

'What are you working on?'

'Still going through the list of potential carjacking suspects. Out of the eight names who fit our images, six have alibis, which I confirmed. There are two left, who are friends, according to their social media presence. We'll bring them in, when you're on duty, and we'll interview them together. I'm assuming you want to be in on it.'

'What a stupid question. Why wouldn't I?'

'Because you're working on Lacey's case.'

'Not during work time. Well … not exactly. You know what I mean.'

'I take it you're here now to do some Lacey stuff. What is it?'

'You know the car we identified? The stolen one from Creaton. We can't prove it yet, but it looks like the cleaner took it. We've traced the woman. She lives with her brother. We didn't see the car on the premises, but we'll find it. It's got to be connected to Lacey. I know it. I'm going to see what I can dig up on the pair of them. I'd better be quick, in case Sarge makes an appearance sooner than expected. It's like he has some sort of sixth sense where I'm concerned.'

She opened her computer and searched in the database for any child born to a Tessa Casey.

'Crap,' she muttered after looking through the birth records twice, to make sure she hadn't missed anything.

'What is it?' Twiggy asked.

'There are no births registered in Tessa Casey's name, nor can I find any record of her being in hospital. Does that mean Lacey isn't hers?'

'Not necessarily. Not everyone registers a child's birth.'

She bit down on her bottom lip. 'You could be right, Twig. And it would account for us being told at the shop that they'd never seen Tessa, or her brother Patrick, with a child. They could've kept Lacey hidden.'

'Why?'

'I can think of one excellent reason.'

'Being?' Twiggy asked, frowning.

'Her brother is Lacey's father. Well, he's her half-brother, as they had the same dad. He's much older than she is, and she's terrified of him. I reckon he beats her. He used to be a priest. Bloody hell. It's all adding up. He fathered the child, had to give up the priesthood, and they moved off the grid to keep their dirty little secret.' She sat back in her chair and folded her arms across her chest.

'Now you have to prove it.'

'I will. Believe me, I will. I'll start by looking into him. Patrick Casey, you won't be able to hide from me.'

She leant forward and began searching in the databases for anything on him, but none of the Patrick Caseys she came across were him. Then … Her eyes widened, and her lips turned up into a broad smile.

'Gotcha. Listen to this. Patrick Casey isn't anywhere in the system, but there was a priest done for child sex offences by the name of *Sean* Casey. I've called up the image, and it's him. He's changed his name. It lists his next of kin as *Sinead* Casey. There's no image of her, but it's got to be Tessa. Does that mean Lacey's birth is registered under that name?'

She went back to the database and went through it again. 'No. Still nothing.'

'Surely he'd be on the sex offenders' register and being monitored? If he changed his name, there should be a note somewhere in his file as it's illegal not to inform the police,' Twiggy said.

'It depends on the crime and how long he had to remain on the register. I'll find out.' Now she had his proper name, it was easy enough to get the details she needed. 'Okay. He was charged with having pornographic images of children on his computer and was sentenced to three years in prison and for his name to remain on the register for ten years. The ten years aren't up and there's nothing on record of his name change.'

'You've got him. Great work. But now you have to think about Lacey and what's next for her.'

'I know. I'm going out to East Farndon to see Clifford. If Sarge asks, you haven't seen me.'

'Why is he going to ask, it's your day off?'

'Good point. No wonder you're a detective. I'll see you tomorrow morning.'

## Chapter 26

Seb opened the door to be greeted by Birdie standing tall with her shoulders back. She held a Manilla folder in one hand, and a bright yellow packet in the other.

'You've had success in your research, I take it?'

'You bet I have. I didn't want to risk a celebration yet, in case it doesn't pan out, so instead of buying booze I stopped at the supermarket and bought these for Elsa. Where is she?' She held up a bag of chicken delight doggie chews.

'In the garden. How did you know they were her favourite snack?'

'You had some when I took care of her that time. Mind you, she's a Labrador, so I'm guessing that almost every-thing is her favourite.'

'True. Come on in and we'll take them to her. Then you can update me on what you've discovered.'

They headed through the kitchen door and into the garden. He spied Elsa sniffing around the lavender. She looked up, saw Birdie and came charging towards them, making a beeline for the officer, who stepped forward to greet her.

'Hey, Elsa. Look what I've got.' Birdie dangled the packet in front of the dog, who sat down and stared up at her. 'You're so well trained.' Birdie took out a chew and held it out. 'Here you are.' Elsa took it from her and then ran off. 'I'm impressed. She didn't snatch it from my hand.'

'Believe me, that took a lot of training, and several sore fingers,' Seb said, grinning. 'Let's go into the study.'

They stopped in the kitchen on the way for some coffee, and then headed to the study, sitting themselves down on the easy chairs facing the French doors which opened out onto the garden.

Birdie opened the folder she'd placed on the coffee table in front of them. 'First, Tessa and Patrick Casey are really Sinead and Sean Casey. They changed their names.'

'Interesting. Do you know why?'

'Sean Casey went to prison for having child pornography on his computer, and his name was put on the sex offenders' register. He was still working as a priest at the time in Gloucester, which is where they both were born, according to birth records. When he was released, they both changed their names and moved here, but he didn't inform the police.'

'There's a loophole in the law, enabling offenders to change their names by deed poll. They risk a five-year prison sentence if they do so without informing the author-ities, but that doesn't appear to deter many. There have been calls for the government to stop them being able to do this.'

'I'm not surprised. How awful for survivors of abuse if their attacker could turn up using a different name. You'd be looking over your shoulder all the time, worrying about it.'

'It's certainly an issue. Did you discover anything regarding Tessa and Patrick's links to Lacey?'

Birdie shook her head. 'I found no birth registered in Tessa or Sinead's name. I also looked at hospital records and couldn't find any trace of her having been there, either. If she's Lacey's mum, then she had her at home and they didn't register the birth. That's all it can be. Unless we've got this totally wrong, and Lacey isn't related to her at all. But how likely is that? We've both agreed on the likeness between them.'

'We could have seen a likeness that wasn't there, based on our presuppositions. You've done excellent work. Now we need to come up with a plan to find out if she is Lacey's mother.'

'Don't forget him. I still think he's the father.'

'Another line of enquiry warranting investigation.'

Birdie stared out of the window, drumming her fingers on her leg, before turning to face him. 'We've already seen how scared Tessa is of Patrick … I'm sticking to their current names for now as it's less confusing. If we want her to confide in us, we need to get her alone, when he's out. I bet I can get her to cave. She looked like she would earlier, before he turned up.'

'I agree we might find out more if she's on her own. I also think it's more likely that she'll confess to you, rather than me, because she seemed scared of men. I could tell by the look on her face when we were there that she was much more comfortable talking to you and didn't like me asking questions.'

'We need a plan.' Birdie picked up her coffee and took a drink. 'I know. We'll stake out the place and wait to see if he goes out on his own. If he does, then we can go to the house and speak to her. Not only that, we can also see if he's driving the silver Golf.'

'That would work, but it's better if we go in separate cars. If we see him go out, I'll follow and warn you when he's on his way back.'

'Perfect. We'll start tomorrow.' She screwed up her face. 'Crap. I'm at work. Unless I phone in sick.'

'Do you have any annual leave owing?'

'Yes, I've got plenty. That's a better idea. I'll see Sarge in the morning and ask for some time off. I'll have to give a few days' notice. If I tell him it's a family thing, he should be okay. It's not like I'm lying because Lacey *is* my family. He won't ask what it is, anyway. He never does.'

'If you can get the time off and it won't get you in trouble, then it's worth us doing. I'll keep watch for the next few days and see if there's any pattern to what they do. I'll position myself on the opposite side of the road from the start of the track. Once your leave starts, we can put our plan into practice.'

'Providing they don't disappear after today.'

'We'll have to take that risk. I'll follow if he goes out, or if they go out together.'

'As long as you keep your distance, we don't want them sussing you out.'

'Birdie, contrary to what you seem to believe, I know how to do this.'

'That's okay, then. Remember to let me know how it's all going.'

Seb arrived at the spot opposite the track at nine-thirty and positioned himself out of sight. Yesterday, Patrick Casey had left the property at ten forty-five, driving the silver Volkswagen Golf, and Seb had followed him into Northampton, where he'd stopped at the supermarket, and bought a trolley full of non-perishable goods. He then went to a pub in St James End, or Jimmy's End as Birdie had informed him the locals called it, where he stayed for an hour and then drove home. He was back by one-thirty and didn't leave again.

Seb had reported what he'd seen to Birdie, but they decided they wouldn't apprehend him straight away for driving the stolen car. That could wait. It was more important to discover whether going out in the morning was a regular occurrence or a one-off.

What worried Seb was the vast amount of food and other goods the man had bought, all of which would be suitable for travelling if they left the area.

His phone pinged, and he picked it up from the passenger seat. It was a text from Birdie.

*Sarge got back to me and approved my leave. I'm off from 5 today. How's it going?*

Excellent. With Birdie with him tomorrow, they might get the chance to speak to Tessa.

*I'm parked opposite the track, waiting to see if Casey leaves again. I'll be in touch.*

Seb returned his phone to the seat and glanced across the road. In the distance he glimpsed the Golf heading down the track. He started the engine and waited. Patrick Casey was driving, and he was alone. He turned left and Seb waited for a few more seconds before following him.

Seb kept his distance as Casey headed along the A508 towards Northampton. Seb was a few cars behind as they drove through Kingsthorpe and, just in time, he spotted Casey turning right at the traffic lights. He remained in pursuit until they reached the car park of a large DIY store in Duston, finding a space in the row behind the Golf.

Thirty minutes later, Casey left the store pushing a trolley. Seb held up his binoculars to see what the man had bought.

'Oh no,' he said to himself, as he saw camping gear in there. Non-perishable goods and camping equipment. A holiday or were they planning to leave? And, if the latter, when?

Casey drove into St James and went to the same pub as the day before, where he stayed for an hour before going home. Seb followed him back to Holcot and then phoned Birdie.

'Anything?' she asked straight away.

'Casey went out again this morning at ten forty-five and bought items one would use for camping.'

'Do you think they're planning to scarper?'

'It's possible. He then went to the same pub as yesterday before going home.'

'We're expecting a storm tomorrow, so surely they won't go then. We'll stake out the house in the morning and hope he goes into town again so I can get to Tessa. I'll meet you in Holcot at nine, by the shop. That should give us plenty of time to talk things through before we go to wait for him.'

'Jay Murphy and Elliot Faulkner are downstairs for interviewing. They were brought in separately. They've both got records for petty crimes. I gather Murphy is being mouthy,' Twiggy said as he replaced the phone on his desk.

'I bet he's the short one. They're always the worst. It's like they're trying to prove something. We'll speak to the quieter one first and see if we can break him. They've got to be nailed today because I'm off on leave from five this afternoon. It's annoying we couldn't get to them yesterday.' Birdie said.

'The sneaky little shits must have realised we were after them. Though I'm not sure how. Still, at least we have them now.' Twiggy picked up his jacket from the back of the chair and pulled it on.

Elliot Faulkner wouldn't make eye contact with either of them when they entered the interview room. He stared at his hands, which were tightly balled and resting on the table.

Twiggy pressed the recording equipment. 'Interview Monday, 18 May. Those present: DC Branch, DC Bird and … state your name.'

'Elliot Faulkner.'

'Mr Faulkner, where were you on Saturday, 9 May at eight in the evening?' Birdie asked.

'Out somewhere. I don't know.' He shrugged.

'Who were you with?'

'My mate.'

'Jay Murphy?'

'Yeah.'

'Where did you go?'

'Just out.'

She glanced at Twiggy, who was tapping his foot impatiently.

'Were you drinking?'

'We might have had a few, I don't remember.'

Birdie opened the folder in front of her and slid it over to him. 'Is this you and Jay? It was taken in the town centre on Saturday night.'

'I don't know.'

'Well, let me help you. This was taken after you and Jay attempted to carjack a woman on Welland Road.'

'No, we didn't.'

'We have your image here and we've got software which can take all the body proportions and compare them with yours.'

'It wasn't us.'

'Do you have an alibi other than each other? If you have, then we'll let you go. It's easy.' She leant forward and stared directly at him.

'Look, we'd had a few, I don't remember. But we didn't carjack anyone.' He rubbed the side of his nose with his fingers.

Classic lying.

'How's your leg?' Birdie asked.

'Still hurts a bit, after I …' He clamped his jaws shut.

'After you jumped in front of the victim's car and didn't land right,' Birdie said.

'No. I … I …'

'If you cooperate, we'll let the Crown Prosecution Service know and it will go in your favour. Whose idea was it to do these carjackings?'

'I don't know.'

'Look, son, you're in enough trouble. Tell the truth,' Twiggy said.

'Put it there,' Twiggy said, high-fiving Birdie.

'I can't believe Faulkner caved so easily.'

'He wouldn't have done if you hadn't mentioned his leg. Great catch.'

'Just doing my job,' Birdie said, waving a dismissive hand.

'Come off it. I know you're pleased. Even with Murphy denying it, we've got enough to lock them up.'

'I'll ask Sarge to arrange some search warrants, and we

can officially charge them later. The rest is down to you until I'm back from leave.'

## Chapter 27

The next day, after stopping at the supermarket on her way, Birdie drove to Holcot to meet Seb, arriving at five minutes after nine.

No surprise that he was already there, so she parked behind him, grabbed her bag, and hopped into his car.

'Look at me, only five minutes late. I hope you're impressed.'

'Five minutes ago, I would have been. Now ...'

'Don't finish that sentence, or you won't get any of the supplies I've bought.'

'I don't see any.'

'That's because they're in my car, for when we're watching the house.'

'In that case, my lips are sealed.'

'I knew you'd be here first, even though I'm not properly late. It's got to be over fifteen minutes before it counts. What time did you arrive?'

'Ten minutes ago. Follow me and we'll drive to a spot opposite the track leading to the cottage. We can't be seen there because of the curve of the road.'

Once they were there, she returned to his car, this time clutching the bag of doughnuts she'd bought.

'Look what I've got,' she said, wafting the bag under his nose.

'Doughnuts?' He grinned.

'I know you love them as much as I do. I take it you're happy with my selection?'

Seb reached into the bag. 'I certainly am. Jam, I hope.'

'It's the best.' She took one for herself and bit into it.

'Was it difficult to persuade your sergeant to give you the time off?' Seb asked between mouthfuls.

'No. I told him it was a family thing, and he didn't ask what it was. I'm due in court next week and I told him I'll be back for that. All I can think is, it's because he's working on budgets, and he's tied up in meetings with the DI. He probably didn't have the time to argue about it. Anyway, I'm not complaining. But we do have to wrap this up quickly.'

'We have no choice if they're planning to leave.'

'It could be a holiday.'

'There were a lot of provisions in his trolley. If they were going on holiday, they could shop at a local supermarket, but it looked like he was stocking up so they could go off the grid for a while. Him buying a tent, and camping equipment yesterday, confirmed it.'

'Maybe we should let them disappear.'

Seb frowned in her direction. 'What made you say that?'

'What if Tessa and Patrick are Lacey's parents? Will she have to return to living with them?'

'That's not up to us to decide, is it?' Seb said gently.

'I don't get it. He's a sex offender. What woman would let her child live with a man who possessed child pornography on his computer? Even if he is the father.'

Had she been right in asking Seb to look into Lacey's background with her? Now they'd got this far she was having serious doubts. She turned and stared out of the window.

What had she done?

'Have you considered that Tessa might have given up Lacey to stop her from being in his clutches?'

'Not really, but—'

'There's a car coming down the track,' Seb said, interrupting her. He picked up his binoculars. 'It's Patrick Casey, and he's on his own again. I'm going to follow him. Give it half an hour to allow him time to be well away from here and then drive up to the cottage and speak to Tessa.'

'If he turns around and comes back early, call me and I'll get out of there quick.'

After Seb had gone, Birdie sat in the car waiting, staring ahead at the winding track which broke up the overgrown grass on either side of it. Each passing minute seemed like an eternity, but finally it was time for her to drive to the cottage to speak to Tessa.

She headed over to the house and gave a gentle knock on the door. There was no reply, so she wandered around the back of the house to see if Tessa was there. In the small fenced off garden, which backed into the fields, she could see the woman picking beans off the plant and putting them into a bowl she was holding.

Birdie didn't want to surprise her, so as she got closer, she made a noise on the gravel which ran alongside the garden. Tessa looked up, fear in her eyes. The sun was shining, but it was at odds with the scared look on her face. The woman had on a short-sleeved shirt, showing bruises on both arms, as if she'd been held in a tight grip.

Was her brother responsible?

Birdie walked over to her, smiling. 'Hello, Tessa. I've come back to have a quick chat with you.'

'I can't talk,' she said, looking around as if expecting her brother to turn up.

'It's all right, I know Patrick has gone out and probably won't be back for a couple of hours.'

'You've been watching us?' she said, her voice barely above a whisper.

'Only to make sure he wasn't going to be here, so we'd have time to talk uninterrupted. I could sense when we were here the other day that you wanted to but you couldn't once Patrick came home. Tell me if I'm wrong, but I don't think I am.'

'You're right,' she whispered.

'Let's go inside. Everything you say to me will all be off the record,' she added, hoping that would push her in the right direction.

'Um …' she said, clearly undecided.

'He'll be gone for ages, and I promise to make sure that I've left before he returns.'

She wouldn't mention that Seb would warn her if Patrick was on his way back, or that he was actually following him. That would only worry her further and make her think she was in trouble.

'Okay, I suppose so.'

They went into the kitchen and Tessa put the bowl of beans beside the sink. Birdie's eyes were drawn to a painting on the wall. She hadn't noticed it before. It was quite abstract and had what looked like a small sun shining through some thorns.

'What does this represent?'

'It's showing the crown of thorns that Jesus wore, to symbolise his sacrifice. We only have religious artwork on the wall. Patrick wants it like that. It stems from him being a priest,' Tessa said, as if she wanted to excuse it.

'Do you share his views?'

The woman shrugged. 'I'm not sure.'

'Why don't you tell me a bit about you and your brother. How long have you lived together?'

'My parents died in a boating accident when I was twelve and there was no one to look after me, so Patrick took me in. We share the same father. We lived in the house that came with his job, in Gloucester.'

'Where did you go when he was in prison?'

Her jaw dropped. 'You know. How?'

'From my research.'

'We went to live with a friend of Patrick's'

'*We?*'

Did she mean Lacey?

'Only me, but I had to take Patrick's belongings. When he lost his job, he lost the house that came with it.' Her face coloured.

Was she lying?

'I also know that you both changed your names by deed poll when Patrick was released from prison. Previously you were Sean and Sinead. Why did you do this?'

'Patrick said it was for the best so we wouldn't be victimised. That's why we moved here, where no one knew us.'

'Did you work when you were living with Patrick's friend?'

'No.'

'Why not?'

'I didn't feel up to it.'

Or she was taking care of Lacey?

'Was there a reason you didn't move into your own place?'

SALLY RIGBY

'I had nowhere to go, and I couldn't support myself. I'm not trained to do anything as I dropped out of university before finishing my course.'

'What did you study?'

'Philosophy and theology. The only job I've ever done is cleaning, but that doesn't pay enough to cover rent.'

'When I was here, the last time and I showed you a picture of a little girl who was left in Market Harborough, you said you didn't know her.'

'Yes, that's right,' Tessa said, averting her eyes.

'I saw the look in your eyes when you were asked. You didn't tell the truth. You know her, don't you?'

Tessa's fists clenched by her sides. 'No, I don't. You've got it wrong.'

Silence hung in the air, and Birdie deliberately remained silent for a while.

'I don't think so, Tessa,' Birdie eventually said, her voice soft. 'Would you like to talk about her?'

'I've already told you I don't know this girl. You'd better leave now. If Patrick comes back, he'll be annoyed to see you here.'

Tessa opened the front door and gestured for Birdie to leave.

On her way out, she turned to the woman.

'I'm going to wait in my car for a while in case you change your mind.'

Tessa didn't reply. She just closed the door.

## Chapter 28

Patrick Casey drove into Northampton again.

Would he do the same as he had the previous two days, shop and then stop at the pub for a drink?

Seb followed him into Kingsthorpe and waited while he went into the chemist. He was only in there for five minutes and then he drove straight to St James, where he parked around the corner from the pub he'd visited the previous times.

Did that mean he wouldn't be away from home as long as he had been before? He hoped not, or that wouldn't give Birdie much time with Tessa.

Seb double-parked further up the road from Casey and monitored him in his rear-view mirror, making sure he actually went into the pub. Once he was in there, Seb looked for somewhere to park.

He ended up driving around the block twice until eventually coming across a vacant spot in the next street. The trouble was, he couldn't stay in his car because he wouldn't be able to observe Casey's movements, so instead he walked down to the main road, turned right and stationed himself outside the pub.

Fortunately, because of his height, he could stare through the small, rather dirty window and see the interior of the pub. He watched Casey take a pint from the bartender, hand over his money, and then head over to a circular table along the side wall where he sat opposite a man in his fifties, who was wearing a flat cap and an anorak. They shook hands and talked. Was it a prearranged meeting? If only he could go inside to watch and listen. But it was too risky. Casey might notice him.

Instead, he leant against the wall and waited.

After Casey had been in there for ten minutes, Seb peered through the window and saw the man he was sitting with slide an envelope across the table. Casey picked it up and started running his fingers through the contents.

Was it money?

What was he being paid for?

Seb pulled his jacket around him and shivered as a gust of wind whistled through. A sign that the storm was on its way, no doubt. He sighed and leant against the pub wall, preparing himself for a long wait.

## Chapter 29

Birdie turned the key in the ignition, letting out a frustrated sigh. Her plan had backfired. She'd been waiting outside the cottage for ten minutes, but Tessa hadn't appeared. She'd been convinced the woman would. *Damn it.*

She put the car into reverse gear, glanced in the rearview mirror and was about to move when there was a bang on the passenger side window, startling her.

The car door opened.

'Okay, I'll talk to you. I want to know about Emily, but you must promise not to say anything to Patrick.'

Emily? Was that Lacey's real name?

'You have my word that I won't.' Birdie turned off the engine and hurriedly jumped out of the car, following Tessa back inside the house.

They sat at the table. 'May I see the photo again?' Tessa asked, her eyes anxious.

Birdie took out her phone, called up a photo of Lacey, and slid it over. 'Here, you are.'

'She's looking well.' Tessa held the phone in both hands.

'She's very well cared for and has settled down a lot, but she's quiet and reserved, and scares easily. Is she your daughter?' Birdie asked, coming straight out with it.

The woman nodded. 'Yes. Yes, she is.'

'We've called her Lacey. Is her real name Emily?'

'Yes. But Lacey's a nice name, too. It suits her.' Tessa held the phone close, staring intently at the photo. 'It seems so long since I've seen her face.'

'Don't you have any photos of her?'

'No. Patrick didn't like me to take any.'

'Do you ever call Patrick by his original name, Sean?'

'It was hard at first because he'd been Sean my whole life. He got angry with me when I forgot because he never got mine wrong. He was right, though. We had to learn to use our new names to make sure we didn't accidentally drop ourselves in it when we saw other people. It took a few months, but eventually I was okay. I only think of him as Patrick now.'

What sort of life had she endured? Constantly living in fear of being reprimanded.

'Will you tell me what happened on the day you left Emily?' Birdie waited a few seconds, but there was no reply. 'Tessa?'

The woman started, and she glanced away from staring at the phone and focused on Birdie. 'Yes?'

'I'd like to know what happened the day you left Emily in the centre of town and why you did it.' It seemed strange to call Lacey that, but Birdie hoped it would encourage Tessa to open up and explain.

'Um …' Her voice faded, and an embarrassed expression crossed her face. She bit down on her bottom lip and couldn't maintain eye contact.

Birdie sensed she'd have to lead this conversation, rather than wait for her to open up, if she was going to find out anything about Lacey's background.

'I'd like to check. Is Patrick Emily's father?' Should she have started with something less contentious?

'Yes, he is,' Tessa whispered with tears in her eyes.

Had he raped her? Was it consensual? What exactly happened between them?

'And was it you or Patrick who took Emily into Market Harborough and left her?'

'It was me. I had no choice.'

'Did Patrick force you to do it? Is that what you mean?'

'No. He didn't want her to leave, but I could see what was happening. Patrick was becoming far too attached to her.'

'Can you be more specific?'

'He'd watch her all the time. Want her to sit on his lap. It wasn't right. You know what I mean, in *that* sort of way. I couldn't bear the thought of anything happening to her. Especially after what I'd been through. I didn't want Emily to suffer.'

Nausea washed over Birdie. How could he?

'Leaving Emily must have been so hard. You were very brave.'

'It doesn't feel like it. I keep remembering the bewildered expression on her face when I told her she wasn't to stay with me.' She squeezed her eyes tightly shut.

'Tessa?' Birdie said gently after a few seconds.

The woman opened her eyes. 'I tried leaving once before and took Emily with me. But he found us and said if I ever did it again, he'd kill me. He threatened to kill Emily, too. That's why I stayed here all this time instead of being with my daughter. I knew he wouldn't go after her. At least, I hoped he wouldn't.'

'When Emily was found, we could tell how well you'd looked after her. She's a very clever little girl, isn't she?'

'Yes. I taught her myself. She talked from a very early age and was curious about everything around her. She learnt to read when she was only three. She's an amazing child.'

'How was she with Patrick?'

'I could tell that the tension between me and Patrick affected her. She didn't speak to him much and was very clingy when he was around.'

'Do you believe he harmed her in any way?' Birdie scrutinised Tessa's face to see if she was going to hide anything.

'No. But I knew it was only a matter of time.'

'When we found Emily, she had a card around her neck with the words *Speak No Evil* written on it. What can you tell me about this?'

Should she have asked? They'd kept the sign secret up to now. But that was to correctly identify Lacey's parents, which they had done.

'Patrick made her wear it all the time because he said it would teach her the right way to behave. Every day he made her pray. We all had to. He spent much of the time preaching at us.'

'Why didn't you take off the sign when you left her?'

'I tried to, but she held on to it and wouldn't let me. I didn't want to force her, because I knew she was going to be upset enough by being left.' Tessa placed Birdie's phone on the table and kept it covered by her hand. It was as if letting go would break the contact between her and her daughter.

How on earth had the poor woman coped?

'Taking Emily to Market Harborough and leaving her

there, was such a courageous move. How did you do it without Patrick realising?'

'He'd gone away for two days to see his friend, so we were alone. It wasn't something I'd planned to do, it just sort of happened.'

'Can you explain it to me in more detail?'

'Patrick left early on the Friday morning and couldn't take me to work. I caught the bus to Creaton and left Emily here.'

'On her own?' Birdie's tone was harsher than she'd intended.

'I know that seems bad, but she was fine and was used to being alone sometimes. I was only going to be away for a couple of hours. Except the bus didn't turn up to bring me home, and the next one wasn't until much later. I went back to the house and borrowed the car. Mr and Mrs Kingston had gone away, so I thought it would be okay. I'd fully intended to take it back later that day, when I had Emily with me.'

'Why didn't you?'

'During the afternoon, I thought about Emily and what might happen to her if she stayed with us, and then a plan formed in my mind. I decided that first thing in the morning I'd take her into Market Harborough and leave her. I wanted to give her a better life. It wasn't a straight-forward decision to make.' Tears filled her eyes, and she brushed them away with the back of her hand.

'And after you dropped her off you drove around a few times looking for a parking spot and then sat in the café opposite, watching her ...'

'Yes, that's exactly what happened. I wanted to make sure Emily was okay. Once I saw the police had arrived, I knew she'd be fine.'

'What did you do next?'

'I left the café a little while later and drove home, intending to take the car back to Creaton in the afternoon. I was too upset to go straight away. But before I could go there, Patrick returned. I wasn't expecting him until the next day. I don't know why he came back early. When he asked where Emily was, I told her she'd run away and I couldn't find her anywhere, even though I'd hunted the streets. He was really mad.'

'Did he ask why you didn't call the police?'

'No, because he knew we couldn't. Emily was a secret. No one knew about her.'

'What about when you gave birth?'

'I had her at home. Patrick, or Sean as he was then, delivered her. I was scared that something might happen to me, or the baby, but it didn't. He knew what he was doing because he helped on a farm in Gloucester when he was younger. He'd delivered calves and lambs before.'

'You were very lucky that it turned out okay.'

'He would've taken us to the hospital if there was an emergency. I'm sure of it.'

Really? Birdie wasn't so sure. She hadn't liked the man when they'd met before. She liked him even less now.

'What about the car you stole from Mrs Kingston? Why didn't you return it?'

'Patrick decided we should keep it because his car kept breaking down. He went out and bought some fake number plates and sold his other one for scrap.'

That reminded her.

'If neither of you works, how do you survive?'

'We inherited money when my parents died. My father only had Sean and me, so we shared everything. It's not a huge amount, but it's enough to cover our expenses.'

'Two weeks ago on the Saturday morning, something happened in Market Harborough town centre, which distressed Lacey. I mean, Emily. Were you in town then? Could she have seen you?'

Birdie knew they were there, but she wanted to hear from Tessa what they were doing, and to make sure she'd been telling the truth.

'Yes, we were in town. We seldom go in, and rarely at the weekend when it's busy, but Patrick needed cash for something he was buying. I don't know what. Emily could have seen him and got scared.'

'Was she always frightened of him?'

'He was very strict, and she'd be punished if she did anything wrong.'

'What sort of punishments?'

'It depended on what she'd done. If she didn't remember her prayers properly, she'd be smacked. If her bed wasn't made perfectly, then she'd have to miss her breakfast. Like I said, it would all depend.'

'Is Emily aware that he's her dad and your brother?'

'Yes. But she doesn't know that it's wrong.' Tessa hung her head. 'What's going to happen now? Are you going to arrest me?'

'I think it's best if you accompany me to the station and we can sort it out from there.'

'Will I be able to see Emily if I go with you?'

'I don't know. I'll have to speak to my sergeant, and he'll need to contact social services. If you cooperate regarding Patrick and his behaviour, then you'll have a better chance, but I'd be lying if I said you definitely could see her, because it's not my decision to make.'

Her insides clenched. Were they about to lose Lacey?

'My bag and jacket are upstairs. I won't be long.' Tessa headed over to the stairs.

'I'll wait here for you.'

## Chapter 30

Seb peered through the pub window again to check what Casey was doing. He was still talking to the man who'd passed him the money earlier. How long was he planning to stay?

His phone rang, and he pulled it from his pocket, not checking the screen before he answered.

'Clifford.'

'It's Rob. Do you have a moment?'

He glanced into the pub again. Casey didn't appear to be in any rush to leave, as his pint glass was still half full.

'I should have a few minutes spare.'

'Remember the syndicate from Singapore you were investigating before they disbanded your squad? Rhetorical question. I know you do. What I'd like to know is whether you discovered anything that showed they were into drug trafficking as well as the illegal betting you knew about?'

'I don't have any proof, but it wouldn't surprise me. Although we were focused on the illegal betting side, we suspected they had their fingers in many pies. What have you learnt about them?'

'One of our informants overseas has given us some information regarding an influx of drugs into the UK, from a gang with links to Singapore. I don't know for certain that this is related to the group you were looking into, but I'd be very surprised if there wasn't a connection. Singapore isn't so large that groups like that work in isolation.'

'I agree with you, it's highly likely.'

'If you've got time, I'd like more information on the people you were investigating. Key players, their teams, any people on the periphery. Anything you know that might assist us. We don't want to waste time by going down blind alleys, as has been the case on many occasions in the past.'

'Mainly because we had an officer leaking information,' Seb said, grimacing as he remembered what had happened to his former squad. It had mortified him when he'd learnt that a member of his team, someone he had trusted, had turned out to have links with the syndicate they'd been investigating.

'Hopefully, we're now clean,' Rob said.

'In an ideal world, maybe. But remember to keep on your guard, because this syndicate has ways of infiltrating the police. I'm out on a job at the moment but when I get back home, I'll let you have everything I think might be useful.'

'Thanks, mate. How's everything going with the Birdie case? Is this what you're working on now?'

'It's going well. We've got ourselves a break, which should bring the investigation to a close.' The pub door squeaked as it opened and Seb glanced up. Casey was leaving. 'Sorry, Rob, I've got to go. I'll call you later.'

He ended the call and walked the few steps to the corner, monitoring Casey while he headed to his car.

Seb then turned and ran towards the street in which

he'd parked, hoping that he'd make it in time to see the direction Casey took. He assumed the man would return home, as that's what he'd done the two previous days, but in case he was heading elsewhere, Seb didn't want to lose him.

He turned into the street and did a double take. What the …

A van with *XYZ Printing Solutions* sign-written on the side was double-parked and blocking him in.

He dashed over, but the driver was nowhere to be seen.

Where had he gone?

He ran back down the street looking for the Golf. As he approached the pub, Casey drew up beside him and turned right onto the main road, heading back the way they'd come. Casey was concentrating on the traffic, looking for a space, and not the pedestrians. Seb was confident he hadn't been seen.

He returned to his car.

The van was still there.

He pulled out his phone. He had to warn Birdie.

It went straight to voicemail.

*Hello, this is Birdie. Leave me a message*, she said in her sing-song voice.

'It's Seb. I've lost Casey. I don't know if he's on his way home or not, and I'm stuck in Northampton. My car's been blocked in by a van that double-parked. Be careful.' He paused. 'Actually, leave now and I'll meet you where we were earlier.'

He also texted her a warning.

*I've lost Casey. Keep an eye out for him. Leave the cottage now.*

He scanned the street. There was a printing shop on the corner of an adjoining road. Could the driver be in there? It was worth a try.

He sprinted over and went up to the counter. A woman

who had her back to him was talking to a man holding a large parcel in his hands.

'Excuse me,' Seb said.

The woman turned around. 'Yes?'

'Does the *XYZ Printing Solutions* van belong to anybody in here?'

'Yeah, it's mine,' the man who'd been talking to the woman said. 'I'm delivering a parcel. I won't be a minute.' He walked through the open door behind the counter into what looked like a large warehouse area.

'I really need to get out now,' Seb shouted.

'Keep your 'air on, mate. I said I won't be long,' the man barked.

'But I need to go *now*,' Seb said, unable to hide his agitation.

'And if you don't let me finish getting my delivery signed for, it's gonna take even longer.'

Seb glanced at the woman, who shrugged.

He marched out of the shop and paced the pavement.

He drew in a calming breath and returned to the shop.

'Could you tell me whether the driver is going to be much longer?' he asked the woman, who was flicking through a magazine.

'There's a problem, because the delivery isn't complete. I don't know how long it's going to take to sort out. Sorry.'

'Can you please ask him to move the van now and then come back to deal with the problem? I'm late for an appointment.'

'Where would he go? You know what it's like round here. Parking spaces are like hen's teeth. Non-existent. Especially for a van the size of his. You were lucky you found one. Give him a few more minutes and he'll be there. I'm sure of it.'

'I don't have a few minutes. Could you move the van for him?'

'Sorry, love, I don't drive. I took my test five times before finally giving up after my husband refused to pay for any more lessons. It don't really matter much. I catch the bus everywhere.'

'Do you have the key to the van, and I'll move it myself.' Though where he'd leave it would be anybody's guess.

'Are you insured to drive a vehicle that size?'

'No.' He wasn't prepared to lie, in case he had an accident.

'Then you've got your answer.'

'If he doesn't move, it will cause a very long traffic jam.'

'It won't because it's one-way and people can take a right, then immediately left to avoid it.'

'Apart from me, because I have parked.'

'Sorry, love. Most people out there stay all day. It's unlucky that you ended up in the wrong place. Don't worry, it won't be much longer. Do you want a coffee, I'm going to make one for myself. It's only instant, but it's okay. I've got a packet of bourbon biscuits, too, if you fancy one.'

'No, thank you.'

The woman left the shop and headed into the warehouse section.

Seb paced the floor, clenching and unclenching his fists. How could he have got himself in such a ridiculous situation? Birdie might end up in trouble and he'd be unable to do anything about it.

He left the shop and tried Birdie's number again. Surely she'd pick up now. After a couple of rings, her voicemail tripped in again.

*This is Birdie. Leave me a message.*

He sucked in a breath. 'It's me again. Why aren't you answering your phone? I'm still stuck here and I don't know for how long. Get out of the house now and meet me at our lookout point. I'll be with you as soon as I can. Be careful. For God's sake, be careful.'

Chapter 31

While Tessa was upstairs, Birdie looked around the kitchen. The Welsh dresser, which ran along the wall to the right of the sink, contained a selection of mismatched plates and bowls and a few mugs. At the back of the room stood an old oak sideboard. There was nothing on top apart from a well-used, navy leather-bound Bible with gold edging and lettering. She opened it and read the inscription written on the inside page:

> *Dear Sinead,*
> *Let the words in here guide you.*
> *We will be together forever*
> *All my love,*
> *Sean*

Were those the sort of words a brother and sister would say to each other? No, they weren't, and she should know. She had two younger brothers of her own. She closed the Bible and pulled open the middle drawer of the sideboard, keeping an eye on the stairs to make sure Tessa didn't see what she was doing.

Much the same as the rest of the house, it was sparse and tidy, containing nothing other than a recent gas and electricity bill and a red wallet made of card. She opened it and found documents in their previous names. There were driving licences, passports and birth certificates. Underneath the documents were photos of a tiny baby, looking only a few days old and then some when the child was older. It was definitely Lacey.

Should she call her Emily now?

No. It seemed all wrong. And it would be confusing to everyone, Lacey in particular.

Tessa had told her there weren't any photos because Patrick hadn't allowed it. Had she been lying, or had he taken these secretly? She'd love to take them to show her aunt. Except she couldn't. Obviously. She took one last look, replaced the folder, and returned to the kitchen table.

She glanced at her watch. What was keeping Tessa? She'd only gone upstairs to collect her bag and jacket. How long did that take? She headed over to the stairs and climbed halfway up.

'Tessa, are you nearly ready? We've got to get going.'

Call it gut instinct or whatever, but they had to get out of the house, and the sooner the better. She didn't want them bumping into Patrick before they could get away.

'Sorry, I got changed because I had mud on my dress. I won't be a sec,' Tessa called out.

'Okay, but be quick.'

Birdie turned and walked down the stairs. She'd almost reached the bottom when the front door opened, and Patrick marched in, kicking the door shut behind him.

She froze. What the …

He headed straight for her.

Where was Seb? Why hadn't he warned her? Now, what was she going to do? The one thing she didn't want was a confrontation, or Tessa would never come with her.

'What are you doing here?' Patrick stood in front of her, his arms folded.

'I came to speak to Tessa.' She deliberately kept her tone calm and matter of fact.

She had a can of pepper spray in her handbag, but it was hanging on the back of the chair by the kitchen table and way out of reach. If he went for her, it could get nasty, and she had nothing to defend herself with. But she was strong and trained in self-defence. It would be fine.

Bloody Seb, leaving her alone. She'd give him what for when he finally arrived.

'What about? If you remember, I told you to go away and not come back.' His eyes flashed with anger.

'I'm here on a police matter. Tessa's coming with me to the police station at Market Harborough.' Being on the second stair meant she was at his eye level, and she stared at him, determined not to let him think she was in any way intimidated.

'Oh no, you're not. I forbid it.' He looked past her, up the stairs. 'Tessa, get down here at once.' His voice wasn't raised, but it was chilling.

The sound of dragging footsteps on the upstairs wooden floorboards echoed around the house, and Birdie turned to see Tessa standing at the top of the stairs, fear in her eyes.

'I'm sorry, Patrick. It wasn't my idea. I didn't want to go, but she said I had to.'

He tried to push past her to go up the stairs, but Birdie stood her ground and stopped him. No way would he harm his sister while she was there.

'Forget it, mate. I'm taking Tessa to the station, and you can come with us, too.'

He gave a hollow laugh. 'You must be joking. I'm not going anywhere with you. No way am I going back to prison. Ever. Do you understand me?'

He made a grab for Birdie, and she pushed him hard with both hands. He tripped and fell backwards off the stair he'd been standing on. There was an almighty crack as his head hit the floor.

She turned to Tessa. 'Lock yourself in the bathroom and stay there until I say it's safe.' The woman stared at her, mesmerised. 'Now,' Birdie shouted.

Tessa ran, and Birdie heard the door being locked. She walked down the remaining stairs and stood over Patrick. He wasn't moving. He must have been knocked out. She was about to get her mobile from the table to call for backup when he stirred, rolled over and took hold of her leg, pulling her down beside him. He swung his leg and ended up sitting on her, pinning her body to the floor.

'You're going to regret ever coming here and interfering with my family. Do you understand?'

'Let go of me,' she said, twisting and trying to pull herself out from under him. But he was too strong.

'Keep still. You'll only end up getting hurt. If you don't do as you're told, you'll *never* get out of here.'

'You're making a big mistake, if you think you can threaten me.' Her breath caught in the back of her throat. 'I'm only here to sort out what's going to happen to Lacey. I don't care about you, or Tessa. Lacey is my only concern,' she lied, hoping it would persuade him to let her go.

'Lacey? I don't know who you're talking about.' His brow furrowed.

'Your daughter. Emily.'

'I don't have any children.'

His eyes glazed over, and in that split second she clenched her fist and thumped him hard in the nuts.

'You bitch,' he yelled, doubling up in pain and leaning over to the side, releasing the pressure on her.

She rolled away and scrambled to her feet. She ran towards the door, hoping it wasn't one that self-locked. But before she could get to the handle, he grabbed her by the shoulder and pulled her back.

'Let me go.' She spun around and thumped him hard on the chest.

'Forget it. You're not going anywhere.'

## Chapter 32

Patrick held the policewoman's arms tight so she couldn't escape. He dragged her towards the table and pushed her down onto the chair.

'Don't move. Or you'll regret it.' He glanced around the room, looking for something to contain her. His eyes focused on the hook beside the front door, where there was a rope hanging. 'Tessa, where are you?'

Footsteps sounded on the ceiling above him. 'I'm here.'

'Fetch me the rope.' He nodded in the direction of the door.

His sister ran down the stairs and got it for him. He tied the officer's arms behind her back and her ankles to the chair legs. He had no choice.

'Don't do this. Kidnapping a police officer will get you more time inside. Let me go and I won't pursue it,' she said.

Could he believe her?

What a ridiculous thought. Of course, he couldn't. She was the police, and he'd experienced plenty in the past.

None of whom helped. If anything, they'd gone out of their way to make his life as difficult as possible.

'Do I look stupid? If I release you, there'll be a dozen cop cars surrounding the place within minutes. You're staying with us until I decide what to do with you.'

'This is a big mistake.'

'You're the one who made the mistake of coming here in the first place and interfering. We weren't harming anyone. You wrecked our lives.'

He gave a frustrated sigh. All this could have been avoided if Tessa hadn't lost the child last year.

'I did it for Lacey as I've already told you.'

He thumped the table. 'Stop calling her that. Her name is Emily. Do you hear me? *Emily*. She's nothing to do with us now, so why are you here? We're not having her back.'

'She was abandoned, that's why I'm here.'

'The last I heard, it's not a criminal offence if the child is over two years old.'

The officer frowned. 'You've researched into it?'

He shrugged. 'When she went missing, I checked all scenarios. I know my rights.'

'Yet you tie me up and prevent me from leaving your house. You're not as smart as you think. And let's not forget that you changed your name without informing the police. That's illegal for anyone on the sex offenders' register.'

He bristled. How did she know that? Was it Tessa? Had she forced his sister into admitting everything?

He couldn't think straight with her staring at him.

'It was an oversight. I can soon put it right.'

'That's what you think. Not informing the police of your name change will be the least of your worries after this. Remember, my fellow officers know I'm here.'

He glanced at Tessa, who was standing close to the table, her hand on her hip. She gave a slight shake of her head.

'I don't believe you.'

'The man who was with me last time knows. He'll come looking for me.'

'Where is he because I don't see him anywhere? Do you, Tessa?'

'No,' his sister said.

'He'll be here soon.'

'If you say so.' He untied her ankles and took hold of her arm. 'You're coming with me.'

She tried to wriggle out of his grasp, but she was no match for him. Her arms were tied, and he was bigger and stronger.

'Where are you going?' Tessa called out.

'I'm putting her in the barn, out of the way. I need to think things through, and I can't with her incessant chatter in my ear.'

'Don't kill her. Please don't kill her,' Tessa said, clutching the lapels of her jacket, fear etched across her face.

'What?'

'You'll end up inside again if you do. I can't be here on my own. Don't do it.'

The officer's fight went out of her. Her body was less rigid. Is that why Tessa had said it, to make sure the woman complied? It had worked.

'Then tell her to behave.'

'DC Bird, please do as he asks. Then you won't get hurt,' Tessa said.

'You're not gonna get away with this, Patrick. Abandonment might not be a crime, but abuse is. I know what you've been doing to Tessa. Were you the same towards Emily, too?' the officer said.

'Shut up.' His body tensed, and he wrenched her by the shoulders until she faced him. He slapped her hard around the face, leaving a handprint on her cheek.

He'd never touched Emily like that. How dare she suggest he had?

He forced her outside and dragged her towards the barn, her feet hardly touching the ground. Once inside, he took hold of a rope from on top of a hay bale and tied her to the pole holding up the rafters.

'You can stay here until I've decided what to do with you.'

'You're gonna regret this.'

'If I hear another word from you, I'll gag you with this cloth.' He picked up a stinky, old, oil-stained cloth and wafted it under her nose. 'Want this in your mouth, do you?'

She winced and shook her head. 'No.'

'Finally, you know what's best for you.'

He made sure she was secure and then marched back to the house.

The kitchen was empty.

'Where are you, Tessa?' he shouted.

'Upstairs.'

'Get down here, we have things to discuss.'

He stood at the bottom of the stairs, tapping his foot impatiently. What had started out as a pleasant day had rapidly turned into one unmitigated disaster and it was down to one person. That bloody policewoman.

Tessa slowly headed down the stairs towards him. 'What are we going to do now?'

'Stick to the plan, only we'll be leaving sooner than I'd originally planned.'

He'd bought enough supplies to keep them out of sight for months. They were going to head for the New Forest and camp for a while. It was illegal, but still possible to do discreetly if you knew where to go. Which he did, as he was very familiar with the area.

'Did you sell the car?'

'I've swapped it for an old Ford Focus, plus some cash.' He tapped the top pocket in his jacket where he'd put the money he'd been given. 'It's not as smart as the Golf, but police won't know the registration.'

'But the old car's still outside.'

'I agreed with Greg to do a swap with him tomorrow when we leave. I didn't want it to be seen by anyone around here. I'll phone him in a minute and tell him we'll be there soon. Go upstairs and pack. Only bring the essentials. Anything else we need, we'll buy. I'll stop at the bank on the way and take out some money. It will save using the debit card for a while.'

'What about the policewoman in the barn? Are we going to leave her here?'

'Do you have a better idea?'

'We could let her go when we leave.'

'That wouldn't work because we wouldn't have time to get away.' He sighed. 'I can't believe you let her in the house, it's not like you at all.'

'I had no choice. She came to the door and practically forced herself inside. She told me I had to go to the police station with her to talk about Emily or she'd arrest me.'

'On what charge? She ...' He paused, distracted by the mobile on the table. 'Who does the phone belong to?'

'It's hers. She was showing me photos of Emily earlier and must have forgotten to pick it up.'

He hadn't even thought to look for her phone when

he'd taken her to the barn, but it looked like luck was on his side. She wouldn't be able to contact anyone.

'Good. It means she can't call for help.' He picked it up and pressed one of the keys, but it was locked, so he dropped it back on the table.

'Thank goodness,' his sister agreed. 'I wish we didn't have to leave. These last few years have been the best.'

'You're not the only one regretting that we have to go, but we have no choice. We'll settle in somewhere as nice as this once the fuss dies down. As long as we're together, that's all that counts.'

Even if they couldn't ever be with Emily again.

'We'll have to change our names, or they'll find us.'

'There's no need for us to do that. As long as we stay off the grid for a few months, everything will be fine. They'll have stopped looking for us by then. It's not like we're murderers on the run. There are far more important crimes to be solved.'

'But we've kidnapped a police officer. Isn't that considered serious?'

'She hasn't been harmed.'

'You slapped her.'

He tensed as guilt flooded through him. That was the last thing he'd intended to do, but her accusations had made him see red.

'I didn't mean to.'

'I'm going to take her some water, before I go upstairs to pack, in case she's thirsty. Is that okay? Then it will look like we had no intention of hurting her.'

'Okay, but don't be long. I want to leave in fifteen minutes, tops.'

# Chapter 33

Birdie wriggled her body and twisted her arms. But she couldn't free herself from the rope, although the knots had loosened a little. Would she be able to reach into her jacket pocket for her phone and alert someone where she was being held?

Should she call Seb?

Or had Casey done something to him, too?

But surely, he would have told her when she'd mentioned Seb coming to the house. Then again, he wouldn't want to alarm her. She'd have to call Twiggy, and he could bring backup. She twisted again, but it was no good. She still couldn't reach.

Was Tessa going to be okay with her brother, or would he turn on her, too? He was a nasty man and clearly flew off the handle at the slightest provocation. Birdie had always been strong for her size, but that man had made mincemeat of her. And as for that slap. She'd thought her face was going to explode. He didn't even look that strong.

She had to get out of there. In desperation, she gave one more determined twist of her hips and finally slid her hand into her pocket. She let out a sigh of relief as her fingers fumbled along the edges. But … there was nothing there. Her pocket was empty.

'Fuck.' She'd left her phone on the kitchen table when showing photos of Lacey to Tessa. Why hadn't she remembered to pick it up? She'd been so busy talking with Tessa, persuading her to come with her to the station that it had totally slipped her mind.

No doubt Patrick Casey now had it and was revelling in his good fortune. Because he hadn't even thought to ask her for it. They were as bad as each other.

Where the hell was Seb? If he'd lost Casey, then surely he'd be here soon. But what if Casey was waiting for him and things got nasty? Would Seb come rushing in looking for her, or would he get in touch with the station and ask for backup? That was the thing to do. He was level-headed enough to know that. He used to be a police officer, for goodness' sake.

The not knowing was killing her. She didn't want Seb walking into a trap. But he wouldn't think to search for her in the barn. Her car was still there, so he'd know she hadn't left.

If only she could release her arms, she could escape. Was there anything within reach that she could use? She also needed a weapon in case Casey came after her. There was a pitchfork close to the door. That would do.

She wriggled her arms for the hundredth time, wincing as the rope chafed against her wrists. It was no good. He'd tied her too tightly.

The barn door creaked and opened.

What did he want now?

Was he going to release her? Or worse?

But it wasn't him. Tessa walked towards her, a tentative smile on her face and a mug in her hand.

'I've brought you some water. I thought you might be thirsty.' She squatted down beside Birdie.

'It's not looking good, Tessa, and you're a part of it. Help me escape. It will go in your favour if you do, I promise. You realise Patrick won't get away with kidnapping me. You could be charged as an accessory.'

'But I didn't do anything.'

'Then untie me. Prove that you had nothing to do with it.'

Birdie held her breath, hoping that the woman would do as she'd asked.

'It's not a proper kidnap. He's not going to hurt you. He told me. But he might if you escape. I'm sorry. I can't let you go, or he'll punish me. I know he will.'

'Does he know you're here?' Birdie forced her voice to sound calm. She didn't want to panic Tessa even more.

'Yes. I told him I was bringing you some water. Would you like a sip?' Tessa held the mug under Birdie's mouth.

Was it water or something else? Casey could have made Tessa come in intending to drug her.

'No, thanks.' She wasn't prepared to risk it.

'You should have something in case you're here for a long time. We're leaving soon, and you might not be found for a while, and ...' Her hand shot up to her mouth. 'I don't think I'm meant to tell you what we're doing.'

'I won't say anything. But why do you want to go with him? We'll find you somewhere to live. Somewhere close to Emily. We could even let you see her again. You'd like that, wouldn't you?' Birdie wasn't sure whether social services would allow it, but they might, if the visit was supervised. And at this precise moment she was prepared to say anything if it got her out of there.

'How do I know you're telling me the truth?' Indecision flickered in the woman's eyes.

'I haven't lied to you up to now. Surely you want to get away from Patrick and everything he's done to you. Look at the state of you. The bruises on your arms and on your face. Do you want to be beaten for the rest of your life? Because that's what will happen if you stay with your brother.'

'He doesn't mean it. You saw what he was like. He has a short fuse. He's always sorry afterwards. It's how he is. He's kind in lots of other ways.'

How could she stick up for him like that?

'You were strong enough to get Emily away from him, why can't you do that for yourself? Come on, Tessa. Think about seeing Emily again. Untie me and let's both of us get out of here.'

'I can't. He'll find me. I know he will.'

'Not if he's in prison.'

'He'll never go back there again. He'll do anything to make sure he doesn't.'

'Untie me now,' Birdie snapped, hoping to shock Tessa into it.

'I can't. Please don't ask me to. Patrick will kill us both if he sees us leave.'

'Has he killed before?'

'I don't think so, but that doesn't mean he won't if we push him too far. I'm going back to the house to pack. If I'm here too long, he'll think we're planning something.'

'Please untie me. We'll leave in my car and drive somewhere safe.'

'I keep telling you, no. We can't do that because he'll see us.'

'He won't realise until it's too late. We can creep over to my car if we go around the back of the barn. My car can't be seen from the kitchen window.'

'Your bag is in the kitchen on the back of the chair.'

'I don't need it. The keys are in the ignition.'

Unless Patrick had removed them. But would he have done? He hadn't asked for her phone. Surely he wouldn't think of her car keys.

The woman hesitated. Was she going to give in and help?

'I'm not sure.' She closed her eyes for a few seconds. 'No. I can't. He'll see us. I'm sorry.'

'Well, untie me and let me go. Please, Tessa. Do the right thing.' She had no intention of leaving without the woman. She'd force her if necessary.

'I can't, so stop asking.' Tessa held out the mug. 'Take a drink before I go back.'

Birdie shook her head. 'No. You go, before he comes looking for you.'

'I'm sorry, but it's for the best,' Tessa said before walking away and leaving the barn.

Birdie sat on the ground, totally deflated. 'This is ridiculous,' she said to herself. 'There has to be a way out of here.'

## Chapter 34

Seb leant against his car, his eyes fixed firmly on the printing shop. Two more minutes and he'd call the police. He'd waited long enough.

He marched back to the shop. The woman had a mug of coffee in one hand and a biscuit in the other.

'I'm going to call the police and ask them to instruct the driver to move his van.'

'Don't do that. We've already been warned about blocking the road in the past.'

'Then I suggest you ensure the driver is out of here in sixty seconds or it's *exactly* what I'm going to do.'

Why hadn't he threatened the police before? It would have avoided all this.

He waited in his car, the engine running, as the seconds ticked down on his watch. With only five to go, the driver left the shop, gave a wave in Seb's direction and then marched to his van. He checked the back and then got into the driving seat.

'Hurry up,' Seb said impatiently, when the van didn't leave immediately.

Finally, the driver pulled away and Seb drove down the street and turned right. The traffic through to Kingsthorpe went at a snail's pace until he was through the worst of it and on the A508 which was free-flowing and would take him back to the turning towards Holcot and the farm.

It would take him at least fifteen minutes to reach the farm. He'd call for backup. Birdie might not like it, but he had no choice.

He'd put the station on speed dial after the last case they'd been working on.

'Market Harborough police.'

'Please, could you put me through to DC Branch, it's Sebastian Clifford,' he said to the woman who answered.

'Just one moment, I'll see if he's available.'

He was put on hold for what seemed like ages.

'DC Branch.' Twiggy made no sign that he knew who he was talking to.

'It's Sebastian Clifford.'

'Yes, I know. What do you want?'

'Birdie might be in danger and I need your help.'

'What?' he said sharply.

'You're aware of what we're working on, aren't you?'

'Yes. Birdie has included me in her investigation into the abandoned child.'

'Good. I was following Patrick Casey, the brother of Lacey's mother, and who we believe is the father while Birdie was speaking to the sister at the farm. Unfortunately, I lost him.'

'How?'

'My car was blocked in by a van.'

'On purpose? Was someone working with him?'

'I don't believe so. If Casey goes home and finds Birdie there with his sister, he might harm both of them. I've phoned Birdie three times to warn her, but she didn't answer. He couldn't have been there when I first called, so I've no idea why she didn't pick up. I've also left messages.'

'Could the sister have harmed Birdie?' The panic in Twiggy's voice echoed Seb's own.

'I doubt it but we won't know until we get there. I should arrive in fifteen minutes at the most, traffic dependent.'

'What's the address?'

'It's a cottage outside Holcot on the Walgrave Road. There's a track leading up to it. You can't see the house from the road. It's the first turn you come to on the right once you're out of the village.'

'With the sirens on, we should make it in fifteen. About the same time as you. Is he armed?'

That thought had been plaguing him.

'I didn't see any weapons in the kitchen, but that doesn't mean there isn't a gun stashed somewhere. It's a farm. There are bound to be implements lying around that he could use to harm her.'

'Jesus, Clifford. How could you let this happen?'

He didn't need reminding.

'There's no time for recriminations. We have to assume he's going to be violent when confronted, so make sure all officers take adequate precautions.' Seb could feel himself slipping into detective inspector mode because of his past, and made a conscious effort to pull back. Angering Twiggy wouldn't get them anywhere.

'Like you did, you mean?' the officer snapped.

'Enough,' Seb said, his voice flat.

'Do nothing without us being there. You're not on the force now, remember.'

'Understood.'

'We'll be there as soon as we can.'

Seb ended the call, and within seconds, his phone rang.

Was it Birdie?

'Clifford.' He pressed the button on his steering wheel while concentrating on the road ahead, waiting for a chance to overtake the vehicle in front, and not paying attention to his screen to see who it was.

'Hello, Sebastian.'

It was Hubert.

'Sorry, I can't talk now. Do you mind if I call you back later? I'm in the middle of an investigation.'

'This won't take long. I've been to see the local doctor, who was very understanding of my circumstances. He's given me some medication and recommended that I speak to a counsellor. He's given me the number of someone who works in Winchester. I made an appointment straight away before I could change my mind.'

'It's a scary step, but you've done the right thing. How was Virginia when you told her?'

'Supportive. More so than I'd imagined.'

Seb hadn't doubted her for a moment. His sister-in-law had showed how caring she was when he'd seen her with the children.

'Let me know how the counselling sessions go.'

'I will. I'll let you go now as you're busy.'

Seb ended the call, pleased that Hubert had taken his advice and hopeful that his brother would soon be back at work.

His thoughts returned to Birdie as he continued along the A508, going as fast as he could without breaking the speed limit, and soon he was close to the Holcot turn.

## Chapter 35

Twiggy left his desk and rushed to Sarge's office. The door was closed, which meant he was busy, but this couldn't wait. He tapped on it three times and waited for a response. Everyone knew you couldn't walk in unless the door was ajar.

'Enter,' Sarge's voice came booming out.

He opened the door and headed over to the desk, not bothering to sit. 'I've had a call from Clifford. That *ex*-officer who worked with Birdie on the Donald Witherspoon case. Do you know who I mean?'

'Yes. What did he want?' Sarge gestured in the familiar circular movement with his right hand, which meant *get a move on, I'm busy*.

'He's been helping Birdie look into the background of the girl who was abandoned last year in the town centre. Remember the case?'

Sarge thumped his desk and stood. 'Birdie will be the death of me. Of course I do. She asked me to reopen it and I refused. Lack of staff and there was no new evidence. Did you know that she'd asked him to help? Is this why she took annual leave? She told me it was a family thing.'

'Well, Lacey does live with Birdie's aunt.'

'Did you know about all this? You still haven't answered.'

He'd save his views on Clifford and the way he seemed to have Birdie at his beck and call for another time.

'There's no time to talk about it, now, Sarge. Clifford thinks Birdie's in danger.'

'Danger? How?' Panic shone from his boss's eyes.

'All I know is they tracked down the little girl's parents, and Birdie went to the house to talk with the mother while Clifford kept an eye on the father who was out somewhere in Northampton. Oh, and he's also the uncle.'

'What?' Sarge frowned.

'Long story short. Brother and sister relationship. Nasty stuff. Abuse. He used to be a priest until being locked up for sexual offences. Anyway, Clifford's lost the brother, and he's worried he'll go back to the house and find Birdie with his sister. Clifford's on his way, but I told him not to approach the house and to wait for us.'

'At least we have someone following protocol. So, what are you waiting for? Take the others and get there fast. Is he armed?'

'We don't know.'

'Take Tasers and I'll inform the DI what's going on. I'm due in a meeting I can't get out of at Wigston, which includes the Chief Constable. Keep in touch. And make sure Clifford doesn't get involved.'

'Yes, Sarge.'

How the hell he was going to do that remained to be seen. But, to be honest, he didn't care whether Clifford joined in or not. Twiggy's prime concern was getting

Birdie out of there unscathed. The rest could be dealt with after.

He ran back to the office, where Tiny and Sparkle were chatting over a mug of coffee.

'What's going on?' Sparkle asked, looking across as he came charging over towards them.

'Birdie's in trouble. Grab Tasers and come with me. We'll take two cars. I'll call uniform and arrange more cars for backup.'

## Chapter 36

Seb parked in the same spot as he had the other times. Where was Twiggy and the backup? He'd expected them to arrive before him. Unless they'd driven up the track. But that wasn't what they'd arranged.

With or without them, though, he wasn't prepared to leave Birdie on her own for a moment longer than necessary. That meant he had to get to the cottage without alerting Casey of his presence. Instead of sticking to the track, he'd walk alongside of it and keep out of view. There were sufficient hedgerows to keep him hidden on his way up. Twiggy would realise where he'd gone when he found the empty car.

Having justified to himself his reason for not waiting for the police as arranged, Seb crossed the road onto the track and then immediately veered off it. He couldn't see the house, and was sure that they couldn't see him. The fact the track was winding went in his favour. With his long strides, it shouldn't take him many minutes to get to the top.

After the final curve, the house came into view. Birdie's

car was outside, and behind it, blocking her exit, was the silver Golf.

Where was she? It didn't bode well that she hadn't answered her phone. If Casey had harmed her he'd have Seb to answer to.

He couldn't go to the front door in case he was walking into a trap. He'd shelter in one of the outbuildings and assess the situation.

There was a small barn to the right of the house, and he crept over, intending to hide and observe for a few minutes. There appeared to be no signs of life. Where were they? He walked along the back of the outbuilding and then up to the side, looking for the entrance. He poked his head out. Tessa was heading out of the barn holding a mug in her hand.

Why had she been in there? To see Birdie? Had Casey imprisoned her?

Tessa remained outside the barn and stared up at the sky for a few seconds. Then she headed to the rear of the house, and he remained stationary until she'd gone inside through the back door.

He knew that from the angle of the kitchen windows he couldn't be seen, so he quickly edged around the rest of the barn, stopping to pick up a broken handle from a farm tool that he'd spotted in the grass, in case he needed to defend himself. He got to the door and nudged it open. It gave a loud creak, and he swallowed hard.

Was Casey in there? He hadn't considered that. His grip tightened around his weapon, and he marched in, his arm raised.

'About time, too.'

He jumped at the sound of Birdie's voice. She was sitting on the ground, with her legs out in front of her, tied to one of the roof supports.

He ran over, dropping the handle on the floor as he went. 'Are you okay?' He crouched down beside her and scanned her face. She appeared uninjured, although one of her cheeks was redder than the other.

'I am now you're here. Where have you been? Why didn't you phone and tell me Casey was on his way back.'

'My car got blocked in by a van for twenty minutes and I lost him. I phoned you three times, texted and left messages. Why didn't you answer?'

'It didn't ring.'

'Why didn't *you* phone me?'

'Because I enjoy being here tied up.'

'Now I know you're fine, as your sense of humour hasn't deserted you.'

'You think I was being funny? Well, I wasn't. I thought I had my phone, and it wasn't until I got my hand in my pocket that I realised it was on the kitchen table. I'd been showing Tessa photos of Lacey. I'd persuaded Tessa to come with me to the station, to make a full confession and find out more about Lacey, when her brother came back. We fought, but he was too strong for me.' She rubbed her cheek.

'Did he do that?'

'He slapped me, but it doesn't sting anymore. Then he tied me up and left me here.'

'You were lucky he didn't do more damage.'

'I wonder if my phone was on silent and that's why I didn't hear it.'

'Did you turn it to silent?'

'No.'

'Then who could have? Tessa?'

'That makes no sense. Unless she accidentally flicked the button when looking at the photos. She came to see me a few minutes before you arrived.'

'Yes, I saw her leave.'

'I tried to persuade her to release me and escape together, but she wouldn't. She's too scared of him. She thinks that wherever she goes, he's going to come after and kill her. She told me she was going to stay with him. What are we going to do? We can't leave her because God knows what he'll do.'

'I phoned Twiggy and arranged to meet him at the bottom of the track, but I couldn't wait. Has Casey got a weapon?'

'I haven't seen one.'

'Our best bet is to stay here until backup arrives, in case he tries to escape. If he does, we can go after him. Where are your car keys?'

'I left them in the car's ignition.' Her eyes narrowed. 'Don't say anything.'

'I won't. For now.'

'Wise move. Are you going to untie me or have I got to wait for Twiggy and the others to turn up?'

'Sorry, I'll do it now.' He slid around to the back of the pole and pulled at the knot, eventually releasing her.

She shook her arms. 'Thanks, my hands had totally gone to sleep.'

'Stay where you are in case Casey comes to check. If we hear the door creak, I'll hide behind one of the hay bales in the corner and you put your hands behind your back.'

'Okay.'

'Except it won't creak, because I didn't close it. I'll do it now.'

'What are you doing here?' Patrick Casey's voice boomed out.

He was by the entrance, glowering at them.

'There's no point in trying to get away with this.' Seb

stood to his full height and marched over to the man. 'You're coming with us to the station.'

'Over my dead body,' Casey snarled.

'The police will be here shortly. It's pointless you trying to go anywhere.' Birdie jumped to her feet and rushed over to where the two men stood. 'You might as well admit the truth and come with us to the station.'

'You've got to be kidding.' He turned around and Seb made a grab for him, holding onto his shirt. Casey shook himself from Seb's grasp and ran out of the barn.

Seb and Birdie chased after him as he made a beeline for the house. Birdie caught up with him, grabbed his arm, and twisted it behind his back.

Casey wrenched himself out of her grasp and pulled back his arm with his fist clenched.

Seb threw himself at the man, determined not to let him harm Birdie. But Casey was too quick, and he avoided Seb's clutches. Casey ran to the back of the house and into the kitchen, with Seb and Birdie in pursuit. He grabbed his car keys from the table and headed out of the front door towards his car.

Seb slowly gained on him and pushed him away from the door. Birdie followed closely behind, and they took hold of Casey's arms and pushed him against the car so he couldn't move.

Out of the corner of his eye, Seb caught sight of Tessa running from the house holding a saucepan. She went straight for Birdie and whacked her on the head.

'Arrrgh. What the fuck …'

'Leave him alone,' Tessa shouted.

Birdie grabbed the saucepan from the woman's hand and twisted her arm around her back.

'Why are you sticking up for him?'

'He's my brother, and I love him. I want to be with him.'

'But he abused you. He beat you. You told me what he was planning to do to Emily.'

'It's not true,' Casey shouted.

'Save it for when we're at the station,' Seb said, pushing the man to the ground and sitting on him. 'We'll stay like this until the police arrive.'

# Chapter 37

Birdie stood beside her car while Tessa and Patrick were escorted from the farm in two separate police vehicles. She'd stayed out of the way during their arrest, as she wasn't on duty and she didn't want to cause any issues down the track. Barristers were well known for using whatever technicality they could for getting their clients off charges.

What a mess the whole thing had become. Had she done the right thing in reopening the case? Would they ever tell Lacey about her parents? How would she react when she found out? How would everyone react? She shuddered at the thought.

'There you are,' Twiggy said as he approached.

'Where did you think I was?'

'Stop it, Birdie. You're not funny.'

'I wasn't trying to be,' she lied, deciding it was the best option, as Twiggy looked about ready to explode.

'You've got some explaining to do. Why did you come here on your own? You had no idea what was going to happen. Call yourself a detective. I can't believe your stupidity. You could've been killed.' He turned his head, but not before she witnessed tears fill his eyes.

She swallowed hard. 'I'm sorry, Twig. But, in my defence, Casey had gone out and Tessa was on her own. We had it all planned. Seb was following him and was going to let me know when he was on his way home so I could leave. It was unlucky the way things turned out.'

'Bloody Clifford. I can't believe how he let you down.'

'I'm sure he feels guilty enough without you adding to it. It wasn't his fault.'

She glanced around. Where had Seb gone?

'Did you even think about the potential outcomes before you went to the house? What if Casey hadn't tied you up and put you in the barn? What if he'd killed you and then scarpered?'

'That ridiculous. Why would he kill me? I accept I put myself in a difficult situation, but—'

'Difficult. Is that what you call it? You wait till I see Clifford. Where is he?'

She caught sight of Seb walking towards them and nodded in his direction.

'Where have you been?' she asked him.

'Back to my car. Did you want me?'

'Yes, I did,' Twiggy said, turning to him. 'I can't believe you let this happen to Birdie.'

'You don't have to remind me, DC Branch. I'm fully cognisant of what might have happened.'

'It didn't stop you stuffing up though, did it?'

'I resent that remark.'

Seb and Twiggy glared at each other. They'd be threatening to fight a duel if she didn't step in. For grown men, they could be extremely childish.

'Look, boys, stop it right now. Seb saved me, and that's what counts. We're all put in dangerous situations, sometimes. It's part of the job. It turned out alright, didn't it? But let's keep this between ourselves. I'm on annual leave so Sarge needn't know what went down here.'

'What planet are you on?' Twiggy said. 'Of course, he's going to know. He does already.'

She sighed. 'Great. What did he say?'

'I'm sure you can work that out for yourself.'

'He'll be pleased when I tell him we've located Lacey's parents.'

'He knows that, too. Did Casey actually admit being her father?'

'Tessa told me.'

'Did he abuse Lacey?'

'It's unclear whether there was any physical abuse, but according to Tessa, the reason she abandoned Lacey a year ago was because she could see the direction in which his feelings towards the child were heading.' Her stomach churned at the thought.

'The dirty bastard,' Twiggy said.

'Tessa was concerned he would sexually abuse Lacey. She wouldn't let the child go through what she'd been through herself with him. I didn't get the whole story from her, but I know that she'd lived with him from when she was twelve after her parents died in a boating accident. I don't know when the abuse started.'

'Yet she ended up fighting you so he could escape,' Twiggy said.

'It's complicated. I tried to get Tessa to come with me to the station and she was about to, but then he turned up and she changed her mind. She's so scared of him, she believed it when he said if she left he'd find and kill her.'

'Did she talk much about Lacey?'

'She wanted a better life for her. One that they couldn't give.'

'Does she want her back?'

'I told her that social services would have to be involved. That they will make a decision that's best for Lacey. Tessa will have to be interviewed by them. She didn't actually say whether she wanted her back. I'm going to text my aunt to let her know what's happened.' She reached into her pocket. 'Crap. My phone's still on the kitchen table. I'll get it, before forensics arrives. They're on their way, I assume?'

'Yes, and you shouldn't be going inside.'

'My prints are already in there.'

She dashed off before he could say anything else. Her mobile was where she'd left it, and her bag on the back of the chair. She picked them both up and checked the side of her phone. The sound was off.

Twiggy and Seb were standing next to each other when she got back, but not talking.

'My phone was on silent, that's why I couldn't hear you, Seb. Tessa must have done it when we were talking? Which begs the question, why?'

'Maybe she isn't quite the victim she's made herself out to be. Could she have alerted her brother that you were there?' Seb asked.

'We'll find out later. Let's get back to the station. You both need to make statements, and I'll be interviewing Tessa and her brother,' Twiggy said.

'I've cancelled my leave, from now. I want to interview with you,' Birdie said.

'You can, but only because no one else is available.'

'Thanks.'

'But let me take the lead.'

# Chapter 38

Seb sat in the observation area waiting for Birdie and Twiggy to go into the room to interview Tessa Casey.

The woman sat there, her head bowed, and didn't even look up when they walked in. She was a pitiful sight. What would happen to her in the future, and how would Lacey fit into the picture?

Twiggy pressed the recording equipment. 'Interview on Tuesday 19 May. Those present: DC Branch, DC Bird and …. please state your name for the recording.'

'Tessa Charlotte Casey,' she said, her voice barely above a whisper.

'Could you speak louder so the recording can pick up your voice,' Twiggy said.

'Tessa Charlotte Casey. Am I under arrest?'

'No, but we'd like to talk to you about your little girl, who you abandoned in Market Harborough just over twelve months ago.'

She glanced up and looked at Birdie, stark tension in her eyes. 'I've already told you about this back at the farm.'

'We'd like to discuss it now, in an official setting,' Birdie said. 'How old is your little girl?'

'Emily's now seven. Her birthday's 20 August.'

'Before you left her, where did she go to school?'

'I taught to her at home with my brother. Half-brother,' she corrected.

'Did you inform the local authority of how she was being educated?' Birdie didn't know what the regulations were for homeschooling, but assumed there would be some.

'According to the legislation, we didn't have to notify anyone of our intention to teach Emily ourselves. But the local authority can check up on anyone if they discover a child is being homeschooled. That won't happen for us because …' Her hand flew over her mouth.

Seb frowned. Tessa's action appeared contrived in that she raised her hand a fraction of a second after he'd have expected from a person who believed they'd spoken out of turn. He might have been incorrect in his assumption, but he would scrutinise her further for other signs. It was entirely possible that she was manipulating the situation, but he couldn't interrupt and let Birdie know. Then again, the woman now had the chance to escape from the clutches of her controlling brother. Perhaps she wanted to make sure he would be dealt with severely.

'Because of what?' Twiggy asked.

'Emily's birth was never registered.'

'So, no one is aware of her existence. Are you registered with a GP?'

'None of us are because Patrick thought it was best not to. If Emily was ever ill, we'd look after her ourselves. She wasn't exposed to germs, so it rarely arose.'

'Did you agree with his decision?' Birdie asked.

'We managed,' Tessa said, shrugging.

'I'd like to ask you more about Emily. How would you describe her?'

'Quiet, but very inquisitive. She's always asked a lot of questions.'

'How did Patrick react to this?'

Tessa glanced to the side and grazed her mouth with the fingers on her right hand. 'Um … sometimes he got irritated by it.'

'Did he ever strike her?'

She looked away and then nodded. 'Yes, he did. But … not all the time.'

'When exactly did he hit her?'

'He'd get angry if he thought she wasn't doing as she was told, or if she didn't remember the prayers, he taught her. If she got any of the words wrong, he'd slap her hard on the leg. I tried to stop him, but then he'd turn on me.'

'How often did this happen? Once a month? Once a week?' Twiggy asked.

'Most days,' the woman said, her voice dropping in tone.

'Would you say that your daughter was scared of your brother?' Birdie asked.

'Yes. We both were.'

'Going back to the day when you abandoned Lacey. What prompted this action?' Birdie asked.

'I had no choice. I could see by the way my brother had begun looking at her that she wasn't going to be safe.'

'Can you describe this look?' Birdie asked.

'Um … the way he did to me when I was younger. I'd catch that same longing expression on his face when he watched her … I had to get her away from him and this was all I could think of doing.'

Seb shifted in his chair. Was he being too suspicious? He didn't doubt that there had been violence in the relationship. He'd seen the bruising for himself. But the entire way she was orchestrating the interview and little by little feeding in aspects of her brother's behaviour. Had she also been involved in Lacey's abuse? Was she ensuring that the blame fell squarely on her brother and not on her? It wasn't uncommon for abused people to become abusers themselves.

'Why didn't you leave with her, then you could have been together?' Twiggy asked.

'What would I do? Where would I go? I knew that if I left Emily in town, she'd have a better life than the one I could give her. My money alone wouldn't have supported us. And Patrick would have found us. We'd never have escaped him.' She pulled out a tissue from her sleeve and wiped her eyes.

'I'm sorry we have to put you through this, but it's important that we have the whole picture,' Birdie said.

'I understand.'

'Can you tell us how you felt when you left Emily in the town centre?'

'Like I'd lost a part of me. It was the worst day of my life. But it was the best thing for her. Every day I think about Emily. She's never far from my thoughts. It helps that I know she's being well looked after and that she's doing well.'

'Returning to your fear of what your brother might have done to Emily, do you suspect anything had happened before you took her away?' Birdie asked.

'No, I would have known. I made sure never to leave her alone with him. But I couldn't have protected her forever.'

'You told me you left Emily in town when your brother was away. How did you explain it to him once he'd returned home?'

'I said she'd run off and I couldn't find her.'

'And he believed you?' Twiggy asked.

'Yes.'

'Why didn't he call the police?'

'We were in hiding. That was more important to him.'

'Was he angry?' Birdie asked.

'Not as much as I thought he'd be. I expected to have been beaten for it, but it didn't happen.'

'Why not?'

'I think deep down he was glad to see her go. He saw her as baggage. A stone around his neck.' She looked at Birdie and then Twiggy, a single tear rolling down her cheek. 'Am I under arrest for leaving Emily?'

'Child abandonment is only illegal if the child is under two. So no, you're not,' Twiggy said.

'It was hard but for the best.'

'Tessa, we need to ask you some personal questions,' Birdie said.

'Okay.'

'When did you go to live with your brother?'

Tessa leant forward and rested her face in her hands. 'After my parents died when I was twelve, I lived with him at his house in the parish where he was a priest.'

'Was he strict with you then?'

'Yes. I would be smacked for anything I did wrong.'

'Your brother is Emily's father. Did you have a consensual sexual relationship?'

'We only had sex once, and I got pregnant. It didn't happen again.'

'And yet you told us you were worried about Patrick and Emily because of the looks he gave her? You said he looked at you in the same way, too, when you were young. Did anything happen between you then?'

'No but that was because he restrained himself, because

of being a priest. He's not a priest now, which is why I thought Emily was at risk.'

This wasn't making sense.

'When Patrick went to prison, what did you do then?'

'I already had Emily, and we went to live with a friend of his until he got out. The house we were living in went with his job, so we had to leave.'

'When Patrick, or Sean as he was known then, was working as a priest, how did he explain the birth of Emily to his employers and parishioners?'

'He said the relationship I was in hadn't worked out.'

'When Patrick came out of prison, you both changed your names and moved to Holcot without informing the authorities. Why did you do this?'

'He thought it would be better. A fresh start. We moved here, and that's where we've been. Renting the cottage.'

'Did you go to hospital when you had Emily?'

'No. Patrick delivered the baby. It was a straightforward birth.'

'So while Emily lived with you, she'd never been checked, vaccinated or had any medical treatment?'

'No.'

'Tessa, my phone had been put on silent when I was with you. Do you know how that happened?' Birdie asked.

Seb focused on Tessa's face, looking for any telltale signs she was lying.

'No, I don't.'

'If you remember, I gave it to you so you could look at a photo of Emily.'

'Yes.' She nodded. 'But I did nothing to your phone unless it was by accident, when I was holding it.'

The woman's blink rate had slowed. She wasn't telling the whole truth.

'Why did you hit me with a saucepan, when we were arresting Patrick?'

'I'm not sure. I panicked because everything was about to change and I got scared. I wasn't thinking straight. Are you okay?'

'Yes, I'm fine, but that's not the issue. Attacking an officer is illegal.'

'But I didn't mean it. Am I in trouble? What's going to happen now?'

'That's yet to be decided.'

'What's going to happen to Patrick?'

'We can't discuss that with you. Before we end the interview, we'd like to know more about the card Emily was wearing around her neck which said *Speak No Evil*.'

'This was something Patrick believed in because he's very religious and we had to study the Bible for hours at a time every day. The card acted as a reminder to Emily of how she was expected to behave.'

'Interview suspended,' Twiggy said as he stopped the recording.

'You're to stay here, in case we need to interview you further. I'll ask the officer on the front desk to bring you something to eat and drink,' Birdie said.

# Chapter 39

Birdie and Twiggy met Seb in the corridor and stopped for coffee on their way to the office.

'When I said, I'll be taking the lead, I didn't just mean the formalities,' Twiggy said as they were in the queue at the canteen.

'I didn't ask all the questions. We shared, like we always do. And that's how we get results. No point in changing that now, is there?'

'I suppose not,' Twiggy agreed.

They bought their coffees and returned to the office.

'What was your take on Tessa Casey's interview?' she asked Seb once they were all seated at her desk.

'There's more to the woman than she's showing and she wasn't being completely truthful.'

'How did you work that out?' Twiggy asked.

'Her body language. Her blink rate slowed right down when Birdie asked about her phone.'

'But why would she have done that?' Birdie asked.

'That's what we need to discover. It's my belief that she told you what she thought you wanted to hear to make sure her brother was incriminated for everything that had happened to her and Lacey. She also implied that her brother had sexually abused her when she was younger but that didn't take place.'

'What about the physical abuse. Do you believe that took place?'

'It would appear so, but we can't take her account at face value. Once you've interviewed her brother, you'll have a fuller picture.'

'That will be as soon as his solicitor arrives,' Twiggy said.

'Are you going to recommend charging her for assaulting you?' he asked Birdie.

'She did it under duress and has been through enough. Although after what you've said … am I being too easy on her?'

'Not necessarily. But if you want to get anything out of him, I suggest you take the softly-softly approach. If you go in heavy-handed, he'll dig his heels in and say nothing. Especially to you, Birdie. He's used to being the domineering one, if Tessa's account is to be believed.'

'I witnessed it myself, so I'd say she was spot on.' Birdie picked up her mug and took a sip of coffee.

The phone rang on Twiggy's desk. 'DC Branch. Thanks, we won't be long.' He replaced the receiver and turned to them. 'The duty solicitor has arrived.'

'Our goal for this interview is for Casey to admit to the physical abuse of both Lacey and his sister, as well as kidnapping me,' Birdie said.

'He's very protective of his sister, so you can use it to your advantage,' Seb said.

'Even though she's hung him out to dry.'

'He doesn't know that.'

'We can handle this,' Twiggy said.

'I can't stop thinking about your view of Tessa. The fact my phone was turned to silent is still niggling at the back of my mind. She said she didn't know how it happened, and I know these things can happen accidentally. But what if she did it on purpose? What if she really is playing us?'

'That's what we'll find out when we speak to her brother,' Twiggy said.

They headed to the interview room, and Seb left them to observe in the adjoining area. Sarge would've gone mad if he'd known. But he wasn't there, and Birdie wasn't going to tell him.

They entered the room, and she pressed the recording equipment. 'Interview on Tuesday 19 May. Those present: DC Bird, DC Branch, and please state your names for the recording.'

'Matthew Black, solicitor.'

'Patrick Casey,' he said, his eyes focussed on Twiggy and not on her.

'Mr Casey, there are several issues we'd like to discuss. First, your kidnapping of DC Bird. Why did you do this?'

'It wasn't intentional. I was angry because she'd come into our home and upset my sister. I'm sorry.' He looked directly at Birdie. 'I shouldn't have done it.'

That surprised her. His whole demeanour was at odds with how he'd been before. Was it an act to get him out of being prosecuted?

'Intentional or otherwise, do you admit to doing it?' Twiggy asked.

The solicitor leant in and whispered something to Casey, who nodded.

She knew what was coming next.

'No comment.'

As expected. That could wait. She'd move on.

'I'd like to talk to you about your daughter, Emily, who is known now as Lacey.'

'I'm not her father.'

'Why would your sister say you were?'

He shifted awkwardly in his chair. 'Okay, I am. We had sex the one time when we'd both been drinking. It was while I was a priest. I broke my vow of celibacy.' He bowed his head. 'It's not something I'm proud of but I resolved to take care of them.'

'And that responsibility involved physically abusing both of them, did it?'

His eyes widened. 'I never laid a hand on either of them.'

'How do you account for the bruising on your sister? I saw it myself.'

'Did she say it was me?'

'It doesn't matter what Tessa said. I'm asking you.'

'My sister is a little … temperamental. She's always been that way. She has so much pent-up emotion that sometimes she can only release it by harming herself. She'd bang her head on the wall, or she'd throw herself down the stairs. Sometimes she'd squeeze her own arms until they bruised. I stop her when I can, but it's not always possible.'

Birdie exchanged a glance with Twiggy. Had the woman totally fooled them?

'Are you a violent man?' Birdie asked.

'No.'

'Yet you slapped me hard across the face and we fought. Do you not consider that to be violent?'

'Yes. It was. I was provoked. Under normal circumstances, I'm not like that. I'm sorry.'

'Going back to Tessa. You maintain that she self-harmed. Did she ever harm Emily?'

'Occasionally she'd get angry with her.'

'Whose decision was it not to send Emily to school?'

'It was joint because of our situation. I regretted it because Emily would've enjoyed the company of other children.'

'And when the child went missing, why didn't you do anything about it?'

He laid his hands flat on the table and leant forward slightly. 'It was hell not having her around, but I knew it was for the best. I'd come back several times and found Tessa had locked Emily in her bedroom for hours without food and water, for not behaving.'

'I'm confused,' Birdie said. 'Why are you telling us this now? I thought Tessa was your priority and you would do anything to protect her. But now you're blaming her.'

'I can't go back to prison. Not again. It almost killed me.'

'So, what you're saying about Tessa is to protect yourself.'

'No.' He drew in a breath.

'What is it then? You might not want to go back to prison, but I can tell you now, it's looking extremely likely after what has happened. Tell us the truth.' Birdie locked eyes with him, ignoring Seb's request that she should tread carefully because she sensed it wasn't necessary.

Patrick stared ahead, and the solicitor sat with his arms folded.

Birdie knew not to speak. Twiggy did, too. They'd often discussed the sales technique *he who speaks first loses* in police interviews. But she nudged him with her foot, to make sure.

After at least a minute had passed, Patrick cleared his throat. 'When I was put inside, it was for having porno-graphic images of children on my computer. I lost my job and my freedom. Except they weren't my images. They belonged to Tessa. I took the blame. I couldn't let her go to prison because she needed to be with our daughter. It was a mess, and that was the best way of solving it. I hadn't realised how awful my time in prison would be. Nonces are fair game for everyone, and some guards turned their back and let it happen.'

Whoa. She hadn't expected that. Surely it couldn't be true.

'And you expect us to believe this? Are you sure you're not covering your back?' Twiggy said.

'It's the truth.'

'Did you ask Tessa why she had these images?'

'She told me it was for research because she wanted to write a book about child exploitation.'

'And you believed her?' Twiggy said.

'Yes.'

'And if we ask her, would she tell us the same?' Birdie asked.

'She might be too scared, in case she was then charged with the offence.'

'That aside, we have a very different picture of events regarding Emily from your sister. She told us she abandoned the child because she was frightened about what you might do to her. What you'd already done to her.'

He raised his hand to his mouth, and behind it said something to his solicitor.

'No comment.'

'Why no comment if you have nothing to hide?'

'You don't want to believe me. I didn't touch Emily. Not physically or sexually, as you're implying.'

'We don't think you did sexually abuse her, although your sister was worried that it might progress to that. But we know you've physically abused her. In the same way as you did to your sister.'

'I've already explained that it didn't happen. Why won't you believe me?'

'Is it true that you delivered Emily into the world?'

He frowned. 'Yes. Why?'

'But you refused to register the birth?'

'We couldn't because I would've lost my job if it was discovered that I was the father.'

'How convenient. Did you threaten to harm Tessa if she told anyone the truth about Emily's father?'

'No. Did she say that?' He sucked in a breath, resignation showing in his eyes. 'You don't understand what she's like.'

'Why don't you tell us, then,' Birdie said, sitting back in her chair and folding her arms, keeping her eyes on him.

'My sister paints a picture of herself as being frail and helpless, and in a way, she is. But she's also manipulative.'

Exactly what Seb had said. Birdie went on full alert. 'In what way?'

'Why do you think I've never left her? Because she threatened that if I did, she'd tell the police I raped and abused her. She knew I'd do anything not to go back to prison.'

'Why should we believe you? Do you have any proof of how your sister is?'

'I have a text on my phone but I can't show you because it was taken when I was arrested.'

Birdie arranged for the phone to be brought to them, and she handed it to Casey.

He called up the text and then slid his phone across the table. 'This is from her when you turned up at the house today.'

Birdie stared at the message on the screen. 'For the benefit of the recording, the text reads: *The bitch is here again. Come home now.*'

'So, let's get this straight,' Twiggy said. 'You maintain that you're the father of the child, but you didn't abuse her. Your sister did. And when your sister abandoned the child, you didn't do anything about it because you thought it was best. Which is the total opposite to what your sister said.'

'Yes.' Patrick drew in a breath and exhaled loudly.

'Two weeks ago, last Saturday, you were in town and Emily saw one or both of you. Who was it?' Birdie asked.

'It could have been when Tessa went to the ATM while I was in the car.'

'When I spoke to Tessa about the incident, she thought Emily had seen *you* and got scared.'

'That's not true. She was the one who was out of the car. Emily couldn't have seen me.'

'Is it true that you made Emily pray all the time?'

'No, it's not. Tessa was more insistent on the prayers because she said it reminded her of our father. He was obsessive about praying.'

'Yet it was you who went into the priesthood.'

'I know. My upbringing rubbed off on me. But I didn't make Emily recite prayers. I don't believe that religion should be used as a threat like that.'

'I saw the Bible you gave to Tessa on the sideboard in your kitchen. It was a strange inscription, implying there was more than a brother and sister relationship between the two of you.'

'Apart from when we conceived Emily, there was nothing sexual between us. I've lived with the guilt since it happened. But ...' His voice faded away.

'Continue,' Birdie said.

'For all my regret, having Emily was the best thing in my life. She was a lovely little girl. Can I see her? It's been so long. I miss her every day.'

'That's a decision for social services to make, and nothing will happen until we have resolved this case.'

'That's what I expected you'd say. But I had to ask.'

'How do you manage for money, as you've been living off the grid?'

Again, she wanted to compare his story with Tessa's.

'We had an inheritance from when our father and Tessa's mother were killed in a boating accident. It's enough for us to rent the cottage and live basically.'

'If this is all true, why did you tie me up and put me in the barn?'

'That was to protect you, because I didn't know what Tessa was going to do. She can be volatile.'

'It didn't seem like you were protecting me when we were struggling, and you slapped me.'

'I wanted Tessa to believe that I would sort it out. If she saw me being weak then she'd try to take over.'

'Why did you let her come to the barn with some water, then? She certainly wasn't acting volatile then.'

'I monitored things from a distance.'

'And when you came into the barn after my colleague had arrived, and then tried to escape, what was that about?'

'I knew you wouldn't believe me. I'd planned that Tessa and I would leave and head for the New Forest.'

'What were you going to do with me?'

'We'd have left you. I assumed that your colleague would come back, and it would all be fine.'

Who to believe? Or were they both lying? But …

'Before we end the interview. I'd like to know about the *Speak No Evil* sign.'

'The what?' he replied, frowning.

'Do you know this saying?'

'Yes. It's common enough. Some people think it has religious connotations, but it doesn't.'

'Is it something your sister would say?'

'I've heard her use it.'

'Who wrote it on the sign?'

'What sign?' he repeated. 'I don't know what you're talking about. I remember one time Tessa making Emily write it out twenty times for being naughty. But this was on paper, not a sign.'

He genuinely didn't know.

'Interview suspended.'

'Is my client being charged?' the solicitor asked.

'Not at the moment. But he'll remain in custody. I'll arrange for someone to collect him.'

## Chapter 40

Birdie and Twiggy left the interview room, and Seb joined them in the corridor.

'Well?' she asked him.

'You have an interesting conundrum.'

'You can say that again. We need to reinterview the sister. Nothing is as it seems, and we need to get to the bottom of it. Do you have any thoughts on who's telling the truth?'

'My money's on her.' Twiggy said.

'But remember, Seb had misgivings about her even before we interviewed him. What made you suspicious?'

'Her body language seemed a little contrived and not as natural as I'd have expected, and she displayed signs of lying as I mentioned earlier.' Seb said.

'What about Patrick?' Birdie asked.

'He was trickier to read, but I didn't spot any inconsistencies. That doesn't mean he wasn't telling the whole truth. He has a lot more to lose than she does.'

'Okay. Let's go back and reinterview Tessa, Twig, and get this sorted once and for all.'

She could usually rely on her gut to know when someone was playing her. If Seb was correct, Tessa had been very clever.

'Watch the timing of her reactions,' Seb said.

'Will do.'

'May I observe again?'

'There's no Sarge here, so it's fine by me,' she said.

They returned to the room, and Tessa was sitting in the same position as when they'd left her, with her head bowed and looking like a victim. An untouched cup of tea and a plate of biscuits were on the table.

Was it all an act?

She pressed the recording equipment. 'Interview with Tessa Casey resumed. Those also present: DC Bird and DC Branch. Tessa, we have just interviewed your brother.'

'Does he know what I said about him? Because if he does, he's going to come after me. I know he will. You have to protect me. I'm not safe.' Her eyes darted from Birdie to Twiggy and back again.

'We have a difference in opinion between the two of you as to what's been going on.' Birdie ignored the woman's pleas.

'What did he say?'

'He's covered for you over the years, hasn't he?'

'No. That's rubbish. He's a good actor. But you don't know him like I do. You haven't seen what he's capable of when he's crossed.'

'Even if that is true, can you explain to us why you sent a text to him when I was there saying: *The bitch is here again. Come home now.*'

Tessa gripped hold of the table with both hands. 'I didn't. It wasn't me who sent it.'

'We've seen the text on his phone, and we know it

came from you. As there was only you and me at the house who else could it be?'

'Um … um …'

Was the truth finally going to come out?

'Do you have your phone with you?' Twiggy asked.

'It's at home.'

'How convenient.'

'The police were there, and they made me come to the station straight away. I didn't have time to get my bag or phone. I brought nothing with me. Believe me. I promise I didn't send the text.' The words tumbled out of her mouth.

'Enough,' Birdie said, holding up her hand to silence her. 'I want to return to my phone and how it ended up on silent after you'd been holding it. It wasn't an accident, was it? You did it intentionally in case my colleague tried to warn me that Patrick was on his way back.'

'I don't know anything about it.'

'I suggest that when I showed you the photo of Lacey, you changed the setting.'

'But that makes no sense. Why would I have come to you in the barn?'

'To cover your tracks. You wanted me to believe that Patrick was the dangerous one.'

'No. You've got it all wrong. I was on your side. Don't listen to what he said. He's very clever at making you see things his way. He's a sex offender and on the register.'

'According to him, it was you and not him who downloaded the pornographic images to his computer. He took the blame to protect you and the baby.'

'Why would I want sick images of children? He's lying.'

'You told him you wanted to write a book about child exploitation and downloaded the images.'

'That's not true. It wasn't me.'

'Why would he tell us that? It's not like he's going to be prosecuted again for the same offence. He's served his time.'

'So he doesn't go back to prison for what he did to Emily.'

'What did he do?'

'I've told you already. Stop trying to trick me.' Her voice wavered. Were they finally getting to the truth?

'Tell me again, why you left Emily in the town centre.'

'To protect her from Patrick. He was getting too close.'

'And not because you were jealous of their relationship. Because you wanted your brother to yourself, and you didn't like sharing him. Even if it was with your own daughter.'

'That's crazy. Why would I do that?' Her breaths were short and loud.

'You tell me.'

'He might have been Emily's father, but I bet he didn't tell you he raped me and got me pregnant. That he made me so scared of him I gave up my daughter.'

'You didn't say it was rape in our previous interview.'

'I didn't say it wasn't.'

'According to Patrick, you both got drunk and had sex one night, resulting in you becoming pregnant. He said that he was the one who stopped you from harming Emily and not the other way around.'

'That's not true. Why do you believe someone who's been in prison for sexual offences?'

'*Your* offences, that *he* covered for.'

'No.' She thumped the table. 'I didn't want to lose Emily, but I had no choice to keep her safe. I don't know what he's telling you, but it's all lies.'

'I don't believe you.' Birdie said.

'I admit I didn't want to be pregnant, and he persuaded me to keep her. But after that I didn't want to lose her.'

'You told me that Patrick abused you.'

'He did. You saw that for yourself.'

'We saw the bruises, but not how they happened.'

'Why are you taking his side?'

'Is it true that you harm yourself and cause bruising to your body?'

'No.'

'Have you ever thrown yourself down the stairs?'

'You don't understand.'

'Did Patrick harm you, or did you do it to yourself?'

'That's crazy,' Tessa said.

'Answer the question,' Birdie snapped, fed up with her avoidance tactics.

'Okay, we fought. But he wouldn't hit back. I couldn't stand it.'

'So you took your temper out on yourself?'

'Yes. No. It's … he was such a *Mr Goody Two Shoes* …' her words faded away.

'Now we have the truth. Do you still claim he raped you?'

She shrugged. 'I don't remember, we'd been drinking.'

'Since we've been interviewing you, not once have you asked to see your daughter. Why's that?'

'Um … Why does that matter?'

'Did you forget about her?'

'Stop putting words into my mouth. I've never forgotten about her.'

'But you don't want to see her.'

'Yes, I do.'

'Why didn't you ask to? Patrick has.'

'Typical. I told you how clever he was. You've fallen for his words. Just like I used to.'

'We're not so gullible as to believe everything we're told,' Birdie said.

'But you still believe him over me, though.'

'Can we return to the sign that was around Lacey's neck? You mentioned Patrick made it and they were his words.'

'Y-yes.'

'Would it surprise you to learn that he knew nothing of the sign?'

'He's making it up. He made it, but I admit to putting it around her neck.'

'Why?'

'I wanted whoever found her to know that she'd been brought up strictly, in terms of religion. It was for her own good.'

'Like your parents did to you?'

'Yes.'

'As Patrick was a priest, do you confirm he was familiar with the religious teachings of the Bible?'

'Yes, and that's why he made the sign.'

'Except those words don't have a religious connotation. Patrick knows that. He also mentioned that you used those words a lot, but he hadn't told you the true meaning. So perhaps now you'll admit that you made the sign and put it around her neck. Also, that you abandoned Emily not to keep her safe from Patrick, but because you were jealous of the relationship she had with her father. One that you wanted but didn't have.'

Tessa shook her head. 'If that's true, then why did I wait to make sure she'd been found? Why didn't I dump her and run?'

'Because you're not totally heartless. You waited until

275

you knew she was safe and then went home, feeling that your duty had been done.'

'You don't understand … it's …'

Birdie stared at the woman. Were they finally going to learn the truth about Lacey and her life before they knew her?

'Why don't you tell us, then? We want to understand.'

Tessa cleared her throat. 'You're right. It was me and nothing to do with Patrick. Are you happy now?'

'You owe Patrick a great deal. He went to prison and ruined his life because of you.'

'He's my brother.'

'Why did you download those images?'

'He said we were not good for each other and that our fights affected Emily. He said he was going to give up the priesthood and go into a monastery. I couldn't have that. The images were leverage just in case. But I didn't realise his computer was connected to a wider network.'

'Didn't you feel guilty about causing the end of his career?'

'What was the point, I couldn't change anything.'

'Why did you pretend he beat you?'

'I didn't want you to think that Emily should come back home to me, she's better off where she is.'

They were certainly in agreement about that.

'We'll be in contact with the Crown Prosecution Service to discuss whether you're going to be charged with being an accessory to the kidnapping of a police officer.'

'That was nothing to do with me, and you know it. It was all Patrick's idea.'

'To protect me from you.'

'What *were* your intentions towards DC Bird?' Twiggy asked.

'I had none. You have to believe me. It was all Patrick.'

'Yet you put my phone on silent, you assisted your brother by fetching the rope and then you whacked me on the head with a saucepan.' Birdie paused. 'It will also be decided whether retrospective charges are to be made for the downloading of child pornography.'

## Chapter 41

'Birdie, my office now.'

She glanced up from her desk, cringing at the expression on Sarge's face as he stared directly at her. She'd known this was going to happen as it was her first day back at work following her annual leave, not counting when she'd interviewed Patrick and Tessa Casey.

'Coming, Sarge,' she said as her boss turned and headed out of the room.

Out of the corner of her eye she saw Twiggy smirking. She turned and glared, but all he did was wink.

'Off you go. You know what's going to happen now, don't you?'

'I can handle it. I can handle anything now we know Lacey's history. It means we'll be able to talk to her about it and that should help her open up and become more settled.'

'Patrick Casey should've been done for kidnap and assault after what he did to you.'

'I disagree. He did it to protect me and was given an

official warning. He's paid enough after being in prison. Anyway, wish me luck.'

'You'll need more than luck. You better dust off your walking shoes, because my money is on you being in uniform pounding the beat from now on.'

'Thanks, mate. You really know how to reassure a person.' She rolled her eyes and left her desk, heading into the corridor towards Sarge's office.

He was waiting for her by the door, and he closed it behind her. She did her usual scan of his room. It never failed to amaze her how anyone could work in such a mess. He swore blind he knew where everything was but, seriously, how could he?

'Sit.' He pointed to the chair in front of his desk.

That was always kept empty. In all the times she'd been called in to his office, and there had been many, the chair never had anything on it.

'Yes, Sarge.'

'You've got some explaining to do. You asked to reopen the case, and I said no, yet behind my back, you carried on.'

'Well, I did end up taking annual leave to work with Clifford after asking him to investigate.'

'Are you telling me you didn't make use of any police resources, because I don't believe you.'

She looked away, unable to meet his eyes. 'I checked CCTV footage and used the databases.'

'This can't go unpunished.'

'What are you going to do?'

'We'll discuss that shortly. How come you involved Clifford in the case? I thought he was in London. Did you ask him back specially?'

'No, Sarge. He's actually living here now, taking care of

his cousin Sarah's house while she travels overseas. You remember, she was the one who was married to Donald Witherspoon? It was luck that he was here and could help me.'

'You do realise he's not part of our team. He's a civilian.'

'He's set up his own PI company, and he's got a job doing investigative work for the Met, so he's sort of still on the force. Does that count?'

'No, it doesn't. You still haven't told me why you disobeyed a direct order not to reopen the case.'

'Well, Sarge … I couldn't leave it. If you'd seen the state of Lacey when she had the meltdown, you'd have felt the same as me. I knew we had to do something, otherwise, her life could have been ruined forever. Now we know everything, with my aunt's help, she'll be able to put this behind her.'

Sarge's face softened. Did he understand?

'It was a complicated case, that's for sure. A mother and father who were related. An ex-priest who's also an ex-con. It would be more than enough for any person to get to grips with.'

'Patrick Casey only went to prison to protect his sister.'

'And now she's facing charges for perverting the course of justice and downloading pornographic images, as you know.'

'He protected me, too.'

'Which is why I recommended to the CPS not to charge him with kidnapping.'

'It was the right decision, Sarge. The official warning he received was more than enough. What he did came from a good place. He wouldn't have harmed me. I can't say the same for Tessa, though. She could have been far more of a threat.'

She'd played down her fight with Patrick in the house,

as she was the only witness to it. And if he'd done it to convince his sister, then she was fine about it.

'Fortunately, we'll never know. When is the social services case conference for Lacey?'

'At eleven this morning, is it okay for me to go?' She hoped he didn't say no, as social services had given permission for her to attend with Auntie Catherine and Lacey.

'Yes, you may.'

'Is that it, can I go back to my desk?'

'No. We haven't yet discussed your future. I've been in contact with HR and there's going to be an investigation into the incident. You can't break the rules and expect there to be no consequences.'

'Am I suspended?'

'No, but until the investigation is complete, you are to be placed on desk duty.'

And she'd sworn to never put herself in a position where she'd have to do that again, after the last time.

'Will I lose my job?' The words caught in the back of her throat as she voiced the unthinkable.

'Not if I have any say in it. You contribute valuably to the team and would be sorely missed.'

'And Twiggy and I have just solved the carjacking cases,' she reminded him. The case had been a top priority for so long that surely it would go some way towards mitigating what else she'd done.

'A massive plus in your favour. Twiggy explained it was down to your quick thinking.'

'He told you?'

Twiggy could've easily shared the credit.

'He's your partner and proud of you. You have a bright future ahead of you, if you'd only learn to curb your impulsiveness. Which is what makes this situation so frustrating.'

'I promise not to break the rules again.'

'My ulcer and I would love to believe you.'

'Am I likely to be put back in uniform for a while?'

'I have no intention of inflicting you on them, but I expect that you'll be put on probation for a period of time.'

That she could live with. As long as she didn't lose her job.

## Chapter 42

'Are you okay?' Birdie's aunt asked, nudging her arm as they were heading towards the social services office for the case conference.

'What? Yes. Sorry, I've got lots on my mind.'

'Do you want to talk about it?'

'No. It's fine. But thanks. We need to concentrate on what's going to happen to Lacey. The other stuff can wait.'

She'd thought of nothing other than her meeting with Sarge. He said that he didn't want her to be fired, but what if HR didn't accept his recommendation? What if they made an example of her? So they could show officers in the police that rule breaking wouldn't be tolerated. What would she do then? What *could* she do?

'The offer's there if you want it.'

'Thanks, Auntie Catherine. I'll let you know if I change my mind. Right now, let's go inside and see what they say.'

She pushed open the door into the building and they headed for the conference room where the meeting was being held. Taking part were Auntie Catherine, Birdie, as she was the contact person between Patrick and them, Valerie Clark, Dr Miranda Watkins, and Stephen Shaw, the social worker.

'Thank you all for attending,' Valerie said once everyone was seated. 'I'd like to welcome DC Bird, Catherine's niece, to the proceedings. She helped to discover Lacey's identity and with her knowledge of the case and the child's parents we welcome her insight.'

'Thank you,' Birdie said.

'We're here because Patrick Casey would like to visit his daughter Lacey, who he knows as Emily. Our role is to decide whether we should allow it, bearing in mind our prime concern is with the child and her well-being.'

'What about the mother?' Miranda Watkins asked.

'We have no request from her. DC Bird, what can you tell us about the situation?'

'Lacey's mother, Tessa, is currently out on bail pending charges laid against her. Tessa and Patrick are half-brother and sister. When we initially found them, we were led to believe that he was a potential threat to Lacey, and that was why Tessa had abandoned her. It turned out not to be the case. Tessa had been jealous of the close relationship between Lacey and her father and didn't want her there. It is alleged that she had been physically abusing Lacey, but these charges weren't added because the CPS believed it too difficult to prove.' Birdie glanced around the table. What were they thinking?

'The father had been to prison and is on the sexual offenders' register, is that correct?' Valerie asked.

'Yes, but he wasn't responsible for the pornographic images on his computer and we expect he will be exonerated. It was Tessa who downloaded them. He took the blame because he didn't want to leave the child, who was a baby, without her mother. He also carried with him the guilt for breaking his vow of celibacy. Which only happened once, when they'd been drinking.'

'Have you asked Lacey whether she would like to see him? It couldn't go ahead without her consent,' Miranda Watkins said.

'No, Lacey hasn't been asked, as we were waiting to hear the outcome of this meeting,' Auntie Catherine said.

'Stephen, have you met the father?' Valerie asked.

'Yes, I have spoken to him.'

'Does he wish to have custody of Lacey?'

'No, he doesn't. He's happy to leave her in the foster care of Catherine. I brought up the possibility of having Lacey adopted, and it's something he'll consider. He'd like to maintain regular contact with the child, but only if it doesn't cause any issues for her.'

'Do you wish to adopt Lacey, Catherine?' Valerie asked, looking at Birdie's aunt.

'We're happy to be full-time foster carers for the long term, and would consider adopting Lacey if we believed it would be in her best interest. We certainly don't wish to see her placed elsewhere as that would be most damaging to her development.'

'Thank you for your input. Her adoption is not a decision to be made at the moment. Our aim today is to decide whether the child should see her father. What's your opinion on this, Miranda?'

'When I last saw Lacey, she was still reserved, but there was a definite improvement. She responded well to Mrs Cooper and was a lot more content. She didn't avert her eyes every time I addressed her. Providing it is Mrs Cooper who does the asking, I believe that she's mature enough to decide whether she wishes to see him. It must be stressed that there is no right or wrong answer and whatever she decides is absolutely fine. If she says yes, then I suggest a meeting is arranged sooner rather than later.'

'Providing Lacey agrees, we could hold the meeting here, with you present, Catherine,' Valerie said.

'I'd also like Birdie to be with us as she knows the father and has a strong bond with Lacey. The child trusts her, implicitly,' Catherine said.

'I'm more than happy to do that,' Birdie agreed.

'If everyone else is okay with this decision, then I suggest Lacey is asked today and the meeting conducted tomorrow.'

# Chapter 43

Lacey gripped Birdie's hand on one side and Auntie Catherine's on the other as they headed for the meeting with Patrick Casey. Birdie glanced at the stoic expression on the little girl's face, and her heart went out to her. Would she have been so brave at that age?

When Lacey had been asked about her father, she'd closed her eyes and remained still for five minutes. Birdie and her aunt had sat there waiting. Eventually, Lacey had looked at them and said yes, she would like to see him. They'd reassured her that they would all meet him together, and she'd happily accepted it. She didn't once ask about her mother.

That spoke volumes, as far as Birdie was concerned.

'Are you sure you're okay about this, because it's not too late to change your mind if you want to,' Auntie Catherine said to Lacey as they approached the social services building.

'Yes, I'm sure,' Lacey said.

Birdie admired the child for how well she was coping. She'd gone through so much, but at least now they knew her background, they could talk to her about it when she was older and help her to deal with it.

'Remember, we'll both be with you all the time, and you can talk to your dad if you wish, but don't feel you have to say anything. He wants to make sure you're doing okay and that you enjoy living with Auntie Catherine at her house,' Birdie said.

'I know.' Lacey gave a shaky smile.

Birdie squeezed her hand. 'He might still call you Emily. Do you want us to tell him it's now Lacey?'

They'd spoken yesterday about changing her name back, but Lacey was adamant that she didn't want to because she liked her new name. Birdie suspected it was more because she didn't want to be reminded of what had happened in the past.

'Yes, please.'

'Consider it done.' Birdie leant down and gave the little girl a hug. Lacey responded by hugging back and giving her a kiss on the cheek.

Warmth flooded through Birdie. If anyone ever did anything to harm Lacey again, she'd make sure it was the last thing they ever did.

'What about me? Can we have a group hug?' Auntie Catherine asked, bending down to join them.

'Yes,' Lacey said, as they all put their arms around each other.

'Okay, kid, this is it.' Birdie flashed a smile in Lacey's direction as they walked into the social services offices and made their way to the room they'd been allocated.

She opened the door and seated on one of the easy chairs was Patrick. Lacey tensed beside her, and she gave her hand a reassuring squeeze.

They walked over to him, and as they got closer a broad smile crossed his face. It changed his whole appearance. There was no sign of the harsh aggressiveness that Birdie had witnessed in the past.

'Hello, Lacey,' he said, remaining seated.

He used her new name. Birdie nodded her respect.

'Hello,' she said tentatively, but keeping so close to Birdie that a sheet of paper couldn't be slid between them.

'Shall we sit down, Lacey?' Birdie asked.

She nodded, and they went over to the green flecked sofa which was opposite the chair Patrick was seated in. Auntie Catherine sat on one side of Lacey and Birdie on the other.

'You're looking very well,' Patrick said, his voice stilted.

'Yes,' Lacey whispered.

'I'm Catherine Cooper, Lacey's foster mother.' She leant forward and held out her hand, which Patrick shook.

'Thank you for taking such good care of her. Do you enjoy living with Mrs Cooper, Lacey?'

'It's Auntie Catherine,' she replied.

'Sorry. Do you enjoy living with Auntie Catherine?'

'Yes. And Birdie.'

Patrick frowned. 'Do you live with them, too?'

'No, but I spend a lot of time there. We're like cousins, aren't we, Lacey? We both have an Auntie Catherine.'

'You're related?'

'Yes. I was with Lacey when she saw you in Market Harborough the other week.'

'I didn't realise.'

She thought she'd mentioned it. But it didn't matter.

'I'm very fond of Lacey.'

'What's happening with her schooling, Mrs Cooper?'

'Call me Catherine. I'm teaching Lacey myself at the moment, as I'm a qualified primary school teacher. We're hoping that one day, Lacey might be ready to go to school with other children.'

'Are you looking forward to that, Lacey?'

'I think so. But not yet.'

'There's no rush. Whenever you're ready,' Auntie Catherine said.

'I like your new name, it's beautiful and suits you. Do you like it, too?'

'Yes.' She nodded and gave a shy smile.

'Is there anything you'd like to ask me, Lacey?'

She glanced to one side at Birdie, and then the other at Auntie Catherine. Then she stood and walked over to where he was sitting.

'I don't want to go back with you. I want to stay with Auntie Catherine and Birdie.'

'I agree. You've got a lovely home now and I can see how happy you are. I wouldn't want to take you away.'

Lacey smiled and returned to where she'd been sitting.

Patrick looked over at Birdie. 'I'll be forever grateful to you for looking into what happened. If you hadn't, I'd have worried forever, wondering how she was. I'm happy that everything's going to be fine for her.'

They continued talking for a while until their hour was up.

'Thank you for taking such good care of Lacey,' Patrick said to Catherine. 'I'd like a word with DC Bird, if I may.'

Catherine and Lacey left the room, closing the door behind them.

'What is it?' Birdie asked.

'I don't think I should see Lacey again. It's best for her if she continues with her new life. She's clearly thriving and being looked after. If she wants to know about us in the future, then tell her. But for now, I'll step aside. I'm going to suggest that your aunt adopts Lacey if she'd like to. I don't wish to shirk my financial responsibilities,

though, so we can work out some financial support for her.
I know that Tessa will agree.'

'Are you still living with your sister?'

'Someone's got to look after her while she's out on
bail.'

'It's likely that she'll do a stint in prison.'

'Because she didn't download the images for sexual
purposes, her legal team believe that she might be given
probation. Although there's also the perverting the course
of justice charge. If she does, then I'll wait for her.'

'Now you're likely to be exonerated, will you rejoin the
priesthood?'

'Too much water under the bridge for that, but I would
like to work with young offenders. Having been in prison,
I've witnessed first-hand how the experience can shape a
person's future.'

'Good luck. I hope it turns out okay for you.'

# Chapter 44

Birdie grabbed her jacket from her bed and headed downstairs to leave for her meeting with Seb. She still didn't know what it was about. All he'd said on the phone was that now Lacey's case was over, there was something he wanted to discuss with her.

It wasn't like him to be so mysterious and she'd tried to drag it out of him, but he point-blank refused because it was best discussed face to face. Whatever *it* was.

'Bye, Mum. I'll be back later,' she called, as she was on her way out.

'Lucie, wait.' Her mum was the only person allowed to call her that, as she refused to call her Birdie.

'What is it? I need to get going or I'll be late.'

'Since when has that ever bothered you?' her mum said as she came out of the kitchen into the hall.

'Normally, not often, but I'm going to a meeting.'

'Work?'

'No, it's with Seb, but I don't know what it's about.'

'I'm worried about you.'

'Why?'

'You put your neck on the block to help Lacey, and I'm proud of you. But you have to consider yourself. If you want a career in the police, then you've got to follow the rules. Like the rest of us.'

'I know, and it won't happen again.'

'Until the next time.'

'Don't worry, I'll be fine.' She gave her mum a kiss on the cheek and headed out of the front door, anxious to get to the pub.

Seb had even suggested they talked over a meal. His shout. Again, most unlike him, as she was always the one to suggest eating and he invariably made some quip if he ended up paying.

Was Sarah coming back, and he was leaving town?

Knowing him, it was his way of telling her, because he still felt guilty about not contacting her straight away when he'd first arrived back.

They'd decided to meet at a pub in Lutterworth at seven o'clock, because he wanted somewhere they wouldn't bump into anyone they knew.

She reached the pub at five minutes past seven and after parking, glanced around to see if he'd already arrived. Of course he had.

She headed inside and spotted him sitting at a table on the far side of the bar. On the table were two drinks, so she walked over assuming that one was for her.

'Thanks for the drink.'

He glanced at his watch. 'What's going on? I wasn't expecting you for at least another fifteen minutes, if not longer.'

'You can be so hurtful. I made an extra special effort to get here on time because I was curious. Okay, I missed it by a few minutes, but seriously you can't count that.' She sat down opposite him, picked up her glass, and took a sip.

'How's work?'

'Great, if you enjoy being chained to the desk with an impending investigation hanging over you.'

'When do they expect it to be over?'

'Don't ask me. I'll be the last to know, even if I am the one being investigated.'

'It's protocol, you know that.'

'It doesn't make it any easier. Anyway, cut the crap and tell me what this meeting is all about. Or should I guess? You're leaving town, and this is our goodbye meal. Yes?'

'No. Whatever gave you that idea?'

'What else could it be now the case is over? I thought you'd be going back to London to give your company the best chance of succeeding. You'll have clients falling over themselves to give you work.'

'You make it sound so easy.'

'Don't tell me you're having a crisis of confidence. If you are, that's ridiculous. You have the connections, the skills and a crazy-memory. You're like a triple threat.'

'It's not that, but thanks. Your praise is important to me as you don't bullshit.'

'You're right about that.' She grinned.

'There's something I wish to ask you. I don't expect an answer straight away because it's a big step. I've been thinking about this for some time.'

'I wouldn't expect anything else from you. Rash decision-making isn't part of your make-up. Well, most of the time, it isn't. I seem to recall you rather quickly moved into Sarah's house.'

This was getting more bizarre by the minute.

'I'll ignore that insult.'

'I'm not insulting you. I'm just … What is this proposition?' Surely he wasn't …

'It's not that sort of proposition, for goodness' sake.'

'How do you know that's what I was thinking? Don't tell me you've now added mind reading to your skill set.'

'Call it an educated guess. I'm under no illusion that you think of me as nothing more than an older, stuck in the mud, man. But we are friends, aren't we?'

'Good friends. Tell me what this is about or the kitchen will be closed by the time you've finished, and we won't have ordered our food.'

'We can't have that. I'll get to the point.'

'Hu-bloody-ray.'

'Stop interrupting. I've been having thoughts about the future of Clifford Investigation Services.'

'You can call it *CIS*, I know what you mean.'

'When we were talking about the company, you mentioned you might join me?'

She jerked her head back. 'You know I was joking, don't you?'

'Many a true word is spoken in jest.'

'You don't have to go all *cliché* on me now. Are you being serious?'

'Never more so. We make an excellent team, even if we drive each other mad sometimes.'

'And my timekeeping drives you to distraction.'

'We can work on that.'

She hadn't for one moment imagined he'd be asking her to work with him permanently.

'Look, Seb. I'm flattered by your offer. Who wouldn't be? But I love my job and I hadn't planned on resigning. Even if I am destined to never leave the office again.'

'Don't dismiss it just yet. Think it through.'

'Are you asking me to be an employee, or an equal partner?'

'That would be entirely up to you.'

'The only money I have is what I've saved for my house

deposit. If I was to be a partner, then you'd need me to invest.'

'Not necessarily. We could work out a payment plan, where you could invest from your share of the profits.'

Her mind was a whirr of thoughts. On the one hand, she'd enjoy working with Seb more. But Twiggy was her partner, too, and she'd hate never to work with him again.

'You say you're going to be selective about the cases you take, but what if there aren't many? Would you consider taking mundane cases? That would make you one of those failed, wannabe coppers whose only skill is to follow adulterous men and women, to quote Sarge.'

'He's not a fan of private investigators, I take it?'

'Is anyone on the force? You weren't either, remember?'

'Which is why I want to be selective about cases and work with you.'

Indecision flooded through her. An alien concept, as normally decisions were relatively clear-cut.

'Would you change the name to *Bird & Clifford Private Investigators*?'

'I was thinking more *JIT Investigators*,' he said, a deadpan expression on his face.

'JIT? I don't get it. What does that stand for?'

'*Just in time*.'

'That's pathetic. Leave the jokes to me.'

'Will you think about it?'

'When do you need to know by?'

'Take as long as you like. Rob wants to employ me for the foreseeable future, and that's the only case I have at the moment.'

'Whatever my final decision, thanks for asking me. I appreciate your trust in my skills.'

'That was never in doubt. Come on, let's order.' He passed her a menu to look at.

While she was deciding, her phone rang.

'I better get this. Hello?'

'Is that Lucinda Bird?'

'Yes, it is.'

'It's Craig Davis. Marie's son. We met the other day at my mother's house.'

'How is she?'

'She's doing very well. Thanks for asking. That's why I'm calling. She asked if you would like to visit next weekend.'

Her heart thumped in her chest, she'd thought that avenue had been closed. 'I'd love to. Where will she be?'

'Back at home in Leicester. She didn't want to leave, and so the family have paid for a live-in carer. It's the best thing for her.'

'That's fantastic. I'm sure she'll be happy in familiar surroundings. Would Sunday at three work for her?'

'Perfect. I'll let her know.'

She ended the call, unable to stop an enormous smile from spreading across her face.

'Good news, I take it?' Seb said.

'Marie Davis is home from hospital and I'm going to see her next week.'

'That's excellent.'

'Yes. Finally, I'm going to learn more about where I come from.'

**Book 3 -** Sebastian and Birdie return in ***Never Too Late*** when they join forces with DCI Whitney Walker, to

investigate the brutal attack twenty years ago which left her
brother with irreversible brain damage.
Tap here to buy

❦

GET ANOTHER BOOK FOR FREE!
To instantly receive **Nowhere to Hide,** a free novella
from the Detective Sebastian Clifford series, featuring DC
Lucinda Bird when she first joined CID, sign up here for
Sally Rigby's free author newsletter.

## WEB OF LIES: A Midlands Crime Thriller (Detective Sebastian Clifford - Book 1)

### A trail of secrets. A dangerous discovery. A deadly turn.

Police officer Sebastian Clifford never planned on becoming a private investigator. But when a scandal leads to the disbandment of his London based special squad, he finds himself out of a job. That is, until his cousin calls on him to investigate her husband's high-profile death, and prove that it wasn't a suicide.

Clifford's reluctant to get involved, but the more he digs, the more evidence he finds. With his ability to remember everything he's ever seen, he's the perfect person to untangle the layers of deceit.

He meets Detective Constable Bird, an underutilised detective at Market Harborough's police force, who refuses to give him access to the records he's requested unless he allows her to help with the investigation. Clifford isn't thrilled. The last time he worked as part of a team it ended his career.

But with time running out, Clifford is out of options. Together they must wade through the web of lies in the hope that they'll find the truth before it kills them.

Web of Lies is the first in the new Detective Sebastian Clifford series. Perfect for readers of Joy Ellis, Robert Galbraith and Mark Dawson.

## SPEAK NO EVIL: A Midlands Crime Thriller (Detective Sebastian Clifford - Book 2)

### What happens when someone's too scared to speak?

Ex-police officer Sebastian Clifford had decided to limit his work as a private investigator, until Detective Constable Bird, aka Birdie, asks for his help.

Twelve months ago a young girl was abandoned on the streets of Market Harborough in shocking circumstances. Since then the child has barely spoken and with the police unable to trace her identity, they've given up.

The social services team in charge of the case worry that the child has an intellectual disability but Birdie and her aunt, who's fostering the little girl, disagree and believe she's gifted and intelligent, but something bad happened and she's living in constant fear.

Clifford trusts Birdie's instinct and together they work to find out who the girl is, so she can be freed from the past. But as secrets are uncovered, the pair realise it's not just the child who's in danger.

Speak No Evil is the second in the Detective Sebastian Clifford series. Perfect for readers of Faith Martin, Matt Brolly and Joy Ellis.

## NEVER TOO LATE: A Midlands Crime Thriller (Detective Sebastian Clifford - Book 3)

**A vicious attack. A dirty secret. And a chance for justice**

Ex-police officer Sebastian Clifford is quickly finding that life as a private investigator is never quiet. His doors have only been open a few weeks when DCI Whitney Walker approaches him to investigate the brutal attack that left her older brother, Rob, with irreversible brain damage.

For twenty years Rob had no memory of that night, but lately things are coming back to him, and Whitney's worried that her brother might, once again, be in danger.

Clifford knows only too well what it's like be haunted by the past, and so he agrees to help. But the deeper he digs, the more secrets he uncovers, and soon he discovers that Rob's not the only one in danger.

***Never Too Late*** is the third in the Detective Sebastian Clifford series, perfect for readers who love gripping crime fiction.

# Also by Sally Rigby

### *THE CAVENDISH & WALKER SERIES*

### DEADLY GAMES - Cavendish & Walker Book 1

#### A killer is playing cat and mouse....... and winning.

DCI Whitney Walker wants to save her career. Forensic psychologist, Dr Georgina Cavendish, wants to avenge the death of her student.

Sparks fly when real world policing meets academic theory, and it's not a pretty sight.

When two more bodies are discovered, Walker and Cavendish form an uneasy alliance. But are they in time to save the next victim?

*Deadly Games* is the first book in the Cavendish and Walker crime fiction series. If you like serial killer thrillers and psychological intrigue, then you'll love Sally Rigby's page-turning book.

Pick up *Deadly Games* today to read Cavendish & Walker's first case.

### FATAL JUSTICE - Cavendish & Walker Book 2

#### A vigilante's on the loose, dishing out their kind of justice...

A string of mutilated bodies sees Detective Chief Inspector

Whitney Walker back in action. But when she discovers the victims have all been grooming young girls, she fears a vigilante is on the loose. And while she understands the motive, no one is above the law.

Once again, she turns to forensic psychologist, Dr Georgina Cavendish, to unravel the cryptic clues. But will they be able to save the next victim from a gruesome death?

*Fatal Justice* is the second book in the Cavendish & Walker crime fiction series. If you like your mysteries dark, and with a twist, pick up a copy of Sally Rigby's book today.

**DEATH TRACK - Cavendish & Walker Book 3**

**Catch the train if you dare...**

After a teenage boy is found dead on a Lenchester train, Detective Chief Inspector Whitney Walker believes they're being targeted by the notorious Carriage Killer, who chooses a local rail network, commits four murders, and moves on.

Against her wishes, Walker's boss brings in officers from another force to help the investigation and prevent more deaths, but she's forced to defend her team against this outside interference.

Forensic psychologist, Dr Georgina Cavendish, is by her side in an attempt to bring to an end this killing spree. But how can they get into the mind of a killer who has already killed twelve times in two years without leaving a single clue behind?

For fans of Rachel Abbott, L J Ross and Angela Marsons, *Death*

*Track* is the third in the Cavendish & Walker series. A gripping serial killer thriller that will have you hooked.

## LETHAL SECRET - Cavendish & Walker Book 4

### Someone has a secret. A secret worth killing for....

When a series of suicides, linked to the Wellness Spirit Centre, turn out to be murder, it brings together DCI Whitney Walker and forensic psychologist Dr Georgina Cavendish for another investigation. But as they delve deeper, they come across a tangle of secrets and the very real risk that the killer will strike again.

As the clock ticks down, the only way forward is to infiltrate the centre. But the outcome is disastrous, in more ways than one.

For fans of Angela Marsons, Rachel Abbott and M A Comley, *Lethal Secret* is the fourth book in the Cavendish & Walker crime fiction series.

## LAST BREATH - Cavendish & Walker Book 5

### Has the Lenchester Strangler returned?

When a murderer leaves a familiar pink scarf as his calling card, Detective Chief Inspector Whitney Walker is forced to dig into a cold case, not sure if she's looking for a killer or a copycat.

With a growing pile of bodies, and no clues, she turns to forensic psychologist, Dr Georgina Cavendish, despite their relationship being at an all-time low.

Can they overcome the bad blood between them to solve the unsolvable?

For fans of Rachel Abbott, Angela Marsons and M A Comley, *Last Breath* is the fifth book in the Cavendish & Walker crime fiction series.

**FINAL VERDICT - Cavendish & Walker Book 6**

**The judge has spoken......everyone must die.**

When a killer starts murdering lawyers in a prestigious law firm, and every lead takes them to a dead end, DCI Whitney Walker finds herself grappling for a motive.

What links these deaths, and why use a lethal injection?

Alongside forensic psychologist, Dr Georgina Cavendish, they close in on the killer, while all the time trying to not let their personal lives get in the way of the investigation.

For fans of Rachel Abbott, Mark Dawson and M A Comley, Final Verdict is the sixth in the Cavendish & Walker series. A fast paced murder mystery which will keep you guessing.

**RITUAL DEMISE - Cavendish & Walker Book 7**

**Someone is watching.... No one is safe**

The once tranquil woods in a picturesque part of Lenchester have become the bloody stage to a series of ritualistic murders. With no suspects, Detective Chief Inspector Whitney Walker is once again forced to call on the services of forensic psychologist Dr Georgina Cavendish.

But this murderer isn't like any they've faced before. The murders are highly elaborate, but different in their own way and, with the clock ticking, they need to get inside the killer's head before it's too late.

For fans of Angela Marsons, Rachel Abbott and L J Ross. Ritual Demise is the seventh book in the Cavendish & Walker crime fiction series.

∼

## MORTAL REMAINS - Cavendish & Walker Book 8

### Someone's playing with fire…. There's no escape.

A serial arsonist is on the loose and as the death toll continues to mount DCI Whitney Walker calls on forensic psychologist Dr Georgina Cavendish for help.

But Lenchester isn't the only thing burning. There are monumental changes taking place within the police force and there's a chance Whitney might lose the job she loves. She has to find the killer before that happens. Before any more lives are lost.

Mortal Remains is the eighth book in the acclaimed Cavendish & Walker series. Perfect for fans of Angela Marsons, Rachel Abbott and L J Ross.

∼

**SILENT GRAVES - Cavendish & Walker Book 9**

**Nothing remains buried forever...**

When the bodies of two teenage girls are discovered on a building site, DCI Whitney Walker knows she's on the hunt for a killer. The problem is the murders happened in 1980 and this is her first case with the new team. What makes it even tougher is that with budgetary restrictions in place, she only has two weeks to solve it.

Once again, she enlists the help of forensic psychologist Dr Georgina Cavendish, but as she digs deeper into the past, she uncovers hidden truths that reverberate through the decades and into the present.

Silent Graves is the ninth book in the acclaimed Cavendish & Walker series. Perfect for fans of L J Ross, J M Dalgleish and Rachel Abbott.

**KILL SHOT - Cavendish & Walker Book 10**

**The game is over.....there's nowhere to hide.**

When Lenchester's most famous sportsman is shot dead, DCI Whitney Walker and her team are thrown into the world of snooker.

She calls on forensic psychologist Dr Georgina Cavendish to assist, but the investigation takes them in a direction which has far-reaching, international ramifications.

Much to Whitney's annoyance, an officer from one of the Met's special squads is sent to assist.

But as everyone knows…three's a crowd.

Kill Shot is the tenth book in the acclaimed Cavendish & Walker series. Perfect for fans of Simon McCleave, J M Dalgleish, J R Ellis and Faith Martin.

∾

## DARK SECRETS - Cavendish & Walker Book 11

### An uninvited guest…a deadly secret….and a terrible crime.

When a well-loved family of five are found dead sitting around their dining table with an untouched meal in front of them, it sends shockwaves throughout the community.

Was it a murder suicide, or was someone else involved?

It's one of DCI Whitney Walker's most baffling cases, and even with the help of forensic psychologist Dr Georgina Cavendish, they struggle to find any clues or motives to help them catch the killer.

But with a community in mourning and growing pressure to get answers, Cavendish and Walker are forced to go deeper into a murderer's mind than they've ever gone before.

Dark Secrets is the eleventh book in the Cavendish & Walker series. Perfect for fans of Angela Marsons, Joy Ellis and Rachel McLean.

## Acknowledgments

This book went through several rewrites before the final version. Huge thanks go to my advanced reader team for their support and persistence in helping me get it right. I couldn't have done it without you.

I'd also like to thank my editing team, Emma Mitchell and Kate Noble for their input. To Stuart Bache, thanks for the cover, it really is spectacular.

Thanks to my fellow writers Amanda Ashby and Christina Phillips for always being available whenever I need to brainstorm.

Finally, to my family, thanks for your continued support and encouragement.

## About the Author

Sally Rigby was born in Northampton, in the UK. She has always had the travel bug, and after living in both Manchester and London, eventually moved overseas. From 2001 she has lived with her family in New Zealand, which she considers to be the most beautiful place in the world. During this time she also lived for five years in Australia.

Sally has always loved crime fiction books, films and TV programmes, and has a particular fascination with the psychology of serial killers.

Sally loves to hear from her readers, so do feel free to get in touch via her website www.sallyrigby.com